Without Warning

Larissa Johns

Published by Larissa Johns, 2021.

To Melanie and Raechel, the two best sisters anyone could ask for. Thank you for always being there for me!

Chapter 1 – Paula

It was a virus.

That was all it was, just a virus. Certainly nothing life-threatening. If Paula had left Oliver sleeping at home, he would be fine now. Hell, she could have sent him to school despite his sickness and he'd still be better off.

Paula had cursed under her breath when Ollie had woken up in the morning feeling worse than he had the day before. She was nearly out of sick pay, but she knew there was no point in sending her son to school in this condition. He wouldn't last an hour before the office lady made the call to send him home, exasperation and judgement in her voice. Her husband, Alfie, had already left for work at the construction company, so him taking the day off to be with his son wasn't an option. Reluctantly, Paula had notified the school and the cinema where she worked that they wouldn't be in, and settled in for a quiet day.

Ollie slept in, with Paula checking in on him occasionally. His face was warm, but that might have been from the blankets bundled around him as much as anything else. He was fine, Paula decided, busying herself in the kitchen. Even though she couldn't really afford the day off, it was quite nice to have some time at home to get things done.

It was nearly ten when Ollie finally emerged, looking sleepy and with a severe case of bed-head. "Hi, baby," Paula said, smiling at her youngest child. "How are you doing?"

Oliver shrugged, yawning. "I'm okay," he murmured, and went over and leaned his body against hers. This was the highlight of sons, Paula thought. They stayed cuddly for longer than girls. Or at least that was the case when comparing Oliver to her daughter, Jasmine. Jazzy was fifteen now, and Paula could barely remember when she had last received physical affection from her. She was sure she had been younger than eight. But then Jasmine and Oliver had always been very different children, from the moment they were born.

Paula made some buttered toast for Oliver, hoping he'd show some interest in food. He munched away slowly at it, not making much headway.

"I have to go to the shops," Paula told him, grimacing slightly. She knew the news wouldn't be met with much joy from her son.

"What? Why?" Oliver asked, suddenly more alert. He hated going to the shops at the best of times, let alone when he was feeling like this.

"I left my wallet at work," Paula sighed. "Lisa told me when I called in saying I was staying home. I'm sorry, buddy, but I can't just leave it there, lying around." She didn't often have much cash on her, but Murphy's Law dictated that she had taken out $200 the day before. In the nature of a cinema, there was a revolving door of younger employees, some of whom she barely knew. She wasn't going to chance leaving her wallet there until the next day, or whenever she was able to return to work.

"Can't I stay in the car?" Ollie whined, but Paula shook her head.

"Sorry, hon, but it's way too hot for that. I won't be long, and the doctor said you're not contagious. I think it's safest for you to come in with me. In and out, I promise."

Chapter 2 – Destiny

Destiny eyed herself in the mirror, smoothing down the front of her dress and trying to calm her nerves. *It's just a date,* she reminded herself. *You've had a million of them, and you'll have a million more.*

It was no use. She had been waiting for Luke, her friend from uni, to ask her out for so long. She couldn't help but think that maybe, just maybe, this would be the last first date she'd ever have.

Destiny was getting carried away, and she knew it. Not many people met "the One" at such a young age. She wasn't even sure it was a concept she believed in, really. But it wasn't like the idea was impossible, and Luke was different from the other guys she knew.

For starters, he was gorgeous, with his slightly curly brown hair and his sexy stubble, but it was much deeper than that. Luke was intelligent, kind, *soulful.* That was the word that always sprung to mind when she thought about him, although of course, she'd die before saying it to anyone else.

They'd been friends for over two years now, but they'd rarely been alone together before. They were part of a group of six friends at uni, and while Destiny enjoyed spending time with all of them, she had always felt differently around Luke. She had never been sure if he felt the same way about her, so him finally asking her out on a date was huge. He'd asked her via text, and she'd opened it expecting to be just the usual chatty message inside. Seeing the words *Hey, Desi. I was wondering if you'd like to come to a movie with me?* made her breath catch in her throat. She knew immediately that it was more than just an outing as friends. For starters, he normally would have sent a group message. Secondly, there was just something about the way it started. *Hey, Desi.* It was stupid, but they didn't often use each other's names in messages. It was small, but it seemed meaningful.

They were studying journalism together, although her mother warned her that it was a dying art. Writing had always been her passion, and she was loving the opportunity to hone her craft. Luke was doing some print journalism subjects merely to round out his degree – photography was his favoured art form, and he was good at it. In her moments of fantasy, which were frequent, Destiny imagined herself writing stories as a freelance journalist, with Luke providing the images to go along with her text. Freelance work was what she wanted to do. Destiny generally disliked commitment, and freelance seemed the safer bet. *But maybe I'll commit to Luke,* she thought dreamily, reaching up to fix a stray strand of loose hair. She smiled at her image in the mirror. She looked... cute. Not amazing, but cute. Luke saw her three days a week at uni, so it was crazy to worry so much about how she looked, but this was different.

Destiny's natural red hair was tied back loosely, her pale skin looking practically translucent against her tiny, figure-hugging black dress. Destiny had always hated how tall and skinny she was, but she was pleased to say that at twenty-two, she was finally starting to fill out a little more. She would always be skinny, but she thought it was starting to look fashionable rather than gawky. A padded bra helped the image, of course.

Taking a deep breath, Destiny grabbed her handbag and headed for the door. She couldn't wait to see what the day would bring.

Chapter 3 – Rosie

A ladies' lunch with my twin sister was nothing out of the ordinary. I always had Tuesdays off, while Betty's schedule changed week by week. When she knew she had a Tuesday off coming up, she would often ask about a catch up.

But this was different, because today I was going to tell her my news.

My sister and I never had the kind of twin telepathy that you read about in books but Betty had always been intuitive to my needs, and I liked to think that she'd say the same about me. There was always the chance she'd guess something was up without me having to say anything.

Despite our enduring closeness, Betty and I didn't get to see each other as much as we would have liked. Life had taken us in different directions. I worked in hospitality; she was a nurse. She was married with three kids; I lived with Tim, my partner of four years. To the outside eye Betty seemed to have her life much more together than I did, but I was content. I had a wonderful family and boyfriend and a job I truly loved. Working at a restaurant wasn't as impressive as my sister's career, but I loved meeting new people and I never had to bring my work home the way so many people seemed to these days. In short, I didn't resent Betty and she certainly had no reason to resent me, but our lives had taken completely different trajectories.

Growing up as a twin wasn't easy, by any stretch of the imagination. Our school years were spent being compared to each other, and no matter how much self-esteem you have, that's never fun. We both had our own talents, but it was hard not to feel like my sister's gifts were somehow better than my own. At school, I was more athletic. Betty was more popular. I was involved in theatre. Betty was more academic, or as the kids saw it, smarter. Nothing much had changed there, except for our ease with being in our own skin. Nowadays, if someone tried to compare me to my sister, I just smiled. I was happy with who I was, and I adored my twin. I didn't need to compete with her. She had her good qualities, and I had mine.

Like something out of a movie, Betty had met Jeffrey on what was literally her first day of uni. They weren't even studying the same thing – they'd been waiting in a long queue at the uni coffee shop and started chatting, and that was that. Betty hadn't dated much in high school, despite a large amount of interest from the boys. I'd been not quite as popular, but definitely more attainable, so I'd scored her share of the dates. The consolation prize when you couldn't score the fabulous Betty Blake.

Betty's general lack of interest in high school boys meant she'd been a virgin when she met Jeffrey, and she'd never had eyes for anyone else. After they got married, they'd wasted little time in having three gorgeous kids. The whole family of five could be the stock photo in a frame, they looked so wholesome and picture-perfect.

Oh, and we're not ninety. Everyone always thinks "little old ladies" when they hear the names Rosie and Betty, but our parents just liked classical names. Rosemary and Elizabeth, actually, but neither of us ever used our full name. In reality, our thirtieth birthday was looming large. That was part of why Betty wanted to get together. We had discussed having a joint party, but I wasn't so sure that was something I was interested in. I might be confident and comfortable in my own skin, but I was also realistic. If you put the two of us together – with Betty looking breathtaking in some expensive gown, with her beautiful family and steady career – the guests would feel sorry for me. They just would.

Betty and I are identical, or at least, we were. As it turns out, being identical twins doesn't mean much when one twin is thirty kilos heavier than the other. I'm sure it's not hard to guess which twin is carrying the extra weight.

"Hey Ro, I'm going," Tim yelled out from the kitchen.

"Oh," I said aloud, startled back to reality. I raised my voice louder so he would hear me. "Okay, babe! Have an amazing day."

"Don't I get a farewell kiss?"

I laughed. "I'm naked," I called back.

Tim strode into the bedroom. "Like that's ever stopped me," he said, bending down to kiss me and giving my left boob a squeeze for good measure. "Maybe I don't need to go to work, after all…"

I slapped his hand away, playfully. "You need to bring home the bacon, good sir, and *I* have a date with my sister."

Tim sighed. "Fine, but we're picking this up tonight," he said, nodding his head towards my naked body. I smiled as he left. There was no ego boost like my boyfriend still loving the sight of me, even when I'd put on a few kilos. I started humming to myself as I got dressed for my outing with Betty, my mood instantly lifted.

Chapter 4 – Fiona

The room was quiet. The house was quiet.

Fiona sighed, listening to the ticking of the clock. It had been a month, and the stillness of the house still took her by surprise.

She hadn't returned to work yet. She couldn't. Working in an aged care facility you had to be fully present to the needs of the patients, and Fiona wasn't there yet. Although her job might not have been as prestigious as that of a fully qualified nurse or doctor, she loved doing it. As a Personal Care Assistant her role mostly involved helping patients with day-to-day tasks, monitoring their medications and providing them with company and good conversation. She wasn't saving lives in her job, but Fiona knew that her visits could sometimes mean the difference between a good and a bad day for the patients she worked with, and that was more than enough for her. Not only that, she was good at it. She had never been sure of what she wanted to do when she was in high school. When her great-aunt was put into a home when Fiona was fifteen, she had realised this was the path she wanted to take. She had never looked back.

Until recently. There was no way she could bring herself to return to work right now.

She knew her boss was getting impatient but it was better to stay away, rather than doing any more damage. One more week, she'd told them, and she'd be back.

She wasn't sure it was true.

It was just past ten but Fiona was still lying on her bed, wondering whether she would even get up today. Was there any point in doing so? The Fiona of old used to be a hard worker. A go-getter, up early each day and ready to tackle whatever life had to throw at her.

That Fiona had died a month ago.

The phone rang. She knew without looking that it was her best friend, Angela. It was routine. Fiona's mum favoured the Thursday night call, while Angela had rung to check in around this time every morning for the last month.

It took all of Fiona's strength to reach over and take the phone, but she knew how much Angela would worry if she didn't answer. "Hi, Ange," she said, her voice a monotone.

"Fi!" Angela's voice was filled with false cheer. "How are you going?"

"Oh, fighting fit," Fiona replied sardonically. "So happy to be alive."

This time, the sadness came through in her friend's tone. "Oh, Fi."

They were silent for a minute – there wasn't much to say. Part of Fiona wondered if Angela would stop bothering with her soon, since her friend was giving so much and getting so little in return. Fiona wouldn't even blame her if she did. But she and Angela had been friends since primary school, and over the years they'd become more like sisters. It was an easy, unconditional friendship and she knew that her friend wasn't going anywhere.

Finally, Angela spoke again. "So, what are you doing to-day? Do you want me to come by after work? I can bring some food, or...?" Her voice trailed off. She made this offer most days, and most days Fiona refused her. It was hard for even Angela to keep up the false enthusiasm.

"Thanks, Ange," Fiona sighed, closing her eyes. "I'll be okay. I'm thinking of going to the shops, actually."

There was a brief pause, and Fiona could tell her response had taken her friend by surprise. "Oh, okay. For groceries, you mean? Are you sure you don't just want me to bring you something?"

"No, to Alpine," Fiona said, naming the largest shopping centre near her. She had really only made the comment about shopping to appease Angela, but suddenly, the idea of an outing was appealing. "I thought it might take my mind off things."

"Oh! Definitely!" Angela agreed, and Fiona winced at the twinge of excitement she heard in her friend's voice. Was she really so pathetic that a mere outing to the shops would impress Angela so much? She knew the answer, though. Her life in the last month had proven that she was precisely that pathetic.

The two women chatted for a few moments more before hanging up, and Fiona looked over at her wardrobe. Yes, she was going to do this. She was going to dress in something other than pyjamas, and she was going to wash her hair. She was going out. For a moment, she even felt excited.

Chapter 5 – Paula

Dragging a sick child to the shops was not high on her list of favoured pastimes. Paula let Ollie stay in his comfy old tracksuit, even though he looked like death warmed up. She was determined to keep to her promise – in and out. She tried to park close to the cinema, but Alpine's car park was surprisingly busy for 11:30 on a Tuesday. She parked near the downstairs coffee shop instead. It was only a short walk up to the movies, and there was an escalator, but she knew it would feel a lot longer with Oliver complaining beside her.

When she got up to the movies, she saw her friend Alice behind the counter. Paula waved and smiled, joining the line. If she had to come in on her day off it was nice to see Alice, at least. Paula had a fairly standard timetable – school hours during the week, aside from a longer day on Thursday, when the new movies were released – but Alice had no children and was happy to take the night shift, saying it was busier and therefore time passed more quickly. Paula felt a twinge of guilt when she realised Alice had probably been called in to cover her, but it went away quickly. Her need for the day off was genuine, and the child on her arm was proof of that.

The line took longer than she'd expected, due in no small part to an older gentleman having great issues with his debit card, and by the time Paula got to the front of the queue Oliver was really dragging his feet. "Just a few more minutes," she whispered tenderly to him, mentally kicking herself for leaving her wallet behind the day before.

"Hey, stranger!" Alice greeted her enthusiastically when she reached the counter. "And hey, Ollie! I heard you were sick," she added sympathetically.

"Yeah, he's been a bit off for the last couple of days," Paula sighed. "We went to the doctor after school yesterday. He said it should go away after a few days of rest, fingers crossed."

Conscious of the line of people behind Paula, Alice went and grabbed Paula's wallet from out the back. Paula grinned as she took it back. "I'd forget my head if it wasn't screwed on," she laughed. "I'm just happy it's safe. Thanks, Al."

"No worries. Feel better, Ollie!"

Hand in hand, Paula and Oliver went down the escalator to the floor below, ready to get to their car and start the journey home.

Chapter 6 – Destiny

Luke was smiling when Destiny approached the coffee shop. They were going to a movie, but Luke had suggested they have a drink together first, so they'd have a chance to chat. Destiny was pleased to get more time with him, but she was worried the conversation wouldn't flow as easily now that they were on an official date. When they'd caught up in their group of friends the conversation had been great, but she was self-conscious today in a way she normally wasn't. Besides, in the time they had known each other they'd not spent much time together as a twosome. She tried to relax. It would be fine.

"Hey!" Destiny exclaimed as she approached Luke, before they did the typical awkward first date greeting. She was just planning to smile, but he leaned in to kiss her cheek, and she put her hand on his arm as they quickly embraced. When they pulled away, her cheeks were bright pink.

"It's good to see you, Desi," Luke said, his dimples flashing. "You look great."

She looked down, as if checking if his statement was correct. "Oh, thanks! You – you do too."

They sat down at the nearest table, mercifully far away from most of the other patrons. Destiny had always thought you could just *tell* when people were on a first date, and she and her best friend Gemma always loved pointing those couples out when they saw them. She didn't relish the idea of other people doing the same to her and Luke. Although, maybe since they were friends first they wouldn't have the first date look about them? She doubted it, though. Despite having been friends for two years, she knew things were different today.

Luke broke the brief silence that had settled over them. "So, this is weird," he said with a light laugh.

"Really?" Destiny replied, hoping she sounded cooler than she felt. "I hadn't noticed."

"I thought it might just feel like another trip to the movies," Luke said. "But... it doesn't."

The two grinned at each other over the table, the tension starting to dissipate. Even though Destiny had known it was a date, there was a part of her, deep down, that was nervous that she'd misread the signs – that Luke only wanted to catch up as friends, or that he just wanted to see this movie and he'd had no one better to ask, no one who was free on a Tuesday. His words, along with his obvious nerves, reassured her that that wasn't the case.

"I've been interested in you for a while," Luke blurted out.

"Really?" Now that did surprise her. She'd suspected Luke might have been interested for a while before he made the move, but it was the fact that he was being so open about it that took her by surprise. Didn't he abide by the same bullshit handbook the rest of the guys used, where they had to pretend not to be interested until a girl practically undressed in front of them? She had always known that Luke was something special, Destiny thought triumphantly. He was so... *mature.*

"Well, you can't blame a guy," Luke laughed self-consciously. "You're pretty amazing."

Destiny's heart skipped a beat. Normally she would have felt self-conscious with a guy being this openly into her, but she couldn't help but feel swept away. It was nice that he didn't feel the need to pretend. And Luke was pretty amazing, too. She tried to put that sentiment into words, but her mouth felt like it was made of sandpaper. She could barely string two words together, let alone say something heartfelt. She had never been great at expressing her feelings.

Seemingly in an effort to lighten the mood, Luke opened his menu. "Do you know what you're getting?"

Destiny shook her head, opening her own menu and pretending to look at it while she tried to stop her head from spinning. Luke wanted to be with her. Luke thought she was *amazing*. She could hardly believe her luck.

Chapter 7 – Rosie

I smiled when I saw Betty, who had arrived ahead of me at the coffee shop. She was reading a book, her blonde hair loosely plaited, wearing a soft red gingham dress. She looked like she'd just stepped out of a catalogue, I thought fondly.

When she saw me, Betty dropped her book on the table and gave me a big, enthusiastic hug. "It's been too long!" she exclaimed.

It hadn't been all that long, really. We'd seen each other just three weeks before, at our dad's birthday celebrations. I knew what she meant, though – it had been too long since it was just the two of us. With Dad, Tim, and Betty's husband and kids there, we didn't get much time to chat.

Betty's children were just adorable. Archer was seven, and Harrison and Poppy were only just over twelve months apart at five and four years old. Poppy was at day care, while the two boys were now both at school, which made Betty's and my catch-ups easier to organise. I knew balancing her work with minding the kids had been tricky for Betty, but she'd made it look fairly effortless.

"How have you been?" I asked when we were both seated and had ordered, and Betty started filling me in on the horror stories from her work. Being a nurse was not for the faint-hearted, I thought for the thousandth time. I certainly couldn't do what she did. My own work at the restaurant was often stressful, but at least it didn't often come down to life or death. She filled me in on the patient who had only a few weeks to live and wanted to track down his estranged son before he died, and about the doctor who was facing down a sexual harassment suit from a colleague.

Even as my sister chatted away, I thought she seemed oddly nervous. I put it down to stress from her job, or to something going on with one of the kids. There was certainly no reason for her to be nervous about catching up with me. I was the one who had the big announcement to make, after all! I was sure she would tell me what it was that was bothering her. We had always had that kind of relationship.

When she'd finished chatting Betty asked about me, and I filled her in on my own work at the restaurant and how hectic it was getting. "Business seems to be booming," I told her happily. I'd had to leave my last job when business got too slow – I was the last in, first out – so the fact that the restaurant was popular was a huge relief to me, as my sister knew. I was really happy there. The staff was great, and my salary was the largest I'd ever had.

"And then there's Tim," I added, smiling as I thought of my boyfriend. "It's going really well. You never know... I think there just might be a proposal ahead of me." I felt butterflies in my stomach as I said it, as though I were a lovesick teenager rather than a twenty-nine-year-old woman.

There was a strange look on Betty's face as I spoke about Tim, but I couldn't place it. It certainly couldn't be envy, since she'd been married for so long. It looked almost like regret, but that couldn't be it. She and Jeffrey were so happy together. She did seem to be in a funny mood today, though. Who could tell?

As soon as I stopped speaking, Betty rushed in, as if she'd been waiting for me to pause for air. She looked down at her hands and spoke in a small voice. "I have something I need to tell you."

I looked at her, surprised. "Oh. I actually have something to tell you, too."

Betty shook her head. "I'm sorry, but... I need to go. I've been putting it off, and... if I don't say it now, I might never be able to," she finished, all in a rush.

So I nodded.

And then she told me.

And I knew my life would never be the same again.

Chapter 8 – Fiona

The shopping trip really did help. Fiona had spent most of the last month locked away in her house, surrounded by silence interrupted only by the regular phone calls from Angela. Being around noise, activity... it lifted her mood. Only slightly, but still. Alpine Centre was where she'd always gone as a kid, and there was something strangely nostalgic about it, even though it had changed almost beyond recognition in the last twenty years. Wandering through the shops reminded her of being twelve and on her first unsupervised shopping trip with her friends. They'd felt so grown up, walking through the centre together with slushies in hand and very little money in their purses. It was funny how the smallest things stuck with you for life.

Today, Fiona didn't really have anything she needed to buy, but that was fine by her. She didn't want to shop for something she *needed*. Her neighbour and Angela had both provided the bare essentials Fiona needed to get by, so this trip out wasn't about necessities. She wanted, she mused, to look at clothes for outings she wouldn't take, to look at jewellery she couldn't afford to buy. She just wanted to have a bit of fun. For the first time in four long weeks, she felt positive.

After less than an hour of wandering through the shops, though, tiredness overtook her. She had to remind herself that she'd spent most of the previous few weeks in bed, or on the recliner. A journey to the kitchen table counted as adventurous for Fiona lately, so a walk around the shops was bound to wear her out. Fiona contemplated her options, looking around the centre. There were some plush chairs designed for patrons to relax on, with phone charging points beside them. She could sit and watch the world pass her by. Or she could go home, but that option seemed surprisingly less appealing now that she was out in the real world. She looked around, trying to figure out what she could do to kill some time. Then she spotted the bright, cheerful looking coffee shop in the corner of the centre. *Perfect,* she thought, imaging allowing herself the luxury of sitting with a scone and tea for a while.

With a smile on her face, Fiona headed towards the coffee shop.

Chapter 9 – Paula

"Do you want a milkshake for the road?" Paula asked Ollie. She knew she might not win any parent of the year awards for offering milky drinks to a sick child, but it wasn't like he had a stomach bug. Besides, she was desperate for a coffee, and knew the offer of a milkshake might be her only chance to get one.

Ollie nodded mutely and she smiled and kissed him tenderly on the forehead, then walked towards the coffee shop at the corner of the centre. It was near their car anyway, so it would only add a minute or two to their trip. "You'll be home in your PJs in no time," she told him as they lined up at the counter. He seemed to be feeling a little brighter, but she knew he'd welcome the opportunity to rug up and watch a movie on the couch. What kid wouldn't? Actually, it sounded like a pretty good afternoon plan to her as well. Maybe she could put aside her housework for a while and snuggle up with him.

The coffee shop wasn't overly crowded for lunchtime, but there were a few groups sitting around, and Paula enjoyed the quiet hum of their voices. She placed their order – a milkshake for him, and a coffee for her, both to take away – and she and Ollie stood by the counter. Paula pulled her phone out as they waited, figuring she could use the brief wait to respond to some texts.

Suddenly, before she'd even finished reading the first message, a voice rang out from the entrance to the coffee shop. "Stay where you are! Everyone *calm down!*"

Startled by the noise, Paula looked up from her phone. She dropped it in shock when she saw the man standing in the doorway, wielding a gun. He had short brown curls and wild eyes, as if he were completely out of control. Which, clearly, he was. Instinctively she clutched Oliver closer to her, her legs nearly buckling under her with the horror of the situation. Her son was wide-eyed and open-mouthed in shock and terror.

Paula couldn't comprehend what she was seeing with her own eyes. This had to be a nightmare, or some kind of hallucination. Things like this didn't happen at her neighbourhood shopping centre. Things like this didn't happen to her.

She wasn't overly religious, but Paula found herself saying a silent prayer. *Please,* she begged anyone who would listen. *Let us walk out of here alive.*

Chapter 10 – Destiny

Destiny and Luke had just started eating when the screaming started.

First it was the man, the... gunman? Destiny could hardly bring herself to even think the word. She stared, openmouthed, wondering if she was dreaming. This was the sort of thing that happened in movies, not in real life. It took a moment to even focus on the man. In a far-off corner of her brain, she pictured herself rubbing her eyes in shock, like a cartoon character doing a double take. In reality, she couldn't have moved if she'd tried. Her limbs had never felt heavier.

Immediately after the gunman yelled out, the chorus of screams began. At the counter, a woman tried to hide her young son behind her leg. One couple dove under their table, the woman already sobbing. Another girl around Destiny's own age put a menu in front of her face, as though it would offer protection, or possibly just to shield her own eyes from the horrible sight in front of her.

Destiny was too shocked to move. Her legs felt like rubber. This sort of thing didn't happen here. It didn't happen to them. She looked over the table at Luke, who seemed to be as stunned as she felt. She reached a shaky hand across the table and Luke grasped it.

"I said *be calm!*" the man screamed, still waving the gun around.

One of the waiters stepped forward, his hands trembling. "We d-don't want any trouble," he said. "We'll give you all the m-money in the till. It's yours, okay?"

Then the gunman said the worst possible words Destiny could imagine.

With a sneer on his face, he said "I don't want your *money.*"

Destiny's heart sank.

She'd watched enough crime movies to know one thing: if the gunman wouldn't just take the money and leave, then this situation was even worse than she'd thought.

Chapter 11 – Rosie

The bombshell of my sister's announcement would have been the biggest shock of any other day, but on this day, it paled into insignificance. Almost.

I was taken aback when we'd first heard the shouting, but my instant assumption was that it was just some noisy teenagers. It never would have occurred to me to think anything else until I saw it with my own eyes. Alpine was in a nice area, and Australia seemed so safe compared to much of the world, that the reality took a while to hit me. Even when I saw him, it felt like something out of a nightmare rather than real life.

There stood, in the entrance to the coffee shop, a man with a wild look in his eyes, holding a gun. He was pointing it into the coffee shop, towards the patrons, but not towards anyone in particular, which seemed somehow more terrifying. The server who was coming towards us dropped our plates when she saw him. When the man heard the smash he flinched, swinging around so the gun was aimed at her. She held her hands up in surrender, a horrified expression on her face. I thought I heard her whisper "don't shoot", but it could have been my imagination. I couldn't be sure over the sounds of the terrified screams coming from all directions. Over the beating of my own heart.

"Stay still," the man screamed, still whipping the gun around in a frenzy. Out of the corner of my eye, I caught a glimpse of the slightest movement. Another of the servers, slipping from his position behind the counter out back to the kitchen, where I prayed he had a phone. I closed my eyes. How the hell had a normal Tuesday turned into this nightmare?

Chapter 12 – Fiona

When Fiona had first entered the coffee shop she had automatically gone to a small table in the corner. She still wasn't overly comfortable sitting by herself amongst crowds of people and didn't want to draw any unnecessary attention to herself. Still, she was feeling content as she ordered her much longed-for scone and tea and looked around. She didn't have her book, but she was happy to just people-watch as she ate. It was the most relaxed she'd felt in a while. She was daydreaming, enjoying herself for the first time in recent memory.

And then the shooter burst in.

Her first instinct was to dive under the table, but then she stopped. She wasn't sure drawing more attention to herself was the best way to go about this. Besides, she didn't think she had the power to move anyway. She could already recognise the signs that she was going into shock. Her body was trembling all over, in a way it hadn't done since that night, that awful night when everything changed. She couldn't even make out the words around her. Everything just sounded like white noise in her ears.

And so, she sat still at the table, and she trembled, and she waited.

While she waited, the same words kept repeating in her head.

If he's going to shoot anyone, it should be me.

And with that, she stood up.

Chapter 13 – Paula

All around her people were crying, screaming, praying out loud. Paula wished they would stop. She understood the urge, but screaming around this loose cannon of a man couldn't be a good idea. Her only priority was keeping Ollie safe, and as calm as possible. She had tried to hide him behind her maxi skirt, but she knew he'd still be partially visible to the gunman. She could feel her son sobbing against her leg and she just wanted to reach down and comfort him, but she thought the movement would just make them more noticeable. She was already regretting not getting a table. Standing by the counter seemed to make them an eye-catching target compared to all of those clustered around or underneath their tables. At least those people had some protection, although how much good it would do them was anyone's guess.

Suddenly, a woman stood up. She was tucked into the corner of the coffee shop, and Paula never would have noticed her if she'd stay seated. She wondered, briefly, if the gunman would have. The other woman's voice trembled, but she still managed to sound strong when she spoke. "If you need a hostage," she said, "take me. Shoot me, if you have to."

Paula stared at her, wondering if she was an off-duty cop or something. It was such a brave statement to make, but it also seemed so... stupid. So premature, when they didn't even know what the gunman wanted or why he was there. It was, she thought, bordering on suicide.

"You don't give me orders, bitch!" the man screamed back, and he swung his gun at the opposite direction, aiming it at a young woman with red hair who stared back, her face pale with shock.

Chapter 14 – Destiny

Destiny had been terrified from the moment the gunman appeared, but it ramped up to something entirely different when he aimed his gun at her.

Oh, shit, a voice inside her head said. *I'm going to wet myself.* Then another, more sinister, voice added *I'm going to die.*

Time seemed to stand still, and she wondered if her life was indeed going to flash before her eyes, the way people said it did at times like this. She shook her head wordlessly, as if that was going to change the man's mind. As if anything could.

She closed her eyes, unable to face what she knew was coming.

She heard the sound of the gunshot, but she felt no pain.

Destiny looked up, still shaking like a leaf, just in time to see Luke crumple to the ground. It took her sluggish mind a while to catch up, and then she gasped in horror when she realised what had happened. Luke had jumped in front of her. Luke had taken the bullet that was intended for her.

Pure chaos erupted then, but Destiny barely registered any of it. With no thought of self-preservation, she leapt off her chair and knelt over Luke, sobbing.

She was still waiting to be shot, but the gunman had moved on to other targets.

Destiny put her hand on Luke's chest, screaming and crying. She wasn't sure if her pressure on his skin was making it better or worse, and she tried desperately to remember what she'd seen in the movies. In the back of her mind, though, she knew it didn't really matter what she did or didn't do. She could already see that Luke was losing too much blood. There was no way he could survive this.

Luke looked at her, his eyes dim. "It was going to be you," he whispered.

"I know," she cried. "I know, you saved me. I was going to be shot. Luke, you saved my life."

He shook his head, barely perceptibly. "No. It was going to be you... for me."

And with that, he fell into unconsciousness.

Chapter 15 – Rosie

It had been chaos since the man entered, which felt like a lifetime ago now, but all hell broke loose when the man at the table was shot. The shrieking and wailing intensified. It all sounded like something out of a horror movie. I looked across the table and saw my own grief and panic mirrored on my twin's face. She'd already been teary from our earlier discussion, but now she had broken out into full-blown sobs. She reached across the table and grabbed my hand.

"I'm so sorry," she said. "I love you."

I shook my head, starting to tear up as well. "It's irrelevant," I replied, and in that instant I meant it. "I love you so much, Betty." There was nothing like fear for your lives to erase past wounds. Despite the situation, the ghost of a smile flickered across Betty's face at my words, and I realised how much she had needed to hear them.

"Hey!" the man yelled, and he waved the gun in our direction. I flinched. I had always hated guns, but I'd never imagined having one pointed at my face. It was beyond terrifying. "Hey, beauty queens! Get up!"

Slowly, looking at each other, Betty and I stood. We kept holding hands as we stood, side by side, facing the gunman. We were both trembling. It felt like I would never stop trembling.

He leered at us wordlessly for a minute, and my mind raced with possibilities. Was he going to take us hostage?

Shoot us there and then? Or – my heart ached with hope – let us go?

I heard, rather than saw, him pull the trigger.

I'll never forget that sound.

I'll never forget watching the blood appear on my twin sister's chest, like a flower blooming.

I let out a primal scream, a sound I was sure I'd never made before.

As if in slow motion, Betty fell. Her hand left mine slowly, so slowly. I stared in horror as she hit the floor, the blood spreading further.

"Betty!" I screamed, falling to her side. At that moment I didn't know what he'd do when I left my standing position, but I didn't much care. He could shoot me, if he wanted to.

I had to be with my sister.

Chapter 16 – Fiona

Fiona stared at the scene unfolding around her, wide-eyed and unblinking in horror.

She had done this. She had started this. She had stood up and tried to sacrifice herself, and in return, two innocent people had been shot.

What would have happened if she'd kept her mouth shut? If she'd stayed seated, like everyone else? Maybe he wouldn't have lost the ounce of control he'd possessed. Maybe the police would have arrived in time, and maybe they would have been able to save everyone.

Maybe. Maybe. Maybe.

Just like that night, the unanswered questions were the worst part.

The gunman raised his arm again, and shot.

The bullet went into the side of the little boy standing near the counter.

He had been nearly obscured by his mother, standing in front of him, but his right side was poking out, and that was enough.

The screams of terror rose to a level Fiona would have previously thought unimaginable. There was something about seeing a child be shot that was even more horrific than watching the same thing happen to an adult. Yelling in pain and clutching his chest, the boy fell to the floor, wailing.

"Stay where you are," a calm, authoritative voice said from the doorway to the coffee shop.

The police had arrived, like something out of a dream. Fiona had never been happier to see anyone in her life. At least half a dozen officers filled the doorway. Two of them stepped forward, approaching the gunman cautiously, guns trained on him.

Fiona nearly blacked out with a combination of relief and nerves. Their potential saviours were here, but what next? Would there be a shoot-out? More casualties on both sides? Would the police be able to take him down without hitting innocent people at the same time? She had heard of that, people surviving siege situations only to be shot when the police came in at the end. She'd always thought it was somehow an even more horrific thought than being shot by the gunman himself. Imagine feeling that sense of hope, only to have the worst thing happen.

As it turned out, the events that unfolded next were shockingly anti-climactic. The police officers continued trying to speak calmly to the man, urging him in measured tones to drop his weapon, but to no avail. The gunman swung his gun around, pointed it at the police and then at the remaining patrons in the coffee shop, his eyes wild. Fiona kept expecting the police to shoot him as he moved his gun around unsteadily, but either they didn't have a direct shot or their training didn't call for it. The man kept standing.

Then, completely without warning, the lunatic turned his gun on himself. One of the officers shouted out for him to stop, but it was done. One quick bullet in his own brain.

The coward's way out, the newspapers would say. He would never see justice done for the shootings.

Fiona didn't care much about justice right then and there. Let him be a coward. The only emotion she felt was relief.

No one else would be shot today. No one else would have to die. Fiona sat down in her seat, dizzy with relief, and sobbed. The tears were filled with relief, regret, and pain. It was the release of every emotion she'd felt in the last month, and all the new ones this had caused. She felt like she might never stop crying.

Chapter 17 – Rosie

Two people killed.

That's what all the news articles would say, and despite themselves, the people reading them would breathe a little sigh of relief. *Only two people,* they would say. *It could have been so much worse.*

And, of course, it could have been.

But what they didn't realise was it didn't matter if only two people died, or a hundred.

Because my twin sister was one of them, and that was the only thing that mattered to me.

My beautiful, intelligent, warm, kind sister died on the floor of that coffee shop. I knew she was gone before the paramedics came, but I was holding on to a vain hope, as if their mere arrival would resurrect her. I just couldn't imagine a world without Betty in it.

I would never again hear her laugh, or her voice. I would never again see her smile, so much more radiant than my own. I would never see her reach for her husband's hand. I would never see the passion in her eyes when she talked about her work, or the love on her face when she was near her children.

My God, her children. Three children left behind, without their mother.

How could I tell them? How could I get through this? How could they?

Chapter 18 – Paula

They had been lucky, Paula told herself firmly on the way to the hospital. The paramedics had said that Ollie's injuries weren't life-threatening. She wasn't sure everyone in the coffee shop had been as fortunate.

But still, if she hadn't insisted on going in to collect her wallet, this wouldn't have happened to them. If she hadn't made the decision to stop for a milkshake. A Goddamn milkshake!

Despite the thoughts spinning around in her head, Paula tried to remain outwardly calm. She smiled reassuringly at her son and squeezed his hands. He was lapsing in and out of consciousness, but she tried not to panic. It was the shock, she told herself. Or the pain, but pain was temporary. He would be okay. *His injuries aren't life threatening,* she repeated to herself, like a mantra. *His injuries aren't life threatening.*

She knew she wouldn't fully believe it until he walked out of the hospital. There was a chance she would never believe it again. How would they ever go back to their normal lives after this?

The bullet had grazed him just underneath his shoulder, not in the chest as Paula had first thought. It had been so hard to tell… she'd been so panicked, and there was so much blood. She wasn't sure if there could still be permanent damage. What if Ollie needed his arm amputated, or had limited use of his hands, or…? At the very least, he would presumably be traumatised by the experience. She tried to stop her mind from going through the limitless possibilities. There was more than enough to worry about another day. For now, she just had to be grateful that they were both alive and for now, they were both safe.

Paula messaged Alfie with trembling hands. It was not the sort of news you should send via text, but she couldn't force her mouth to form the words required to tell him over the phone. Alfie tried to ring almost immediately, but she declined the call, feeling like the worst wife in the world. It wasn't fair to him, but she couldn't face talking to anyone right now. Besides, there was no way she could put this horror into words.

When they arrived at the hospital, she finally let her shoulders slump, unaware until then of the tension she had been holding onto. Paula was a worrier by nature, but the things she'd worried about in the past seemed inconsequential now. Who cared about whether they could pay the electricity bill, or afterschool sports, or whether the food she was making was healthy enough, when Ollie might never come home again?

Not life threatening, she told herself again, more firmly this time. *Not life threatening.*

Soon, she might even start to believe it.

Chapter 19 – Destiny

L uke had taken a bullet for her.

In high school, when she and her friends talked about boys, they had swooned about the idea of finding someone who loved you so much they would *die* for you, and how romantic that thought was.

It wasn't so much fun to think about, now.

Destiny had known he was dead straight away, but a small part of her still didn't believe it. Luke was so sweet, so smart, so full of life. He was so damn *young*. How could he be... gone? She wondered if their friends from uni would blame her. If Luke's parents would. She blamed herself.

The nearest police officer, a short muscular woman, introduced herself as Constable Jones and asked Destiny some questions about what she'd seen. With a trembling voice, Destiny told her how the gunman had been aiming at her; how she'd been chosen as a target seemingly at random; how Luke had stepped out in front of her and taken the bullet that was intended for her. The police officer nodded as she noted this down. "That must have been very difficult for you," she said. "Are you hurt?"

Destiny shook her head. *Not physically,* she thought. "Do I need to let his parents know, or...?" She couldn't imagine making that call.

Thankfully, Constable Jones shook her head. "No, we'll handle that. You just need to get looked over by the paramedics and they'll let you know once you have the all-clear."

"Tell them," she said softly, "that he was a hero."

Some of the other patrons at the coffee shop had been taken to the hospital to be treated for shock, but Destiny just wanted to get home as quickly as possible. Once the paramedics had checked her over, she called her mum to pick her up. She realised when she picked up her phone that her mother, Janet, had tried to ring her several times, and when Destiny finally got through her mother's voice was filled with panic. "Baby! I saw – on the news – you're at Alpine, aren't you? Oh my God, I'm so happy to hear your voice," she cried, sniffling. "I'm on my way now. I got in the car as soon as I heard the news."

The sound of her mother's voice broke the wall of denial that had held back the flood of tears, and Destiny burst into gasping sobs. "Mummy," she cried, a moniker she hadn't used for over a decade. All she could think about was Luke's mother, whom Destiny had met a few times before. She would be just as worried as Janet was, but she wouldn't receive the reassuring phone call.

"You're okay? They said people were shot, but there weren't any more details. Baby, you're okay, aren't you?"

"I'm okay," Destiny affirmed through her tears. "But Luke – he – "

She couldn't get the words out, but the sharp gasp on the other end of the line told her that her mother understood anyway. "Oh, Desi," Janet sighed. "I'm so sorry, sweetheart."

When her mother finally arrived at Alpine Centre Destiny threw herself into her arms, weeping. She had never needed her mother more.

Chapter 20 – Paula

Alfie met them at the hospital, and Paula ran into his arms in a way she hadn't done since they were first dating. She let herself let go, sobbing into his shoulders. Alfie was crying, too. He was a blokey bloke, and she'd never seen him cry before. Not that she needed any reminders about the gravity of the situation, but that certainly helped to drive it home. With both her and his beloved son at the coffee shop, she knew Alfie would have been beside himself with worry.

The doctors, thankfully, didn't take long to pronounce Oliver relatively healthy. The bullet had grazed his shoulder, just as the paramedics had said, and he was going to be okay. It was hard for Paula to believe, but she was so grateful. She'd always been a hands-on mother but now she felt like she'd spend the rest of her life clinging on to Ollie, never wanting to let him go. Seeing him get shot in front of her had been more terrifying than anything she could have imagined.

"There can be other repercussions after a situation like this, though," Dr Tyson warned them. "Many people in such a traumatic situation can experience depression or PTSD afterwards, particularly children. Add to that the fact that Oliver was in fact shot himself, and it's likely he might experience night terrors or other emotional concerns. You both need to prioritise your mental health, and lean on your family and friends for support. Further to that, I would recommend Oliver see a therapist to help him sort through his response to this." He nodded towards Paula. "I'd recommend it for you as well, Mrs. Warner."

Paula nodded mutely. Unlike many in her age group, she'd never seen a therapist, but then she'd never experienced anything like this before, either. She didn't have an issue with talking to someone about what had happened, but she was still unsure about Ollie. Was making him relive the experience really the best way to help him get over it? Still, if that was what the doctor recommended, she was willing to do it. She was willing to do anything if it was going to help her son.

Ollie hadn't spoken since before they arrived at the hospital, and her gentle attempts to coax some words out of him had failed, so Paula let him be. He clearly wasn't up to conversation just yet, and she understood that. She just hoped he would be back to his happy, normal self sooner rather than later. She hoped this wouldn't change him forever.

After just a few hours, they were released from the hospital. On their way home, Paula stared numbly out the window. They'd gone out for a quick outing, and lived a lifetime since leaving the house that morning. Now they would be home in time for dinner, just like it was a normal day.

In reality, though, everything had changed.

Chapter 21 – Fiona

More information was released over the next few days, but each story was even more difficult to read. The shooter was clearly unhinged, which was no surprise, but he seemed to have no real motive as to why he had chosen Alpine Shopping Centre as the target of his rage. He'd been fired from his job over aggression towards a customer, and his ex had taken a domestic violence order out against him. In short, he was a ticking time bomb, Fiona thought as she learnt more about him. She didn't want to see pictures of him, or hear his name, although of course it was impossible to avoid. Fiona would never use his name to refer to him. He didn't deserve to be humanised in that way.

The media focussed mainly on an agenda they pushed that this mentally unstable individual had been able to obtain a firearm. People online talked about the failure of Australia's gun control laws, which had long been hailed as so effective. They tried to politicise the issue.

Fiona was tired. Too tired.

She'd gone to her own GP in the aftermath of the shooting, to see if there was anything he could advise her that would help some of the pain to go away. He had been her doctor for ten years. "Stay away from the news as much as possible," he told her. "Reading about the case will only exacerbate matters. And, Fiona..." he sighed, looking concerned.

"Try not to blame yourself for this. There's only one person at fault, and he's dead now."

Fiona tried to take his advice, but it was proving impossible. She'd ruined everything one month earlier, and to compound that pain and grief, she'd ruined everything again.

Angela had come over the night of the shooting. She'd insisted on staying, leaving her husband and children to fend for themselves for the night. Fiona was grateful, but she couldn't deny that she also felt pathetic. She had no one else to turn to, so Angela had had to leave her own family to look after her. This wasn't a position she'd expected to be in as a grown woman.

Always a true friend, Angela had brought a big lasagne and salad from the nearby Italian restaurant, and a huge bunch of cheerful-looking flowers. She also set about organising ice cream to be delivered the second they'd finished eating. Fiona was mostly silent, but Angela kept the conversation going for them both. She bustled around the house, tidying things, putting the flowers in Fiona's favourite vase, and even placing a quilt over Fiona's lap when they finally settled down in front of the TV. It was as if Fiona were a sick child and Angela, her protective mum. Fiona had to admit it felt nice.

The next morning Angela had to go to work – she'd offered repeatedly to take the day off, saying her boss would certainly understand given the circumstances, but Fiona was quite looking forward to spending the day in bed. True, it was where she'd been for a while anyway, but now she had all the more reason to hide away from the world. She called her boss at the aged care centre, who was horrified to learn

Fiona had been a part of the situation that had dominated the news for the past day. To Jennifer's credit, she sounded understanding as she said that of course Fiona could have an extended leave of absence, but she added that it would be unpaid. Fiona wasn't surprised. Her sick leave had been exhausted weeks ago, and she was still over a year away from being able to access her long service leave. Realistically, she knew that in order to make ends meet she would soon have to return to work. Her savings would only take her so far, and Jacob's money hadn't come through yet. She may have been about ready to give up on life, but at only thirty-seven, she presumably had a lot more of it to come. She couldn't afford to lose her job.

For now, though, she told her boss she would need two more weeks, and she went back to her bed.

Chapter 22 – Rosie

Fortunately, the job of telling Jeffrey about Betty didn't fall to me. The police made that visit, although I imagined it in my head enough times that it felt as though I'd been there. Once I knew that he knew, I messaged him and asked if he wanted any help telling the kids what had happened.

"Thanks, R," he wrote back. "But I think this is one I'd better handle myself. Besides, you've been through enough."

His words were a relief. My heart broke for Jeffrey having to do that job, but I didn't want to take it on myself, either. It was unimaginably awful.

I didn't ask how he was coping, and he didn't ask about me. We both knew there were no words, and there was no point asking.

Tim came to collect me from the hospital. I wasn't physically hurt, but I was in shock and needed to be looked over. When Tim saw me, he grabbed me in a huge embrace. I stared straight ahead, dazed.

"I'm so sorry about Betty," he whispered into my neck. "I can't imagine how you must be feeling right now. You guys have always been so close."

Unsure of how to respond, I eventually just nodded. 'Close' felt like something you'd say about a neighbour or a workmate you were particularly fond of. It didn't even begin to cover the bond between Betty and me. Sometimes, it was as if I didn't know where I ended and she began.

"Does your Dad know?" Tim asked.

I nodded. I'd asked Jeffrey to tell Dad. Perhaps it was spineless, but I couldn't face breaking my Dad's heart like that, and I wasn't sure that hearing me break down would be beneficial for him at all. At any rate, Jeffrey seemed to understand and he'd called back to tell me, in a sombre tone, that Dad had been informed. "I should go to him," I said suddenly.

"To your dad?" Tim asked, and I nodded. "If you're sure," he said dubiously, rubbing my back. "Are you sure you don't just want to go home?"

"No," I said adamantly. My main priority was making sure Dad was okay, but I couldn't deny my other, more selfish motive. I didn't want to go home. Not now.

"Alright," said Tim, walking me to the car with his arm around me, as though I might collapse at any moment. "Wherever you think is best."

I called Dad to ask if it was okay for me to come and join him, and he said yes between gasping sobs. If possible, my heart broke even further. Mum had died four years ago, and Betty and I, along with his grandkids, were Dad's world. I didn't know how he'd cope now. I made a promise to myself that I'd go and see him more often, now that I was his only living child.

His only living child. I shivered involuntarily. It was such an alien concept to live with. However hard I tried, I couldn't make any sense of it. I wondered if I ever would.

Teddy, Dad's silky terrier, greeted me at the door, and the sight of him set me off again. Why? I had no idea. Betty liked Teddy, but it wasn't as though they had a particular bond. I think it was just seeing something so sweet and innocent that made me crumble. Between what had happened to Betty and the terror I'd gone through in the siege, the world seemed so much bigger and scarier than it ever had before.

Dad and I tearfully embraced, and then he and Tim exchanged an awkward hug, as men do. "I'm so sorry for your loss," Tim said, his voice husky, and Dad nodded wordlessly in response.

I looked at Tim. "Do you mind going to get me an overnight bag?" I asked him. "I don't need much, just some PJs and some clothes for tomorrow. I'll come home then." I paused, then added "no need for you to stay." I begged him with my eyes not to argue.

Tim nodded. "Of course. Do you want anything, Phil?" he asked, and my dad shook his head.

Our place wasn't far from Dad's, just a twenty-minute journey each way. Dad was silent for a while, then hesitantly asked me about what I'd seen.

"If you're not ready to talk about it, I understand," he said softly. "But I just wondered... was it quick?"

I closed my eyes, flashing back to the coffee shop. I didn't blame Dad for asking. If I hadn't been there I would need to know, too. I couldn't stop thinking about it anyway, so there was no harm in telling him the basics.

"It was, actually," I replied. "Quicker than I expected. One minute she was there, and the next she was on the floor." It had been one of those moments that was both instantaneous and seemed to last forever, actually, but I didn't need to go into all of that. For Betty, it had probably been quick. At least, that was what I had to tell myself.

"And you? You weren't hurt?"

I shook my head. "Not physically. A bit of shock, but I'm okay. I guess I'll be a little traumatised for a while," I added with a shaky laugh. "I mean, I would have been even without what happened to Betty." I felt tears sting my eyes once more as I said those words.

I paused a minute, collecting myself, and then continued. "But I'm going to get counselling. I'll be okay." I grabbed his hands, wanting to feel human affection again. "I'm so sorry, Dad. I can't imagine what you're going through." Losing a sister was hard enough, but I couldn't imagine what it was like to lose a child.

"We're going through it together," Dad replied, squeezing my hands in return. "You can stay here for as long as you like."

I smiled, leaning in closer to him. "I just might take you up on that."

Chapter 23 – Destiny

The first week was rough. She slept surprisingly well most nights, thanks to a cocktail of exhaustion and newly-prescribed sleeping pills, but the mornings were hell. Destiny would lie awake for five or ten glorious seconds before everything came rushing back.

The gunman. The bullets. Luke.

After all of those memories, it was tough to leave her bed.

Of course, everyone had rallied around her. She hadn't seen many of her uni friends yet, aside from Gemma, but they'd sent her nice messages to let her know they were thinking of her. Her mum barely left her side and had even taken the week off for "carers' leave". Her older brother Ben was surprisingly gentle with her.

It all just made her feel worse.

"Stop being so *nice* to me!" she exploded to Gemma one afternoon.

Gemma had stopped by with a hot chocolate, Desi's favourite, and was asking her too many sympathetic questions about how she was coping. Destiny knew it came from a good place, but enough was enough. She and her best friend had never been hesitant to share sarcastic banter before. She needed at least one thing to be normal.

Gemma looked surprised, then smiled. "Okay, you stupid bitch."

It was enough to force a slight laugh out of Destiny. "See?" she said. "That's all I ask for."

"Treat 'em mean, keep 'em keen," Gemma quipped, lying down on the bed beside Destiny as she seemed to relax. "Thank God. I mean, I've had enough of being nice to you to last a lifetime."

Destiny laughed softly. "You really didn't need much convincing to turn on me, did you?"

Her friend shrugged. "Nastiness is my natural state. Why deny it?"

Gemma hadn't asked anything about the day of the shooting, and Destiny was grateful for that. She didn't want to share the details, to relive the moment any more than she already did every time she was alone with her thoughts.

"Anyway," Gemma said, popping a Malteser in her mouth and speaking through her food, "I have a present for you."

Reaching into her bag, she pulled out a package, and Destiny burst out laughing.

A while ago, one of the more obnoxious girls in their unit tutorial, April, had received a "care package" from her long-distance boyfriend, which she'd decided to bring to uni with her instead of leaving it at home like a normal person. She'd made a big show of displaying the teddy bear and cards he'd given her, cradling the bear tenderly in her arms and reading the notes over and over throughout the lesson, sometimes aloud to the people around her.

The notes had been "activity cards" for her to do when she was missing him. Things like "take a bubble bath", "go for a long walk" and most hilariously, "look at photos of us together". Destiny and Gemma had giggled together about how repulsively saccharine the couple obviously were. What sort of twenty-something guy wrote those sorts of activity cards for their girlfriend, or even thought that way? Gemma had even suggested the "boyfriend in Perth" might be entirely fictional, although Destiny wasn't really convinced about that. Of course, April was all besotted by it but from an outsider's perspective, it was truly revolting.

Gemma had taken the activity card idea and run with it. She presented Destiny now with a cute teddy bear clutching a little envelope, and Destiny knew what the contents would be before she opened it.

The envelope was filled with notes, written on plain lined paper with uneven cutting, clearly an attempt by Gemma to make the whole thing look as lame as possible. Her version of "activity cards" included such activities as "eat a whole cake by yourself #selfcake", "conduct an exorcism" and "burn the whole damn city to the ground".

"It's great advice," Destiny told her friend, nearly crying with laughter as she read through the cards. She gave her an impromptu hug. "Thank you!" It was the first time she'd laughed since it had happened.

Destiny and Gemma had met on their second day of uni, three years earlier, and they'd been close ever since. They always found a way to giggle together, even in the most boring of lectures. One day, they'd made a list of the people in their tutorial group and picked the order in which they'd vote them out of their classes. They didn't know all their names, so they dubbed them things like "girl with the big eyes" and "too many questions guy". It wasn't intended to be mean-spirited; it just made the girls laugh, and it passed the time. Destiny actually loved learning, but some of the lecturers just seemed to like the sound of their own voices too much for her.

Another day, their group of six friends had tried, with a moderate amount of success, to start a stadium wave in their lecture. It had taken a few rounds for the people around them to start noticing what was going on and begin to join in, but it had never really taken off the way they'd hoped.

Then there was the lecturer who said "okay" at the end of virtually every sentence. Once they'd noticed the pattern, they'd started keeping a tally of all the "okay"s in their notebooks. It got to the point where they had to resolutely look away from each other every time the lecturer uttered the word, so they didn't break out into hysterics in the middle of class.

Destiny had always been grateful to have Gemma in her life, but until now, she hadn't really known what a true gift her friendship was.

Chapter 24 – Paula

Paula and Ollie spent the first week after the shooting practically catatonic.

"I'm worried about you," Alfie said when he came home from work for the fifth day in a row to find Ollie slumped in front of the TV, Paula lying on the couch staring blankly into nothingness.

"You try going through a siege and see how you feel afterwards," Paula griped.

Alfie sighed. "I'm sympathetic, Paula, I'm not criticising you. I'm trying to *help* you here. This isn't healthy for you or Ollie." He paused. "I think you should see someone, like Dr Tyson suggested."

Paula nodded mutely. It wasn't that she was opposed to seeing someone, as such. But when it took all your strength just to get up and put clothes on in the morning, the thought of scheduling therapy appointments seemed like an insurmountable challenge.

As if reading her mind, Alfie said "I can make the appointment for you, if that's easier."

"Sure," she sighed, relenting. "A family therapist or something would be good, if you can. I'd like us both to attend together."

Alfie nodded. "I'm sure I can find someone."

True to his word, Alfie lined up an appointment for all three of them with a family counselling centre two days later.

Paula was glad her husband was there so he could do some of the talking, but she hadn't really gone into the details about the day of the siege even with Alfie. And, of course, there was Ollie. Paula had thought the family therapist idea made sense, but now she realised just how hard it was going to be to share her emotions in front of her son, who had already been through so much. She didn't want him to take on the burden of her feelings as well as his own.

Ollie's teacher and the kids in his class had sent hand-drawn cards and little gifts, which was sweet, but Paula couldn't imagine him ever returning to school. She never wanted to let him leave her side again. Not that being by her side was any safer, she thought glumly. She hadn't been able to protect her boy. She'd let him get shot! Thinking about that day kept her up at night. When she finally did sleep, she had horrendous dreams that sometimes felt worse than just being awake. It wasn't what she would call restful.

The therapist, an older man named Harold, had a gentle nature which put her somewhat at ease. More importantly, Oliver seemed to warm to him when Harold gave him a mock-formal handshake and sat him down on the chair right next to the doctor's own. When they were settled, Harold looked at Paula and said "Mrs Warner, your husband mentioned that you and young Oliver here were involved in the siege at Alpine Shopping Centre."

Paula nodded; Alfie had made a point of explaining the situation when he made the appointment, so the doctor was aware before they met. She was grateful. It was going to be hard enough to talk about without her having to start the conversation.

"Can you tell me more about that?"

Paula took a deep breath, pondering the question. "Well, I'm sure you know all the logistics of it from the news," she said. "It didn't take long... less than half an hour all up. It felt like a lifetime." Her voice started trembling, and she took another breath to steady herself before continuing. As she spoke, she forgot her concerns about saying too much in front of her son. She couldn't have stopped the words coming out if she'd tried. She explained how the gunman had taken them all by surprise; how she felt like she and Ollie were sitting ducks, standing out in the open by the counter; how she'd looked directly at the gunman and seen how out of control he appeared. She didn't mention how she still saw his face every time she closed her eyes. "My only saving grace is that he committed suicide," she finished off, exhausted. "I can't imagine having to go through a trial on top of everything else. I don't think I would have the strength."

Harold nodded his understanding. "That must all have been very difficult for you," he said. "Now, Oliver, can you tell me about your experience that day?"

Ollie glanced at his mum, who nodded at him. "If you feel comfortable, buddy, you can talk," she said in what she hoped was a soothing tone. "That's what we're here for." Paula smiled, rubbing her hands up and down his back in comfort.

"It's like Mum said. There was a man with a gun," Ollie said in a small voice, looking down at his hands. "I thought we were all going to die."

Paula's heart went out to him. It was far from a surprising revelation, given the circumstances, but hearing her son articulate his feelings like this was gut-wrenching. As a parent, you couldn't help but want to shield your child from the horrors of the world, but one simple outing had changed all of that.

She just hoped Ollie would recover.

Chapter 25 – Rosie

In the end, my one night at Dad's turned into several. I didn't even go home to collect more things, but I took a trip to the shops near Dad's house and bought enough casual clothes, pyjamas and toiletries to last me for a while. I bought a few chick lit books, too. I normally gravitated towards crime and thrillers, but I was avoiding those for a while, for obvious reasons. It was a wasted effort, though. Even the most light-hearted of my new books couldn't hold my attention, so I started spending my downtime in front of the TV, watching mindless sitcoms and reality TV shows. I couldn't even really concentrate on them.

It wasn't just Dad's TV that got me through that week. Dad and I leaned on each other, which gave me the kind of support I wouldn't have received at home. Dad, being on his own, needed me, too. In the few years since Mum had died, I'd considered asking Dad if he wanted to move in with me, and now it seemed even more imperative that I do so. I didn't say anything to him now; I would need to talk to Tim first, but that wasn't something I wanted to do right now. He kept calling, of course, but I didn't pick up. I couldn't. I had nothing to say.

Two days after Betty died, Jeffrey and the kids came over. My stomach had sunk when I'd heard they were coming. Of course I adored my niece and nephews, and my brother-in-law and I had always been quite close, but I couldn't stomach the idea of seeing them without Betty. Just knowing I would never see the family of five together again made me want to throw up.

When their car pulled up and they walked to the door, though, the feelings disappeared. Despite everything, I was happy to see them. The children walked slowly, their heads bowed. Normally happy, energetic little kids, I was certain I'd never seen them so sombre before. I let Dad greet them first. As miserable as I was, I knew he had to feel even worse. I hugged Jeffrey while Dad went to the children, then I greeted each of my nephews and my niece in turn. Archer looked particularly troubled. He'd always been a serious child, quiet and observant. At seven, he now looked like he had the weight of the world on his shoulders. Harrison was also quiet, for him. He was the livewire of the family, but now he didn't say much, and his brown eyes were filled with tears. My heart went out to him.

Of the three kids, Poppy seemed to be faring the best. She was quiet, yes, but she was the only one to greet me with a smile and when I went to hug her, she threw her arms around me with more exuberance than I'd expected. I wondered how much she understood, at only four years old. Did children of that age really grasp the permanence of death? Of course, Harry was not yet six, so might not be much better off, but he seemed to have an awareness his sister didn't. I also wondered, all of a sudden, whether the children would be affected by my appearance, so similar to that of their beloved mother. They didn't seem to be, though. It wasn't as if they'd ever confused us before. Somehow, even when they were really little, they always seemed to be able to tell the difference

between us. The small subtle differences must be more noticeable to a child, or maybe the bond with their mum was
just that strong.

Betty had always been a great mum. She'd married young
and become a mother not long after. Archer had been an
"oops" baby soon after the wedding, and she was just shy of
twenty-three when he was born. To no one's surprise, she'd
handled it with grace and seemed to take motherhood in her
stride, despite juggling finishing her studies and then beginning her career at the same time. She confided in me about
how the sleepless nights took their toll on her, and how she
felt constantly torn between being a good mother and being a good nurse. No one else would have known, though. I
wasn't even sure she'd told Jeffrey how hard it was on her. At
any rate, she'd ended up with three beautiful, sunny-smiled,
well-adjusted children, so she must have done some things
right. It would be so hard for Jeffrey to raise the kids without
Betty. I had always thought it was a tragedy that my own
mother got to see so little of her grandkids' lives, but this was
something else entirely.

Now, Dad and I ushered the kids and Jeffrey inside.
"Would you guys like a soft drink?" Dad asked them, and
they all responded eagerly. Betty had hated the kids drinking
anything sugary, but Dad loved spoiling them, so she had
eventually made a deal that they could have a soft drink at
Grandad's, as a special treat. It was something they'd come to
expect.

While Dad fixed the drinks for the kids, I made tea for
the adults and we all settled in on the comfy lounges in Dad's
living room. "How have you guys been?" I asked, careful not

to ask too much in front of the kids until Jeffrey led the conversation that way.

"We're okay," Jeffrey replied tiredly, and Harrison said softly "Mummy died."

My stomach twisted again at the sad simplicity of his words. "I know, baby," I said sadly. "But you know your Mummy loved you all very, very much."

The kids nodded – there was no doubting that. "And she was brave," I added. "She was so brave." I thought of Betty, standing strong in front of the gunman, gripping my hand.

We all talked for a few minutes, before Jeffrey suggested the kids go and play on the iPad in Dad's rumpus room. Once they were settled, Jeffrey said "we need to talk about the funeral arrangements."

Dad and I nodded. We'd said the same thing the day before, but neither of us could begin thinking logically about it yet.

In a strange way, I'd always kind of liked funerals. Well, 'liked' was a strong word, but they were so cathartic, such a wonderful way to say goodbye. My mum's funeral had been hard, but there'd also been a sense of healing. 'Beautiful', everyone had said afterwards. But Mum had died at the end of a long cancer battle, and she'd been nearly seventy at the time. Death was always hard, but at least for Mum, it had felt like she was truly better off. Betty was young, healthy and in the prime of her life. It was impossible to make sense of.

THE FUNERAL ENDED UP being held exactly a week to the day of Betty's death. It was the first time I'd seen Tim since he'd dropped me to Dad's place a week earlier. He tried to sit by me but I kept him at arm's length, explaining that I needed to be there for Dad and for the children.

"Someone needs to be here for *you*, though," Tim argued back with me.

I shook my head. "I'm okay. Today, I'm a daughter and an aunty. Today, I'm a sister," I told him, and I went over to pick up Harry, who was sitting on the step at the church entrance and crying his little heart out.

The funeral was a nice farewell to someone we didn't want to say farewell to. Some of Betty's favourite songs were played, and Jeffrey and I had put together a slideshow of photos of her. There were so many happy memories behind the photos that I found myself smiling, in spite of myself. In the eulogy Jeffrey tried to tell as many funny stories about Betty as possible, to lighten the sombre mood. Dad had suggested we ask guests to wear a touch of pink, Betty's favourite colour, and almost everyone did so. Despite the horrible circumstances of her death the day felt like a celebration of her life, rather than a day of mourning. It was just the way Betty would have wanted it.

I looked at the framed photo of Betty on top of the coffin. There were so many pictures to choose from, but for this one we had selected a photo of her on her wedding day, all dressed in her gown and veil. She looked so radiant and so happy. I stared at it, trying to commit that to memory.

I hoped that one day soon I would remember Betty like that, rather than thinking about her lying on the floor on that awful day.

Chapter 26 – Fiona

After the siege, Fiona's doctor prescribed her anti-depressants. She'd been refusing them since that horrible night a month ago but now her doctor was more insistent, and Fiona was less inclined to resist. She'd grown up with a sort of stigma around anti-depressants or any kind of therapy, because her mother hadn't believed in either, and had scoffed at people who were 'weak-willed' enough to require intervention. Well, now Fiona was one of them, but she was old enough to make her own decisions.

Somewhat to her surprise, the drugs didn't make her feel weak at all. In fact, they helped her get through the day. She wasn't squealing with *joie de vivre* and taking up gymnastics or anything, but it became easier to leave her bed. Or maybe it was simply the passage of time that did that.

She had a few therapy appointments, too. They helped a bit, but she didn't rush to go back. Against all reason, she had hoped that the first appointment would cure all her issues and make her feel like herself again. When not only the first, but also the second and third appointments, failed to do that, she decided to call it quits. She could be miserable talking to a therapist about her problems, or she could be miserable at home. It didn't seem to matter much. At least at home she got to wear her pyjamas.

Fiona had always had a small circle of friends. Of course, there was Angela. Her neighbour, Katie, had also become invaluable to her more recently. Adam, her closest friend from work, was great, and he'd been in regular touch since everything had happened. He and his husband Julian had even invited her to stay with them, saying she shouldn't be alone in an empty house. She'd declined the invitation, but she'd been grateful for it. Still, there were very few people in her for life for her to lean on, particularly with her parents and brother in Canberra. She'd never been particularly close to her brother, Chris, anyway.

Fiona's lack of a social circle had never really bothered her before; she'd always been introverted, and she'd always thought that quality was far more important than quantity when it came to people around you. She had to admit, though, even as she hid from the world, that it would be nice to have a few more people notice that she was missing from it.

When telemarketers called, Fiona never ignored the calls the way some people did, or hung up on them, or strung them along for her entertainment. She always gave them the time of day and let them make their spiel. If it was a survey, she would complete it. If they were selling something, she would give it serious consideration. Fiona had always assumed it was because she was, simply, a nice person. These people were just doing their jobs, and there was no harm in letting them do so.

It took her a while to consider that maybe the reason she was so eager to talk to them was just because she was lonely.

A week to the day after the shooting, Angela came over in the morning. Fiona was surprised when she opened the door to see her friend standing there. "Why aren't you at work?" she blurted out. Angela worked at an accounting office, so it was unusual to see her on a weekday.

"Called in sick," Angela said with a quick grin, breezing in past Fiona without waiting to be invited.

Fiona closed the door behind her and looked at Angela in surprise. "That's not like you."

Angela shrugged. "I mean, it's not like me to just take any old day off, but today is not just any old day."

"It's not?" Fiona tried to think what she was forgetting.

"It's not. This, my friend, is the first day of the rest of your life."

Fiona frowned. "Are you writing greeting cards now or something?"

Angela laughed. "I knew you'd be cynical! No, I've decided you've wallowed long enough, and it's time to move on and start living your life. I'm here to make it happen."

"It's only been a week," Fiona pointed out pragmatically.

Angela turned more serious. "I'm not talking about the shooting."

Chapter 27 – Destiny

The first time Destiny saw the rest of the uni group was at Luke's funeral, and that thought was so ludicrous it almost made her laugh despite herself. They were too young to be at a funeral, unless it was a grandparent's or something. Luke was too young to die. But here they were.

Courtney, Ed, Nate and Gemma were gathered around together, all looking quiet and solemn. They'd arranged to come together, but Destiny had travelled with her mum. She swallowed a sob when she saw her friends. It had always been the six of them, and being together like this now, as a group of five, truly made the loss sink in.

She ran to them, and Nate was the first to greet her, his long, thin, brown limbs wrapping around her own. "I'm so sorry, Desi," he whispered in her ear, and she let go and started sobbing in earnest. Nate was always quick with a grin, and more laidback than most of the other members of their group of six. She'd never before seen him looking so serious. It was devastating to see.

Courtney and Ed came up to greet her as well. They were the two members of the group Destiny had always been a little more removed from. They were a couple, having partnered up in their first year of uni. All six of them got along well as a group, but one-on-one, Destiny always felt a little awkward around them. She always felt like they thought they were better than everyone else. Team Co-Ed against the world. Still, the two gave her hugs now and whispered about how awful it all was.

The five of them all had tears on their faces by the time they'd finished their greetings. They looked at each other wordlessly for a minute, then Gemma said hoarsely "we should go in. The seats will be filling up fast."

Like most funerals for young people, Luke's was packed with people. It was only a small chapel, and by the time the service started there were rows and rows of people standing behind the chairs. Desi's mum sat with the group as well, squeezing her daughter's hand. Destiny started sobbing in earnest before the service started and didn't stop until she was on her way home with her mum. The reunion with the uni group had been short but sweet. They said they would all catch up for a burger the following week. Burgers were Luke's favourite, so it seemed only fitting, though it seemed so wrong that he wouldn't be there with them.

After the funeral, Destiny started to heal a little more. Of course, there was no getting over something like that, but things were a little brighter. Routine was her friend. She got up in the morning and went for a jog, or blasted music loudly and danced along in her room to it. The endorphins helped. After her morning exercise, she had breakfast, writing in her journal as she ate. She hadn't kept a journal since primary school, but it was astonishing how much difference it made to her mental health. She bought a mindful colouring book, which she'd always dismissed as a silly fad, and coloured it in each night when she got home. She returned to her uni classes, even attending the ones she didn't really need to in order to pass. She even took some shifts at the clothing store where she had a part-time job. Anything that kept her mind off things for a little while was helpful.

She was doing as well as anyone in her circumstances could be. But then she had her planned lunch with the uni group, and all of her good work was undone.

Chapter 28 – Rosie

On the Thursday after the funeral, I went home.

There was no choice, really. I couldn't stay at Dad's forever, as much as I might have liked to right then and there. In the long run, it wasn't good for either of us. Dad would get too comfortable having me there, and I would just find it harder and harder to face my real life if I didn't return to it soon. His neighbour, Brenda, a lovely lady not much younger than Dad, had promised to check in on him now and again, so at least I knew he had someone around looking after him.

Following the same line of thought about life going back to normal, I called my boss and arranged to return to work the following Wednesday. I didn't want to go back, but I didn't want to sit around the house merging with the couch, either. I wanted the pain to go away, and perhaps work would provide a distraction. I deliberately picked Wednesday for my first day back, since it was one of our quieter days. The idea of going back for the weekend rush wasn't appealing.

When Tim came home after work, he seemed surprised to see me. I hadn't messaged and told him I was coming, and I'd barely acknowledged him at the funeral. "Hey, hon," he said, coming over and kissing my forehead. I was curled up on the couch, having showered and put pyjamas on the minute I got home, even though that had been only just after midday. "I didn't know you were coming home."

I shrugged. "I didn't really plan it." That was true. I'd given it some thought the night before, but hadn't made my final decision until that morning.

"Well, I'm definitely happy to have you," Tim grinned. "Can I get you a drink or something? I was just going to have a toastie for dinner, but this calls for something a bit more 'real', I think."

"I'm fine, thanks. And I'm happy with a toastie." I hadn't had much appetite since that awful day.

Tim shook his head as he opened a fresh bottle of wine. "No, we're celebrating," he said, pouring himself a glass. "It's so good to have you home! Let's get pizza or something."

"Sure." It really didn't matter to me one way or another. I waved away the wine as he held it up to offer me.

He came and sat down beside me on the couch. "Have you given any more thought to returning to work?" he asked. I nodded, filling him in on my planned return the following week. "I'm not sure how I'll go," I said, "but it shouldn't be too awful."

The thought had crossed my mind that going back to a dining establishment might bring back memories of that day, but our classy Italian restaurant was far removed from the open, casual coffee shop. Besides, I couldn't just avoid eating out for the rest of my life and I wasn't about to change careers now, either. Throwing myself back into things was possibly the best solution.

Tim ordered pizza as promised, and kept up a steady stream of chatter as the evening went on. I was quiet, but he didn't seem to mind, likely putting it down to my trauma or the strangeness of returning home after more than a week away.

I knew I was shutting Tim out, but I couldn't help myself. If our relationship was to continue I knew I needed to work through my feelings, maybe talk to him about them. But I couldn't face it right now and for now, at least, he seemed to tolerate that.

Of course, part of my problem was watching my sister die in front of me, while fearing for my own life. That was enough to throw anybody off for quite a while. I would never get over the loss of Betty. But there was more to it than Tim knew, and I wasn't ready to tell him yet.

When I'd got dressed that morning, I had planned to tell Betty my own little secret. But what she'd told me was far more devastating.

Chapter 29 – Paula

Things weren't going well in Paula's house.

Ollie's arm still wasn't back to regular use, and between the pain and nightmares, he was waking up screaming most nights. Paula was barely able to sleep and usually only managed to doze off around one in the morning, only to be awakened again by her son's cries. No parent ever wanted to hear their child upset, but now his screams instantly sent an icy shiver through her veins, in a way they never had before. She wondered if that, too, would be permanent.

And then there was Jasmine.

Jasmine had trembled all over when they'd got home and told her that they were part of the siege she'd been hearing all about on social media. She had thrown her arms around both her mother and brother, and Paula had noticed her eyes had even become a little teary as she pulled back from the embrace. It had touched Paula. Of course she had known that her daughter would be horrified to hear she was in danger, but getting affection from the often-moody teenager had been difficult at times, so for it to be given so easily now made Paula want to cry.

As if to make up for the unexpected show of emotion, Jasmine had pulled back from her even further in the week afterwards.

Three days after the shooting, Paula had received a call from Jasmine's school. Jasmine had returned to school only that day, after having a couple of days at home with the rest of her family following the shock of the incident. In a solemn voice, the school principal informed her that Jasmine and her friends had been caught smoking in the school toilet.

Paula had been shocked – perhaps it showed that she lived a sheltered life, but Jasmine had never really been in trouble at school before, and Paula had no idea that she'd even tried a cigarette. The fact that she was willing to light up in the toilets on her lunch break was... well, it was shocking.

Alfie had been more relaxed about it, saying it was normal to experiment and that the principal was making a mountain out of a molehill. Paula supposed there was some truth to that – she'd tried cigarettes as a teenager, and had passed out from drinking too much at a party one time when she was seventeen. But it was different when it was your own child. Besides, she wasn't prepared for something like this so soon after Paula and Ollie had been through such a traumatic event. This was the last thing she needed. Didn't Jasmine *think*?

Things only got worse after that. The school gave Jasmine detention and Paula and Alfie had lectured her about it for a long time, but Jasmine didn't seem particularly fazed by either. She'd been surly to both of her parents for most of the time since, and was even snarling at her brother, who had already been through so much.

Now, Paula sat downstairs with a book in front of her. Theoretically she was reading, but the words just swam in front of her eyes. Ollie was watching TV, but Paula suspected he wasn't paying much more attention than she was. Suddenly, the front door slammed. Paula and Ollie both jumped in their seats at the sound.

"Jasmine!" Paula griped, turning to frown at her daughter. "You nearly gave us both a heart attack!" Ollie had instantly turned white as a ghost. Paula had noticed over the last few days that loud noises seemed to scare him now in a way they never had before. It was natural, of course, but also heartbreaking for her kind, curious little guy. She hoped it was only temporary.

Jasmine rolled her eyes. "Whatever," she muttered under her breath, throwing her schoolbag down and going to walk upstairs to her room.

"Not *whatever!*" Paula said, frustrating rising in her throat. "It's not that hard to say *sorry, Mum.* Actually, it doesn't take any more effort to say that than your fucking *whatever!*"

Jasmine and Oliver were both staring at her now. Paula didn't often swear, and she'd almost never done it in front of her kids. It was enough to shame a quiet "sorry" out of Jasmine before she ran upstairs.

Paula knew she was overreacting, and that her response to her daughter's behaviour was only going to escalate an already unpleasant situation. But she was only human. She hadn't been in control of her emotions since the shooting, and she wasn't sure she ever would be again.

Chapter 30 – Fiona

At the sound of Angela's words, Fiona was transported back in time.

Everyone had come to the funeral – Jacob's friends, her friends, his workmates, her workmates. Her parents and brother had flown up from Canberra. It was a huge gathering.

Afterwards, everyone disappeared.

Not immediately, of course. Most people offered their support in the days before and after the funeral, but by the time a fortnight had passed, almost everyone had dropped out of touch. Her family had been good to her, but they'd eventually had to resume their own lives in Canberra, which she couldn't blame them for.

Fiona knew part of this was human nature – people rallied around you in a time of grief, but there was an expiration date. Plus, it was partly her fault, and she was willing to acknowledge that. She hadn't taken anyone up on going out for a lunch date or bringing dinner to her place, so why would they keep offering?

Her husband had been her entire world, and now he was gone.

If it wasn't love at first sight, it was definitely the next best thing. They'd met online and she'd been instantly drawn to him, and the feeling was clearly mutual. Aside from a physical attraction, they seemed a perfect example of the old adage of opposites attracting. He was as gregarious as she was quiet, and it was the first time in her life that she'd had so many conversations that flowed so easily. She loved that feeling.

Neither of them had wanted kids. They'd both been pretty clear on that since the moment they'd met, twelve years earlier. They were both in their twenties at the time, and when they got engaged people had said they'd change their mind, that they'd realise a marriage was nothing without children. They were wrong. Their marriage was all they needed, and they'd never regretted it.

Now, though... she wasn't so sure. A part of Fiona, a large part, was grateful that she didn't have children to look after. Their children would still be relatively young, and she was having enough trouble getting through life herself, without being responsible for little people. On the other hand, they would have been a tangible piece of Jacob that she could still hold dear to her. A daily reminder of him, running around the house. Maybe then, she wouldn't feel quite so alone.

Of course, it wasn't simply grief that she was feeling. There was guilt, too. Soul-crushing, soul-destroying guilt.

If it weren't for her, Jacob would still be alive.

Chapter 31 – Destiny

Destiny had seen some of the uni group at classes in the two weeks that had passed since the funeral, but this was the first time they had all been together. She felt a shiver down her spine at the thought of catching up now as a group of five, with a gaping hole where Luke should be sitting. She tried to put on a brave face when they arrived at the American-style diner, smiling and greeting her friends as though everything was normal. Destiny knew that the fact that she and Luke had been on a date the day of the shooting had been common knowledge, even though they'd never officially announced it to the group as such. She'd told Gemma, of course, and Luke had told Nate and somewhere along the way the word had spread to the other two. She knew Nate and Ed were pretty tight.

Once they'd ordered their cheeseburgers and shakes, Nate asked how she was coping. "Yeah, okay," she said with a small smile. "It's been weird, but this week has been a little better. I mean, I'll always miss him." With those words, she looked down at her lap and bit her lip, trying not to cry. She was so sick of crying.

"Sure," Ed muttered.

Destiny frowned, her heart rate instantly accelerating in a fight-or-flight reflex. Ed hadn't said much, but she knew him well enough to know that it wasn't a consoling kind of "sure". She tried to stay calm. "Ed?" she ventured.

Her friend looked over at her. "I mean, it just seems like you've gotten back to normal pretty quickly. You're already back in classes... and you don't exactly look like a basket case." Destiny's face instantly flushed. She'd been making an effort with her appearance every morning, but it was all a front. All of it. She'd convinced herself that if she looked good, she'd feel good. It hadn't worked so far, but she kept trying. It was probably shallow, but her physical appearance was one small part of her life that she felt like she still had control over.

"Ed," Nate said softly, his voice a warning.

Ed glared hotly back at him. "You of *all* people know how into Desi Luke was," he snapped. "I'm just saying, he literally took a bullet for her. Obviously, he didn't mean as much to her. She hasn't even stopped putting on makeup."

At that, the tears that had been threatening Destiny spilled down her cheeks. "Luke meant everything to me," she cried, her voice coming out sounding weaker than she wanted. She hated that she was crying, but she couldn't stop herself. "I think I actually... loved him." She hadn't said the words out loud before, but they were true. She had been besotted with Luke, had fantasised about being with him, for so long. It felt like love to her.

As soon as the words were out, though, she wished she could take them back. They sounded so melodramatic, like she was a cheesy character in some romance novel. Even though the words were true, she knew Ed wouldn't be convinced.

Ed snorted again. "Bullshit. You were on your first date, and you were *in love?*" His tone was scathing. "I wish he hadn't taken that bullet for you. You aren't worth it."

"Ed, you arsehole!" Gemma looked like she was about to start crying, too. "Can't you see how upset she is? Just shut up!"

"Ed," Courtney said quietly, putting a hand on her boyfriend's arm. "You need to chill."

Destiny was surprised, but grateful, that Courtney was coming to her aid. She never would have picked that Courtney would side with Destiny over her own boyfriend, even when Ed was being unreasonable.

Ed shook his head. "I'm out," he snapped, walking out with his hand in a fist by his side.

Courtney threw a last look at them, muttered something that sounded vaguely like an apology, and took off after Ed.

The remaining trio sat in stunned silence for a minute, trying to come to terms with what had just happened. "I can't believe that," Nate said finally, shaking his head. "I'm sorry, Desi. He's just upset about Luke. He didn't mean any of it."

Destiny shook her head, still choking on her tears. "He did, Nate. You don't just say those things because you're upset. You could tell he meant it."

Nate fell silent again. He was trying to be a good friend to her, but there was no denying the truth of her words. There was pure poison in Ed's voice, and nothing but contempt on his face when he looked at her. He had meant every word.

"Did you mean what you said?" Nate ventured. "About being in love with Luke?"

Destiny nodded wordlessly, and Gemma reached across and put her hand on Desi's. Nate didn't say anything, but Destiny could see the sadness on his face. She was glad to have them both in her corner.

Their food arrived, but none of them were hungry.

Chapter 32 – Rosie

The rest of my first week at home continued in much the same way as my first day. Tim was trying his best to make things as normal as possible, but nothing was working. I kept him at a distance, which I guess he put down to some kind of post-traumatic stress response. It was easy enough to let him think that.

We had dinner together each night, but I was quiet, rather than my usual chatty self. When we watched TV together, I stared blankly ahead and then I would go upstairs for an early night. He didn't follow. He hadn't even tried to initiate sex since the shooting, probably because he knew how that would end for him. For the last fortnight, I'd barely let him kiss my cheek or put his arms around me. It was like we were simply roommates, and not particularly close ones at that.

Finally, after a week of dealing with my moody solitude, Tim asked me about it. I'd known the question was coming and he broached the topic gently, which I appreciated. Still, I didn't want to delve into anything.

"Do you think you should see a therapist?" he asked me quietly, stroking my arm. "I'm concerned about you, babe. You're not –"

"Don't you *dare* say I'm not myself."

"I wasn't going to," Tim said, but I could tell it wasn't true. "Look, don't keep pushing me away. I feel like I'm walking on eggshells around you at the moment! I'm worried about you, that's all. I know how close you and Betty were, and I get that I don't know what you're going through. But I'm here for you, Ro."

"I know you are," I said quietly. "But I don't need to see a therapist. And I don't want you." I knew I was hurting him, but I couldn't bring myself to feel anything about that, one way or another. "I only want Betty."

When I finally looked at Tim, I could see the pain in his eyes. "I'd give anything to bring her back for you," he said. I remained silent, not voicing the bitter thoughts that filled my mind. "But I can't, baby. I'm so sorry. I just wish there was something I could do to help you out. Just don't push me away."

A long, uncomfortable silence stretched out between us, and then I heard something astonishing. Tim was crying. Tim was not a crier. He'd shed a few tears at Betty's funeral, which was the first time I'd ever seen him so much as tear up, but now he was crying in earnest, his head in his hands.

"Tim," I breathed, reaching out to him. It was the first time I'd initiated physical contact since it all happened. I don't know whether I was moved by his tears, or touched by his obvious concern for me, or whether I was just taken aback. Whatever the cause, I was surprised at how good it felt to reach out to him, despite myself. I took him in my arms, burying his head against my shoulder. It felt so strange to be the one comforting him, but the role reversal felt strangely nice. For five minutes, I didn't have to be the basket case. I could be the strong one.

"I'm sorry," Tim said miserably. "I just wish I could make everything better for you. I feel like I'm losing you, and I... I can't do that."

You have to tell him, a voice inside my head urged me. And so, I said the words I'd been putting off.

Chapter 33 – Fiona

It had been a normal Saturday night when Jacob died, over a month ago now. It wasn't ominous, or stormy, or even overcast. There was no celestial warning about what was going to happen, and she couldn't blame it on the weather.

Jacob's friend Mike had invited them over for his 40th. It wasn't Fiona's idea of an ideal Saturday night, particularly so soon after all the socialising they'd done over the Christmas and New Year period. Jacob had been pretty insistent that they go, though, and Fiona had always liked Mike's wife, Colette. Finally, Fiona had started to look forward to it. She'd bought a new dress for the occasion, and had talked herself into having a good night.

Jacob had asked her before they went if they should get a taxi or if she'd be the designated driver, and she hadn't hesitated before saying that she was happy to drive. Fiona wasn't a huge drinker – she hated beer and spirits, and while she loved curling up on the couch with a wine at night, it always made her sleepy.

Jacob walked up behind her as she was getting ready and wolf-whistled. Fiona smiled at him, then at her reflection. She did look pretty good, actually, in her form-fitting charcoal dress. It had been a while since she'd got herself glammed up, and she was liking the effect. Clearly Jacob was, too. He sidled up beside her and kissed her neck, running his hands down the sides of her body.

Fiona sighed, feeling her body respond to his touch, but she pushed him away before he could go any further. "No point starting something now," she laughed. "We're going to be late."

"Not even a quickie?" Jacob asked, but Fiona shook her head. "Not after I've already done my hair and makeup." She wondered when sex had become something she thought about in such practical terms. There was a time when she would have needed to have him right then and there.

Jacob sighed. "Fine, but let's make it an early night, then," he said, a wicked glint in his eyes.

Fiona felt a stirring in her belly. Their sex life had always been pretty consistent, but it had certainly been a while since Jacob had looked at her so hungrily. At least she'd have something to look forward to all evening, she thought, smiling as she got her handbag and got ready to leave. She knew from past experience that the sex would be all the better after a night of anticipation.

The party turned out to be better than she'd expected. They normally were, honestly. She always had to talk herself into going out, but when she did, she was almost always glad she had made the effort. She chatted to Colette throughout the evening, as well as making small talk with a few other people she'd met before, and she and Jacob had given each other mischievous looks every so often. It made her feel like they were naughty teenagers, rather than a couple over ten years into their marriage.

Eventually, Jacob came up behind her and put his hand on her neck. "Ready to go?" he whispered in her ear. He'd had a few drinks, but hadn't gone too crazy, and she was grateful for that. She was so ready to jump on him when they got home, the last thing she needed was for him to pass out from exhaustion the way he often did when he'd been drinking. She hated the grumpy hangover that usually followed the next day, too.

The couple said their goodbyes and got into the car for the drive home. It was only a twenty-minute drive.

Jacob chatted amicably as they got into the car, filling her in on Mike's new job and their mutual friend Stu's new girlfriend, who was only in her early twenties. So many of the men she knew barely opened their mouths to speak, but Jacob had always been the chattier of the two of them. It was one of the things that had first attracted Fiona to him.

After a few minutes in the car, Jacob grinned at her. "You *do* look hot, you know," he murmured in her direction.

She laughed. "I must... or you're just horny," she teased.

He nodded. "That I am," he said, and moved a hand over to her thigh.

Fiona laughed, slapping his hand away. "Stop it, Jacob! I'm driving."

"Oh, really?" he asked. "Then I guess you don't want me to do this."

Fiona stared straight ahead, hands gripping the steering wheel more tightly as Jacob's hand found its way up her dress, reaching between her legs, pulling her underwear to the side.

"Uhhh," she sighed after a moment. "Okay, you really do need to stop. We'll get pulled over!"

"There's no one around," Jacob pointed out, his fingers still exploring.

She should have resisted more, but her resolve was slipping away. Jacob's hands on her body felt amazing. Besides, when was the last time they'd had a little harmless fun like this?

That was her last thought before she ran the red light.

Chapter 34 – Paula

In the three weeks since the shooting, Paula had grown to not only tolerate, but actually enjoy, going to therapy. She had never expected that, but it was a nice bonus. There were so few things she actually enjoyed nowadays. Something about sitting in the therapist's plain office, talking about herself, seemed like self-care. It was an odd sensation, but a welcome one.

Ollie seemed to be handling it well enough, too. Paula had been concerned about the effect of reliving the experience, but the therapist didn't ask them to go into too much detail about the day of the shooting itself, which was a relief. Instead, he talked about strategies they could try in the future to move them on from the events of that day. He also gently lectured Paula about the fact that Ollie needed to go back to school. She knew he was right; it had been too long already, and the longer he was away, the harder it would be for him to return. Keeping up academically seemed like an insignificant issue at the moment, but she knew in the long run it was really more important than she was giving it credit for. Besides, he should be with his friends. But it was hard for her to let her baby go, even to a supposedly safe space such as his school. After all, the local shopping centre had always been a safe space, too.

On the fourth Saturday after the shooting – the fourth Saturday of what she'd started to think of as her new life –

they went to a wedding. The kids weren't invited, so Alfie thought it would be a good opportunity for some quality time together, just the two of them. Paula wasn't in the mood for a wedding, but she went along, regardless. They'd accepted the invitation a long time ago and it wouldn't be right to cancel now. Besides, she reasoned with herself, she would probably start to enjoy it once she was actually there. Even if she didn't, it wasn't as though she'd be enjoying herself at home, either.

At the reception, she started getting into the swing of things. There were some lovely speeches, the meal was good and after the dinner came the dancing. At every wedding Paula had ever been to, she'd declared at the start of the night that she wouldn't be dancing this time, and at every wedding, she quickly gave in and got carried away. This wedding was no exception. Convinced that this was the time she'd stick to her guns, Paula had been surprised when the mood to join the crowd on the dance floor overtook her. She jumped up and started joining in on the Macarena and the Nutbush with everyone else. She was swirling, laughing, acting dizzy.

It took a while for the thought to hit her: she wasn't actually enjoying herself.

If anyone saw Paula, they would assume she was having the time of her life. Her mouth was open in a broad smile and she was giggling with her friend Rebecca as they danced together. (Of course, Alfie and Scott, Rebecca's partner, were both still seated.) But the realisation hit her like a tonne of bricks. She was playing a role, pretending to be the light-hearted party girl enjoying the wedding. Her mind was elsewhere.

It was a sobering realisation. At that moment, Paula wondered if she would ever actually, truly enjoy anything ever again.

Chapter 35 – Destiny

After her lunch with the uni group, Destiny slid back into her depression.

She could barely get out of bed in time for her classes, so her exercise routine was done for. She still went to uni, but only to the classes that marked attendance. Instead of having any form of a social life, she went to her classes and came home. Luckily the one class she had with Ed didn't have mandatory attendance, so she skipped out on those lectures and tutorials. All of the hard work she had done over the past couple of weeks had been undone.

Destiny knew it was crazy to let one person's words upset her so much. But the negative thoughts kept nagging at her.

Ed had been the only one to say it, but what if everyone else was thinking it, too? She'd never been convinced she was good enough for Luke, and Ed had basically said exactly that. His words were her worst fears coming true. Luke had made the ultimate sacrifice for her, and even she wasn't convinced it was a sacrifice worth making. If Destiny herself couldn't believe it, well, she couldn't expect anyone else to, either.

Gemma, of course, had been amazing. Destiny was still going to the class they had together, and Gemma usually dragged her out for a drink afterwards. Destiny didn't particularly want to go, but she didn't want to be alone with her thoughts, either. A few times a week Gemma would drop around some brownies or a casserole for dinner. She'd always loved cooking but had never made anything for Destiny before. Destiny was grateful for the gesture. Nate had tried to reach out a few times, but Destiny was avoiding him, too. He hadn't done anything wrong, but she still couldn't face him. He and Ed were too close for comfort right now.

"You can't go on like this," Destiny's mother told her after her fourth straight day of lying around the house.

Destiny sighed, rolling over to look at her mother. "I'll be fine." They could both see it wasn't true, but Destiny hadn't told her mother about Ed's harsh words, so she didn't know the half of it.

Janet sat down beside her on her bed, putting her hand on her daughter's arm. "I know you went through a horrible thing," she said, starting to choke up as she spoke. "I wish I could take it back. But sweetheart, I can't. I know Luke was special, and he meant a lot to you. But he wouldn't want you to go on like this. If he cared for you like I think he did, then this would break his heart like it's breaking mine."

Destiny knew that that was true, but she still couldn't help the way she was feeling. Sitting up, she told her mother what Ed had said.

Her mother gasped, putting a hand to her mouth. "That little bastard," she cried. Janet had never been a huge fan of Ed's. "I'll kill him, I swear. I knew you came back from that lunch worse than you had been, but I just thought it was because it was strange not having Luke there. Oh my God, Desi, how *dare* he!" Her fists were balling up with fury. Destiny put her hand on her mother's arm to try to calm her.

"I'm angry too," she said, "but he's got a point. I came in looking like nothing had happened to me, and his friend had just died for me." It hurt to say, but it was how she felt. "I'd have been upset, too, if I were him."

Janet frowned, her eyes still flashing with anger. "There's a difference between being *upset* and saying what he said to you. There's no excuse for that."

They talked it over for a while longer, and Destiny was surprised to find that opening up to her mother actually did make her feel a little better. She wasn't exactly sure why she'd been keeping it to herself. She didn't want to upset her mother more? Well, Destiny's forlorn appearance did that well enough. In case her mother sided with Ed? Of course she knew Janet would never do that, but the brain isn't always rational.

At the end of their conversation, Janet stood up. "I need to pick your brother up from footy, but are you sure you're going to be okay?"

Destiny nodded. "I'm fine. You can go."

She wasn't, of course, fine. But after her conversation with her mum, she had a newfound resolve to make herself that way, as soon as she could. She just had to figure out how to do that.

Chapter 36 – Rosie

Tim's face changed in an almost comical way when I told him about my pregnancy.

"You're – you are? But – how? When? Rosie!" he cried, scooping me up in a hug. I was slightly surprised by his exuberance. My pregnancy wasn't unplanned as such, but it wasn't planned, either. When we'd become serious, we'd briefly discussed whether we'd have kids or not. He, like me, was mostly ambivalent about the thought. I'd gone off the Pill for my own health reasons a while earlier and we hadn't used anything for protection since, figuring if it was meant to be, it would happen. Apparently, it was meant to be.

I laughed despite myself. "How – the usual way. When – I'm ten weeks along," I told him, and registered the surprise that came into his eyes.

"Ten weeks? Wow! That's a fair length of time, isn't it?" I knew what he meant. It was a fair length of time without telling him about the pregnancy.

I nodded. "I guess it took me some time to get my head around it." I'd never been great at tracking my cycle, and because we hadn't been actively trying it had taken a while to realise what was happening. I actually hadn't known myself for too long before that day in the coffee shop, when I had planned to tell Betty my news.

It had never occurred to me to tell Tim before my sister, even though it was his baby. I knew most people would have found that strange, including Tim, most likely. But Betty and I told each other everything first; we always had. It was a habit that long pre-dated Tim, and old habits are hard to break. My only regret was not getting the words out before she died. Aside from everything else, it was so strange living in a world where I was pregnant and Betty didn't know about it.

I had reflected on it often in the time since the shooting. How different would my life have been if I'd said "no, let me go first"? What would Betty have said and done afterwards? Would she have been able to get her own secret out before the gunman came in? Or knowing my news, would she have rethought the whole thing and decided to keep her secret to herself? If she hadn't told me, would I be better or worse off now?

Tim started chatting beside me, excitedly asking about my due date, talking about what our families would think and discussing what he'd need to do to the spare room to turn it into a nursery. For a moment everything felt so normal, as if we were just another couple sharing exciting news. I liked the feeling, and so I decided to keep it going for as long as I could. I leaned my head against Tim, feeling my shoulders relax. It felt strangely nice to let myself be a normal girlfriend again. I wondered how long I could keep that feeling going.

To be honest, when I'd first found out I was pregnant I wasn't sure how to feel. That was the other reason I had wanted to tell Betty first. Talking it over with her would get all of the confusing feelings out of the way before I had to deal with Tim's reaction, which I hadn't been sure about either. But seeing his excitement now, it was hard not to get carried away. Maybe this baby would be the symbol of hope we so desperately needed.

Chapter 37 – Fiona

"So," Angela said briskly, pulling Fiona back into the present, away from her thoughts about Jacob. "I present to you today, your four-step plan in becoming a new woman." She spoke in a mock-formal tone, as though she were doing a work presentation.

Fiona nodded, feeling a little dazed. "Is there a point to asking what this four-step plan entails, or should I just go with it?"

"Both," Angela laughed. "I'll happily fill you in on the finer points, but you *are* going along with it, so there's no point arguing. I told you," she added mock sternly, "this wallowing thing has gone on long enough."

Fiona knew that Angela was being cruel to be kind. Her friend had a point; it had been nearly two months now since Jacob had died, and Fiona had barely seen daylight since then. Of course, adding the siege in didn't help anything, but Fiona secretly knew she wouldn't have been all that much better off even if that hadn't happened.

"Step One: we're going shopping," Angela said, and held up her hand as Fiona started to protest. "I know what you're going to say, you can't face a shopping centre after what happened, and I've prepared for that response. You *can*, however, face a Sunday market, and you can definitely face online shopping. We're getting you some new clothes and makeup.

You're a gorgeous woman, so you might as well look like one."

Fiona smiled faintly. Gorgeous was a generous term – she'd never been one to worry too much about her appearance, and she'd always thought of her body as more of a way to get around than something to be flaunted. But then she thought of Jacob's eyes on her when she'd stepped into her form-fitting dress that night. She'd definitely felt gorgeous then. Despite everything that happened afterwards, that had been a special moment.

"Step Two: you're going out socially at least once a week."

"Who with?" Fiona grumbled, aware she was starting to sound like a petulant teenager.

"Well, me, of course, and I've been speaking to Katie and Adam with you and they both agree they'd love to see more of you, so there's your first three weeks all lined up. You can rotate us if you want to."

"And Step Three?"

"Step Three: you're going to start exercising again."

Fiona nodded. Her work at the aged care home had always provided plenty of incidental exercise, but she'd also enjoyed a weekly swim at the gym pool as well as a couple of weight-lifting sessions. It now occurred to her that she'd missed the rush she got from exercise. Also, even her tracksuit pants were starting to feel a little too fitted. The thought of getting back into an exercise routine didn't really excite her, but she knew it was probably necessary. This was one step she didn't have too many objections to, so she let Angela continue.

"Step Four: The one I'm personally most excited about," Angela said triumphantly. "We're going to an animal shelter!"

"A what?" Fiona stared at her friend. "Why on *earth* would I want to do that? Just to see creatures more miserable than me?"

"Welllllll." Angela drew out the sound for effect. "I thought maybe the house would feel a little bit more like a home if it had a four-legged friend in it, and I knew you'd be tough to convince. So, I thought perhaps if you actually went and *saw* some adorable dogs and cats in person..."

Fiona shook her head, ready to protest in earnest. She'd never – literally never! – owned a pet. She didn't know what was involved in it. She certainly didn't have the energy to give a pet the love and affection it deserved. Having a dog or cat in the house would just make things even harder than they already were.

But the stern look on Angela's face stopped her from saying anything. "Pointless to resist, remember," her friend said. "There's no harm in just going and seeing some animals. It's not like I'm *making* you adopt a pet."

Fiona sighed, relenting. "So, given you've taken the day off and everything, I assume Step One starts today?"

"Oh, don't let the numbers fool you," Angela replied breezily. "They're not in order. We're going to the animal shelter today."

"I can't today," Fiona protested weakly, and Angela arched an eyebrow at her. "Hectic schedule?" They both knew Fiona's plans didn't extend past the living room.

Fiona rolled her eyes. "Fine, but don't expect me to fall in love with some animal."

Chapter 38 – Rosie

As sweet and warm as the loved-up feeling I had with Tim was, I had known it couldn't last. Still, even I was surprised by how quickly it faded away. Well, not faded, so much. 'Fading' implied something that gradually disappeared. In reality, it was shocking in its abruptness. It wasn't so much that I didn't feel it anymore. It was that I couldn't let myself feel it.

Tim noticed, naturally. He had his faults, but he had always been fairly perceptive, especially when it came to me.

"You're pushing me away again," he said quietly one night as I was making dinner.

I wasn't sure how to respond, so I didn't. I thought of that horrible night when Tim broke down in front of me and I felt sympathy for him, but I still couldn't get past the wall of ice that had lodged inside my chest. It was a detached kind of sympathy – not the typical feeling you should have when it concerned your partner and the father of your unborn child.

"I really think you should see someone." This wasn't a new suggestion, but every time he said it, I just as quickly shrugged it away. This was one particular ache that therapy couldn't help. Losing your sister would be enough to strike anyone down with grief; seeing it happen right in front of you was clearly going to be traumatic; fearing for your own life would keep anyone awake at night. Having all three things happen at the same time was a concept most people couldn't even fathom. Hell, it had happened to me and I could barely fathom it. It all still felt so unreal.

And what Tim didn't know was that those things weren't even the extent of my current problems.

Tim let the issue drop, but I knew it wasn't done for good. Sure enough, it was later that night, when we were watching a movie on the couch, that he brought it up again.

"So, I get that you don't want to see anyone. But is there anything I can do to help?" he asked. "If you need to stay with your Dad again or something, it's okay. Or you could take a trip away? The stress isn't good for the baby."

I don't know why it was those words that made me snap, but it was. I'd been holding this secret inside of me for weeks now, carrying the burden of what Betty had told me. It wasn't fair. It was time to share the load.

"Oh, you've done enough, believe me," I said with a humourless laugh.

Tim threw his hands up, helpless. "I don't know what that means, Rosie! I love you so much, and I've tried to look after you as much as I can. I don't know what else I can do to help you."

I stared at him, feeling cold steel in my gaze. "I haven't been pushing you away because I can't deal with my feelings," I said. "I haven't been pushing you away because I'm traumatised. Although I am. I've been pushing you away because the last thing my sister told me before she died…" I paused, and in that moment I saw understanding start to reach his eyes. "The last thing she told me was that you fucked her."

Chapter 39 – Fiona

It took approximately a minute and a half at the animal shelter before she fell in love with an animal.

The animal in question was a tiny, sweet-faced beagle named Burleigh who, according to the animal shelter, was two years old. That put him past the annoying puppy stage that everyone seemed to like so much but Fiona couldn't imagine going through. He seemed quiet and calm, and she knew almost instantly that she wasn't leaving there without him.

Besides, Burleigh Heads happened to be where she and Jacob had gone on their first weekend away together, and the name just put the icing on the cake. This, Fiona told herself, was clearly fate.

Angela grinned triumphantly as Fiona cooed at the little dog. "Excuse me," Angela called out to the staff member nearby, without pausing to consult with Fiona. "My friend is interested in adopting this dog."

"Angela!" Fiona laughed. She was, of course, but she hadn't expressed that to Angela yet. Still, there was no point in arguing. As always, Angela had read her like a book. This dog had her wrapped around his paw, and she hadn't even held him yet.

"Oh, Burleigh's a sweetheart," the staff member said cheerfully. "I'll just talk you through what beagles need in terms of care, and we'll check that he's the right fit for you.

There's a $100 fee if you do wish to adopt him, and if we think he's right for you."

Fiona became suddenly nervous, thinking about her small, modest home with its tiny backyard. She hadn't considered that she might fall in love with the dog and then be rejected by the animal shelter. As it turned out, though, the adoption interview was fairly informal. Karen, the staff member, explained a bit about Burleigh's nature as well as some general information about beagles, and asked some questions about Fiona's living situation. She seemed happy to hear that Fiona was home fairly often. It was pretty much work and home for Fiona – without the work part at the moment, although she knew that needed to change soon.

Before Fiona knew it, she was a pet owner!

Karen told her she couldn't take Burleigh home until the next day, which suited Fiona fine. She needed to collect some necessities for the little dog, which Angela told her they could do right away. They drove to the pet supply shop, Fiona chattering excitedly away the whole time. She saw Angela smirking out of the corner of her eye, clearly pleased with herself and how well her plan was working so far. Fiona had to admit, she was grateful. She hadn't felt this good since before Jacob died.

When they got to the pet supply shop she told the sales assistant that she'd never owned a pet before, and the assistant was all too happy to oblige, making suggestions about crates, harnesses for the car and different food and water bowls she could buy. Fiona put it all on her credit card, feeling a twinge of guilt. She really did need to get back to work – her funds were running dangerously low. But she pushed the thought out of her mind. Burleigh's needs came first right now, and Fiona wasn't going to let her financial situation ruin her happy mood. She deserved at least one completely happy day.

The next day she brought Burleigh home and he walked around the house, sniffing at everything and seeming entirely content with his new living situation. She smiled tenderly, watching her new baby take everything in. He saw her looking and bounded towards her, leaping into her arms. Fiona laughed as the little dog licked her face. She was completely besotted with Burleigh already. It was the first time in a long time that her house had felt like a home.

Chapter 40 – Paula

The return to work would be hard for anyone after a traumatic event, but for Paula, it meant returning to the literal scene of the crime.

She put it off for as long as she could, before deciding that waiting any longer would probably result in her never making it back at all. She scheduled her return for a Monday, and was thrilled when her friend Alice messaged to say she was working the same day. At least a friendly face would make it easier to return, even though they wouldn't get to talk much if things got busy.

When she got to Alpine Centre she drove around until she found the closest possible park to the cinema. Staff members were supposed to leave the closer spots for patrons, but Paula figured if anyone had the right to take one, she did. She certainly never wanted to step foot on the escalator down to the level below again. Besides, she wanted the quickest possible escape route in case anything happened. That was nonsensical; she knew all too well from personal experience that if anything terrible did happen, she wouldn't be able to reach the safety of her car before things escalated. Still, it gave her a sense of security.

When she walked into the cinema, Alice came rushing over to greet her with a hug. "It's so wonderful to see you!" she cried. The cinema staff had sent Paula flowers when it all happened, but she hadn't seen any of them in person. Alice had offered once early in the piece to come over and visit, but Paula had put her off, and Alice hadn't tried again. As much as she liked the other woman, Paula simply couldn't face much company outside of Alfie and the kids. Sometimes even putting on a brave face for her family was exhausting.

The day passed relatively easily. There weren't huge crowds, and the other staff members who were there seemed genuinely happy to see Paula back. "I thought we might never get you back," her manager told her, but Paula smiled and shook her head. "I could never leave," she told him. In truth, of course, she'd thought about doing exactly that, just so she didn't have to ever go into the centre again. But she needed the job security, and she couldn't start anywhere new while she was in this fragile emotional state. After completing her day of work, she knew she'd made the right decision. It was nice having the comfort of her familiar workmates around her, and she had been working there so long that she could complete most of her tasks without much thought required.

"Do you want to go for a coffee?" Alice asked when they had finished their shift. Alice had said it was a happy coincidence that they were working the same hours, but Paula suspected her friend might have called in a favour. She was grateful for it.

"I'm not sure," Paula hedged, but Alice insisted.

"Please? It's been way too long!"

"Fine, but not here," Paula said, and Alice immediately nodded her understanding. "We'll go to Bayside," she said, naming the small coffee shop around the corner from Paula's home. Paula smiled. Bayside was small, homey and familiar. Maybe a drink with her friend was exactly what she needed.

Before leaving the centre Paula sent a quick message to Alfie to ask if he could pick Oliver up from after school care today. As she drove to the coffee shop, Paula realised she was smiling and humming along with the radio. It had been a surprisingly good day.

Chapter 41 – Rosie

When I dropped my bombshell, Tim's face dropped. "Rosie," he gasped. "I'm – I had no idea."

"Had no idea you slept with her?" I asked bitterly. I'd tried to push my feelings to the side since that day in the coffee shop, but now the full force of the devastation came rushing back to me. I was angry and sad, and just so tired. It felt like the world was too much for me and there was nothing I wanted to do except lie down and pull the covers over my head.

"I had no idea..." His voice trailed off. He had no idea I knew, obviously, but he had the common sense not to say the rest of that sentence out loud.

When Betty first told me, I'd been furious with her, but everything that happened after had overtaken those feelings. It was hard to feel truly angry when you were dealing with grief. The full force of my fury now, be it right or wrong, was at Tim. I knew, obviously, that Betty was just as culpable as my partner, or possibly even more so, but I couldn't bring myself to think that way.

"I'm so sorry, Rosie," Betty had told me the day of the shooting, tears filling her eyes. "I have no idea what we were thinking."

I was staring at my hands, stunned into silence.

"It was... stupid," she went on. "We both regretted it immediately. We said we were never going to tell you, but it was eating me up inside. I've always told you everything. And now that you're talking about marrying him... oh honey, I just had to tell you. I couldn't let you make any decisions like that without knowing the truth. I'm so, so sorry."

I finally looked up. Betty's cheeks were bright pink, the tears making her eyes look even greener than usual. She even looked lovely right here and now, in these circumstances. I hated her for it.

"Why?" I asked, simply.

She shook her head. "I don't know. I mean, we were both drunk... I know that's no excuse... But Jeffrey and I haven't had sex lately. I know I never told you that. But ever since Poppy came along, it's kind of been one long dry spell. And he's the only guy I've ever been with." She was rambling now, her words falling over each other as she tried to excuse the inexcusable. "And then you left and Tim and I ended up alone, and we were being kind of flirty, and I guess one thing just led to another. It was..." She took a deep, shuddering breath. "The biggest mistake of my life. Rosie, I love you so much. I never wanted to hurt you. Neither of us did."

"Do you love him?" The words coming out of my mouth surprised even me.

Betty looked startled. "No! Not at all. Like I said, it was stupid. It was, I guess it was a moment in time or something. It will *never* happen again. Tim regrets it as much as I do."

"I'm sure," I snorted. I'd always feared I was the lesser sister, and here Tim was, proving exactly that. He'd had the chance to get his rocks off with the prettier, more successful Blake twin, and he'd leapt at it. I almost couldn't blame him, really.

"It's true. Oh, Rosie, I wish I could go back in time and take it all back, but I can't. But you have to know, I'll spend the rest of my life making it up to you. Please forgive me."

Now, looking at Tim, her words echo in my head. *The rest of my life...* Right after that statement, the man with the gun had burst in, and the rest of Betty's life had turned out to be far too short. She couldn't make it up to me, and I was finding it almost impossible to live with what I knew.

Tim told me the same basic story as Betty had. I'd left them alone after our family dinner, going to sleep because I was exhausted and I'd trusted them, like the idiot I was. It would never have occurred to me to question whether it was safe to leave Betty and Tim alone together like that. And the story was true, they *had* been drinking. But alcohol was no excuse. It didn't just make you have sex with someone who was practically family.

"Where did you do it?" I asked suddenly. I remembered the night in question. Jeffrey had taken the kids home early and we'd partied on, so to speak. Eventually, I'd asked if they would mind if I went to bed. It was a Saturday night but I, unlike the two of them, had to work the next day. They'd said it was fine. Had they been planning it, even then? Or was it truly as spontaneous as they both said it was?

"I don't know if that's helpful-"

"Tim!" I snapped. "You banged my sister. I get to decide what's helpful and what's not, if you *ever* want me to forgive you for that."

Tim nodded, and at least had the grace to look embarrassed as he mumbled "on the couch."

A sharp, bitter laugh rose up from my chest. "On the couch! Our couch? *This couch?*" I leapt up, as if it was still tainted from that night. I knew immediately that I would never sit on the couch again. Tim might have been right; this wasn't helpful. Knowing where it happened just made it all so much more real.

"I told you, it wasn't planned," he said. "It was just some kind of weird moment, and we just... did it."

"Well, that makes it so much better," I sighed. I could feel the fight going out of me, and I just felt exhausted. I was far from forgiving him, but I couldn't keep going around in circles about this. Not tonight.

"Well," I said, still standing over him. He was looking up at me, pleading with me with his eyes. I crossed my arms in front of myself, a defence mechanism. "I hope you enjoy the couch, because that's where you'll be spending the night." And with that, I turned and walked out of the room.

Chapter 42 – Destiny

When Destiny opened the door, she was expecting a mailman or a Jehovah's Witness or something. Her stomach leapt a little when she saw Nate and Ed at the door instead.

"Oh... hey!" she gasped, looking from one to the other. Nate was meeting her gaze head-on, but Ed was looking down at his feet.

Destiny instantly wrapped her hands around her body, as if her arms could shield her from their vision. She was wearing a fitted cream shirt with no bra underneath, and her running shorts. Her hair, which normally fell in gentle waves, hadn't seen a brush for weeks and she knew it now looked more like a bird's nest than anything else. She was momentarily embarrassed by her appearance, until she remembered Ed's harsh words the last time she saw him. Well, if he thought looking too glamorous was a sign that she wasn't grieving, then she was showing him now how she actually felt. Destiny dropped her arms by her side, deliberately, and stared the two down.

"I brought Ed here because he's been a dickhead and he wants to apologise," Nate said bluntly. It was almost enough to force a smile onto Destiny's face. Almost.

"Does Ed actually want to apologise, or are you just making him?" Nate was a good friend to her, but Destiny wasn't really interested in hearing some apology that he had strong armed Ed into making.

"He wants to," Nate replied firmly. "Oh, believe me, he wants to."

Destiny stared coolly at Ed, who finally muttered, "I was out of line."

"Heart-warming stuff," Destiny said, ready to slam the door in his face.

"No, wait!" Nate said. "Can we come in? Please?"

Destiny considered this for a moment, before turning and walking into the house, leaving the door open for the two guys to come in.

"I'll go get some food," Nate said, walking into the kitchen. He'd been over enough times to make himself at home, but Destiny knew his real motive was to leave her and Ed alone for a while. Normally she would have appreciated the gesture, but her only thought now was that she didn't want to be alone with Ed.

Ed and Destiny started at the ground for a while, neither of them seemingly willing to speak first.

Finally, to her own surprise, it was Destiny who broke the silence. "You can wear makeup and still be grieving."

Ed nodded, still not meeting her eyes.

Destiny went on. "You can go out with friends and still know your life will never be the same." Her voice was rising now, getting angry. "Just because I'm not curled up in my tracksuit on the couch, doesn't mean I don't miss him. I'd give anything to have Luke back. Look, I don't think he should have done what he did, either." The words hurt to say, but it was true. She was grateful, so grateful, that she hadn't died that day, but she knew deep down that she could never have taken a bullet for anyone, even someone she adored as much as Luke. And as grateful as she was to still be alive, there was a part of her that would have to live with the guilt forever.

"But if I curl up in a ball and refuse to face the real world, then Luke's sacrifice was for nothing. I'm not, like, ruining his memory if I go on living my life. I *need* to go on living my life for his sake." She paused, picturing Luke's face in her mind. His beautiful face, his kind eyes. "Otherwise, two of us died that day. You can't tell me that's what Luke would have wanted."

Ed continued his silence for a moment, and then he sighed heavily. "You're right."

"I'm what?" Destiny wasn't trying to rub it in. She really couldn't believe that he was admitting it.

"You're right," Ed said, snapping the words in her direction now. "I shouldn't have said what I said. I mean, it's not just you this sucks for, though." He held up his hands as she started to protest. "I get it – you guys might have been a thing, and you were actually there when it happened, I *know*. But I lost a friend, too. One of my good friends. And no one really seems to care how I feel about it."

Destiny nodded, mulling it over. There was some truth to his words. The attention from people they knew at uni had all gone to her – partly because she'd been involved in the shooting as well, but mostly, she had to admit, because of the potential romantic connection between herself and Luke. It wasn't really fair that his other friends got overlooked, just because she and Luke had been attracted to each other. Besides, grieving had to be a little easier for girls, who were 'allowed' to express their emotions more freely. It had to suck to be expected not to cry. It wasn't so surprising, really, that Ed's emotions should come out as anger and aggression instead.

It didn't make it right, what he'd said to her. But maybe she didn't have to hold on to her anger quite as tightly as she had been doing.

And she knew her own words were true, too. She didn't have to stop living her life because of what Luke had done for her. In fact, she *needed* to do exactly the opposite to make his sacrifice worthwhile.

Destiny hadn't realised until now exactly how much guilt she'd been carrying around since Luke had died. She needed to let herself start to move on.

It wasn't a magical switch, and Destiny knew it. She couldn't suddenly go back to the person she'd been before the shooting. But she was giving herself permission to try, and that was enough for now.

Chapter 43 – Fiona

Life with Burleigh was... not the same as before Jacob died, certainly, but it was a lot better than life without him. Every day, the little dog made Fiona laugh. It was nice in the morning to wake up with his little furry body huddled in beside her. And she didn't realise until now how much she'd missed having some company around the house. Years before, her neighbour Katie had commented on how she never felt alone when their dog was in the house, and Fiona had thought she was delusional. How could having a dog around possibly the same as having real company? Now, though, she realised how wrong she'd been. Burleigh made the house into a home again. His presence comforted her and made her feel somewhat whole again.

Burleigh also brought human company to the house once more. Her cousin brought her kids around to see the dog, who seemed to love them as much as they loved him. Katie and her son Sebastian visited, and Adam came over, exclaiming over how much Burleigh looked like the beagle he'd had growing up. It made Fiona's heart feel like bursting to have so many people around. She thought at first that it had taken a dog to bring company back to her, but then she remembered how many of Adam's invitations she'd turned down; how Katie had asked her over at least once or twice a week since Jacob died. Perhaps the difference was in Fiona, rather than the people around her.

One morning Fiona got up and found herself sitting on the floor with Burleigh, stroking his soft ears. She normally played music or put the TV on when she first woke up to distract herself from her thoughts, but she had noticed she was doing it less and less after adopting the dog.

To her surprise, she found herself talking to him.

"The truth is," Fiona told the little dog in front of her, "that the shooting was horrible, but it wasn't the worst thing I went through this year."

She paused, as if waiting for the dog to interrupt her. He nuzzled his head against her stomach, and she continued.

"Honestly, if you gave me the choice I'd go through the shooting every day, and all the trauma that came with it, if it meant I got to come home to Jacob at the end of the day."

She started crying then, but it was the good kind of cry, the kind that felt like there might be some healing involved. Burleigh cocked his head to the side, startled, then curled up even closer to her. She stroked his head as she went on.

"But I don't get that choice. I had to go through the shooting and I still can't come home to Jacob. And that sucks." Fiona began crying in earnest now. "It's just so unfair."

Fiona sat on the floor, cradling Burleigh, for the next half hour. When she got up and went to wash her face, she was surprised to discover that she felt better than she had in a while.

She thought of her failed therapy attempts after the shooting and then looked at the beagle who was now asleep on the couch, his work clearly done.

It seemed she had finally found a therapist who worked for her.

ANGELA SEEMED QUITE self-satisfied with how successful the first step of her plan was going, but it wasn't enough to get her off Fiona's back. She came around after work, a week after Fiona got Burleigh.

"I'm here for step two," she announced proudly, and Fiona immediately groaned. "What's step two?" she asked, tiredly. "Can't I just keep focusing on step one for a while?" She motioned to Burleigh, who was walking in excited circles around the pair.

Angela shook her head. "The first step – well, it was the fourth step, remember – has been a *smashing* success, I must say. Better than I could have hoped for. So, I'm assuming step two will be just as fabulous. It's 'going out socially at least once a week'. So, here I am!"

Fiona stared at her friend, who was still in her work shirt and black pants. She looked fine, but Angela hated going out in her work clothes. As if reading her mind, Angela held up a tote bag. "I thought I'd get ready here, if you don't mind," she sang out, as if Fiona had a choice in the matter. She reached into the backpack and pulled out a flowy pink dress. "I know we haven't done the shopping step yet, but we're not going anywhere fancy, so you can wear whatever you like. And I've brought makeup!" She sounded quite delighted with herself about this fact.

"A little warning would be nice," Fiona grumbled, but she knew it would do no good to complain any further. "I'll get ready," she muttered, walking out of the room. "Just remember I do have a dog now. Going out isn't as easy as it was before."

Angela just gave her a withering look.

Forty-five minutes later, they were at dinner. It was the first time Fiona had left Burleigh alone, but she knew he had to get used to it before she went back to work. She actually loosened up and started enjoying herself over dinner, happy to be out of the house. Maybe Angela was on to something after all.

Over dessert, Angela gently broached the topic of the shooting. "How are you coping with it all?" she asked, and Fiona shrugged.

"It feels a bit like a one-two punch, I guess. I was still healing from Jacob's death, and then that happened. I mean, it would be a lot to deal with at any time, but..." Fiona paused. She had never actually put her feelings about her guilt into words. She'd told the police that she'd been distracted and that's what had caused her to run the red light, but she'd never told them exactly what led to her 'distraction', mumbling vaguely about how she thought she'd seen an animal on the road. As for the shooting, she'd given the statement about how she'd tried to volunteer to be shot herself, but the police officer she'd spoken to hadn't seemed terribly concerned about that. He had only murmured something about killers being unpredictable, and moved on to talk to someone else.

"The thing is," she said quietly, "I'm to blame for both of them."

Angela stared at her, her mouth open and fork dangling in mid-air over her piece of chocolate cake. "What do you mean, you're to blame?" she demanded.

Quietly, Fiona began to fill her in on the events of the night of Jacob's death. To her surprise, Angela's lips started twitching, as though she were trying not to smile.

"What?" Fiona demanded, angry tears pricking behind her eyes.

"I'm sorry," Angela said. "I mean, it's awful, and I'm so sorry you've been going through this alone. I just... I mean, Jacob *knew* you were behind the wheel of a car at the time. He made his choice. I get how you must feel, but you need to forgive yourself. You even said you told him to stop."

Fiona was surprised at the reaction. All the time she'd been dealing silently with her shameful secret, she never would have imagined that the first person she told about what really happened would absolve her of it. Fiona would still need to work through her emotions herself, naturally. But she'd always assumed that Angela would be disgusted to hear the truth, so to get this reaction from her was... well, it lifted some of the burden from her.

"And the shooting?" Angela asked. "Don't tell me you were giving him a hand job when the gun went off." She snorted out a laugh.

"Angela!" Fiona lectured. "No, it... well, I told him to shoot me. I told him to take me hostage because if anyone should die, it should be me. And he turned and shot someone else, straight away."

Angela's face turned more serious now. "Well, you're *definitely* not responsible for that. You were trying to be a hero, and he was a loose cannon with a gun. But I'm a little worried that you feel so badly about yourself that you think he should have killed *you!* Fiona! What on earth would I do if he'd listened to you?"

Angela's simple words were far from enough to assuage Fiona's guilt, but they did put things in a new perspective. Fiona had replayed the events of the day countless times, but had never thought of it from the point of view of one of her loved ones. Between her guilt and her grief, she'd assumed she didn't have much to live for anymore, without Jacob. She'd never stopped to consider that her family and friends might not want to live without *her.*

Chapter 44 – Rosie

I knew, of course, that it was unfair of me to pin all the blame on Tim. He and my sister had been equally responsible for what they'd done to me, and under normal circumstances I'd have been just as furious at Betty as I was at Tim. More furious, probably. Cheating on a partner was a great betrayal, but sleeping with your own twin sister's partner was, at least in my eyes, even worse.

But these weren't normal circumstances, and I couldn't possibly be expected to act rationally.

I continued to give Tim the silent treatment for the rest of the week. One night he asked me if he should stay with his mate Jordan, rather than continuing to sleep on the couch. I glared at him. "What? So you can go out and get some action?" I demanded. "You'll be lucky if I ever let you out of the house again." It might not have done much to heal our fractured relationship, but it shut him up and he didn't leave.

At the end of the week, Jeffrey called me out of the blue and asked if Tim and I wanted to join them for lunch on the weekend. The invitation was lovely, but it stung. I hadn't been to Betty's house since it happened. It was my suggestion that the wake be held in the garden area at the cemetery, and while I sold it as me wanting to save Jeffrey the effort of hosting, it was largely because I couldn't imagine facing Betty's house knowing she would never be there again. Still, I didn't want to stay away forever, either. I missed her kids, and the feeling of having family around me.

After the phone call with Jeffrey I flounced into the living room, declaring "you're getting a day off." When Tim looked at me blankly, I added "we've been invited to lunch with Jeffrey and the kids. Dad's coming, too. So, we're going to play happy families for a day."

Tim's face broke into a huge smile, which I had to put a stop to immediately. "*Playing* happy families, remember. This doesn't change anything, but I'm definitely not about to go explaining to everyone why I didn't invite you to family lunch."

I knew I was being a bitch, and the way Tim's face fell confirmed it for me. I just couldn't bring myself to really care about that. What he'd done to me was far worse than the way I was treating him.

I had to admit, I hadn't stopped to consider Jeffrey in all of this. Betty's only crime wasn't cheating with my partner. She'd cheated on her own husband, the father of her three kids. How could I justify that? And did Jeffrey deserve to know?

The truth was, even if I did decide he should know, I wasn't sure if I had the strength to tell him. His wife was gone, and he would be left dealing with the same emotions as I was battling with every day. He, like me, would have to deal with loving someone and hating them so much at the same time. And it would be even worse for him. At least she'd told me before she died, even though the timing couldn't have been worse. If she hadn't spoken to him about it, I didn't know how to break the news. It would surely be impossible to get over something like this when you couldn't talk it over with the person who had betrayed you.

I knew that was why I was putting all of the blame on Tim. It was my coping mechanism. It was so much easier to rage at someone who was standing there in front of me, that stupid guilty expression on his face, than to focus my anger on a ghost. My beloved sister, at that. Maybe it wasn't fair to Tim, but I just couldn't bring myself to feel the same level of rage towards Betty as I did towards Tim. Maybe one day I would. I almost hoped that I would, for reasons I couldn't quite put into words. Maybe because I thought it would make my life easier. Or maybe I thought it would dilute the rage a bit, to share it between the two of them. The 'why' of it didn't really matter. Things didn't have to make sense right now.

Walking into Betty's house was jarring, as I'd known it would be. Somehow, even more than seeing her children, walking into her house was like proof of her life, a life that had finished too early and so abruptly. Jeffrey hadn't done much packing away since she'd died, so signs of her were everywhere. Her adult colouring book was still lying open on the table, a few markers strewn messily on top. There was a small pile of books on the coffee table. Betty always had a few books in her 'to be read' pile. She didn't have enough time to read them all, but that wouldn't stop her from buying more. I had no doubt that if I went upstairs I'd find her childhood stuffed toy sitting on the armchair in the corner of their bedroom, the way it always had. Looking around, you could be forgiven for thinking Betty had just stepped out and would soon be back, smiling widely, serving up lunch for the family. I would give anything for that to be true.

In the end, lunch was actually quite nice – surprisingly so, given the circumstances. The fact that my situation with Tim wasn't public helped, and I was doing my best to make things appear normal for Dad's sake. The last thing in the world I wanted to do was worry him more. When we were alone together in the kitchen, I even brought up the topic of him moving in with us, but Dad insisted he was fine. As much as I would have loved to have him living with me so I wouldn't have to worry about him all the time, a part of me was happy that he turned me down. It would be too hard to pretend things were fine all the time if he was living with me, and I wasn't prepared to actually forgive Tim just yet.

I also hadn't yet broken the news of my pregnancy to anyone other than Tim. I knew they would be thrilled, but it would also be bittersweet. Having a new baby come into the family wouldn't be the same without Betty being there. I was still coming to terms with my own emotions about it, so I didn't need to see Dad and Jeffrey getting their heads around the same thing. When I was used to it myself, I would tell them.

On the way out the door, I let Tim put his arm around me. I did it mostly for show, but it felt quite nice, and when we got to the car, I didn't push him away.

Chapter 45 – Paula

"Everything's a mess," Paula sighed to Harold at her solo appointment. Exactly five weeks had passed since the shooting, and nothing seemed any better than it had been immediately following that horrific day. Some things seemed worse. "Ollie's gone back to school, which was tough, but he seems to be coping okay. But everything else..." She paused, trying to put it into words. "I'm fighting with Alfie. He says I've become a different person since the shooting." Paula blinked back tears. "I mean, he's right, but what does he expect? I'm the one who's been picking the fights, and I guess he's losing his cool with me."

Harold nodded. "There was always going to be a period of adjustment after a traumatic event such as this," he said in his usual professional manner.

"It's not just Alfie. There's Jasmine – she's been acting out, hanging out with the wrong kinds of kids. She says it's all about Ollie. I said he needs me right now, and she said -" Paula paused, trying not to cry. "She said it's been all about him for the last eight years, ever since he was born. I don't think it's true, but..." She trailed off. The truth was, there was a part of her that thought Jasmine's point might have been a fair one. She loved both of her children equally, of course, but Ollie had always been her special guy. As Jasmine pushed her away more and more as she got older, it seemed only natural for Paula to hold Ollie closer. Maybe she should have been trying to pull Jasmine back to her, instead.

"You need to care for your family, of course, but you can't really help them until you look after yourself," Harold said gently. "How's your support network?"

Paula shrugged. "Good, I guess, but small. Alfie's been doing what he can – I know I haven't made it easy for him, but he's trying. Not much family around here – I'm originally from Melbourne, and I'm an only child," she added. "But my parents have been checking in with me, so I suppose I'm luckier than a lot of people in this situation. I'm back at work, so I'm seeing more people outside of the house now, which is nice." Actually, she was surprised by how smooth the transition back to work had been. Somehow, she didn't associate the cinema with the shooting, but still as the place she'd called her second home for so many years now.

"I wonder if it might be beneficial for you to reach out to some of the other survivors," Harold suggested. "You could organise a meeting and discuss your shared experiences. Having a strong support network is paramount, of course, but none of the people you've named have actually lived the experience you went through."

Paula mulled this over. She tended to keep her social network small at the best of times, and she couldn't imagine putting herself out there in this situation. On the other hand, talking to people who understood – truly understood – what she'd been through that day did have a certain appeal. The only person who really knew the horrors she'd been through was Ollie, and he needed her to protect him, not use him as an unpaid therapist.

"How would I even arrange that? It's not like I know any of the other survivors' names," she mused, and the psychologist shrugged.

"Social media? You could even contact the local paper and see if they'd run something. Anything to continue their coverage of the siege, I suppose," he said with a light chuckle. He had a point – the media had been all over the story for as long as possible before reluctantly letting it drop. "Or just a good old-fashioned flyer on the shopping centre billboard."

Paula wrinkled her nose. "At Alpine? Do you really think people would keep going there?" She knew she would never step foot in there again if she didn't have to for work.

"Maybe, or maybe not. But they don't need to see it directly, remember. You just need someone who knows the people involved."

In the end, she did both a public social media post, encouraging readers to share it, and a simple flyer on the bulletin board. Where to hold the meeting was the hardest decision. She wasn't going to put her home address on the internet for public viewing, but she couldn't very well suggest they all meet at a coffee shop. In the end, she chose a park only a few streets away from Alpine. She wasn't sure if the proximity would be a problem, but you couldn't see the shopping centre from the park and she presumed it was a spot that everyone was relatively local to.

While she had no way of tracking the flyer's reach, Paula was both surprised and pleased by how many shares her post attracted in a short amount of time. She didn't necessarily want to attract a huge crowd but she also didn't want to sit alone, waiting for people who were never going to show up.

She set a date for two weeks in the future, hoping that would give her fellow survivors enough time to see the invitation.

Paula left her email address for anyone with questions, but didn't ask for RSVPs. She would be turning up either way. It wasn't as if she had anything better to do.

Chapter 46 – Destiny

Destiny wrinkled her nose when she saw the social media post her aunty had sent her. It was an invitation for survivors of the Alpine shooting to meet at some park and 'share their experiences'. *No thanks,* she thought, clicking off the post. She couldn't imagine anything worse than a bunch of sad people sitting around complaining about their feelings.

Destiny felt like, after her talk with Ed, some of the wounds inside had started to heal. She needed to send Nate a thank you message – she knew he would have been largely responsible for getting Ed to come and apologise. She wasn't back to the old Destiny, by any stretch of the imagination, but any progress was good progress. She couldn't help thinking that life at the moment seemed like one step forward, one step back, though. One day she'd feel like she was starting to get better, and the next day it would take all her strength just to get out of bed. Destiny knew it was going to be tough for a while, but the good days just felt like false hope, which was even harder to live with. She wished grief was like a scab on your leg. It would start out bad, but get steadily better each day. You knew there was a time limit on it.

Grief was infinite.

Destiny went about her day, going to the one class she attended on a Thursday, which she actually enjoyed, and going for a jog when she got home. After the jog her calves felt like they were burning, and she was short of breath, but she felt a lot better than she had before. She thought again about the survivors' meeting. With endorphins running through her system, it suddenly didn't seem like the terrible idea it had been just a few short hours ago.

Her mum had wanted her to see a therapist, but Destiny had no interest in doing so. She talked to her friends about what had happened, of course, but none of them had been there. Besides, she felt like their patience with her neediness was running out. That probably wasn't true, since they'd been nothing but supportive, but it didn't really matter if it was true or not. It was her perception, and it meant she had started to keep her thoughts to herself rather than sharing them with her friends.

The only person who would have understood was gone. Maybe it wouldn't hurt, after all, to talk to some people who had been through the same thing she had?

And so Destiny took a screenshot of the post, and entered the date in her phone calendar just to make doubly sure she wouldn't forget about it. Maybe the day of the meeting would come and she'd completely chicken out, but maybe not. It didn't hurt to have the details saved, just in case.

By the time the day of the meeting arrived a fortnight later, Destiny's mind was made up. Going to the event might not help at all, but it probably wouldn't hurt, so what was the harm? The worst thing she had to lose was a couple of hours, and it wasn't as if she was filling her time particularly wisely lately anyway.

The invitation had asked attendees to bring a plate, so Destiny cut up some fruit and made it into a basic fruit salad. She dressed in her favourite red dress – perfect for a picnic, and all the better to give her a little self-esteem boost. Grabbing the fruit salad, she walked to her car, surprised to find that her heart rate had accelerated. There was nothing particularly scary about going to meet a bunch of people in a park, but in a weird way, it somehow felt like they were revisiting the day it had all happened.

Destiny shook her head to herself, as if she could clear away her own thoughts. She was safe and life was getting back to normal. Going to the meeting could only help.

Chapter 47 – Fiona

Life was slowly improving for Fiona, so when she saw the flyer for the meet up, she felt like she'd been punched in the stomach. It was like a sick joke. Who could possibly think that revisiting that day would help anything? She shook her head and kept walking.

Still, the thought of it kept intruding on her brain throughout the day. The idea of meeting up with people who understood what she was going through was somewhat of an appealing one, providing they weren't sitting around analysing the whole thing. It wasn't as if she had a huge support network, and she didn't want to spend the small amount of time that she did socialise by talking her friends' ears off about the shooting. The anti-depressants were continuing to help her mood, but there was only so much they could do. Maybe this would give her a boost.

On her way back to her car, she saw the flyer again. This time she took a photo of it on her phone, just in case, and it wasn't long before she'd talked herself into going.

The day of the picnic, Fiona took the chocolate trifle she'd made and balancing it carefully, made her way to the park. It wasn't far and it was a nice day, so she'd decided to walk, but as she held the dessert firmly in her hands she wondered if she'd made the right choice. What the hell was she thinking, bringing trifle, anyway? It was hardly portable. Besides, it was such an old-fashioned dessert now, wasn't it?

Everything was mud cake or molten lava things these days. Come to think of it, what the hell was she thinking, turning up at all?

When she got to the park, her already accelerated heart rate felt like it was going to go through the roof. Fiona hadn't been so nervous to meet anyone since... well, since her first date with Jacob, funnily enough. Somehow, she had her doubts that this little meeting would be quite as life altering as meeting Jacob for the first time.

When she turned up at the meeting spot, there was one woman there, a blonde woman in her 40s. "Are you here for the Alpine meeting?" the other woman asked tentatively, and Fiona was rewarded with a bright, beaming smile when she nodded her affirmation. The smile changed the other woman's whole appearance. Fiona held out a hand. "I'm Fiona," she said, and the other woman shook it.

"I'm Paula."

Fiona recognised the name from the flyer. "You organised this, then?" she asked, although she'd already suspected that from how early Paula was. It was still five minutes until the starting time, but Fiona had decided she'd rather be early than rushing in late.

Paula nodded. "I'm so happy to see you! I was worried no one would turn up."

Fiona smiled awkwardly. Paula seemed friendly, but there didn't seem to be a lot to say just yet. She was always shy around people she didn't know well. There was a momentary silence, but then Paula took the lead. "Please, put your bowl down. Oh, that looks amazing! I brought cheese and salami and some sweets, too," she went on, gesturing to the cooler beside her. "I didn't ask for RSVPs or anything, so I'm not sure who else will be coming along."

Fiona shrugged, taking a seat beside Paula on the picnic blanket. It had been years since she'd sat on the floor like this, but it was a beautiful autumn day, and she felt suddenly comfortable. "I guess we'll wait and see, but at least we have each other for company."

Chapter 48 – Rosie

It hadn't taken me long to decide to go to the picnic. When I saw the Facebook post, I quickly saved the details into my diary. It was a Tuesday so I had the day off anyway, but honestly, I would have swapped a shift if I had to. I don't know why, but the idea of meeting other people who had been through the same thing as me seemed so important. So did meeting people who might have remembered Betty.

Nearly two months had passed since the shooting. Naturally I still missed Betty every day, but things were starting to look up, ever so slightly. At fourteen weeks' pregnant my bump was beginning to show, and I was loving having it on display, even though to everyone else it probably just looked as though I had had a big meal. I could tell, though.

Everyone had taken the news of the pregnancy well – even my workplace, which I was the most worried about. Having had a fair bit of time off already I wasn't sure if they would be happy to hear that they were going to lose me again, but everyone seemed so concerned by my mental state that they were happy to hear any kind of good news. Actually, I was surprised by how overwhelming the support was. I hadn't even been that convinced of my own happiness when I found out about the unexpected pregnancy, but everyone seemed thrilled.

Well, my brother-in-law's reaction hadn't been exactly overwhelming. Jeffrey had said all the right things, but I thought I detected a wistful note in his voice. I figured he was thinking of how much Betty would have loved having her first niece or nephew. I thought of that often, too. She had always loved babies, had cooed over their smell and their tiny hands. She would have been such a doting aunt, and the thought of raising a child of my own would have been less daunting with her in the world.

Dad, on the other hand, seemed to see it as a new beginning. Nothing could bring Betty back, but this baby would give him something to look forward to, at least for a little while. I was pleased to be able to provide him with that.

The scan had gone well. Not just in terms of the baby and its health, which was obviously the most important thing, but it was a nice moment for Tim and me. We were having so few of those lately. I was still so angry that I had considered not even letting him come along for the scan, but it turned out to be a lovely afternoon. After a few more nights on the couch I'd finally let him move back into our bed, but I still made a little wall of pillows between us. It was juvenile, but it made me feel better, and Tim was willing to put up with it. I felt like he was willing to put up with almost anything if it meant the slightest chance of reconciliation.

As I walked towards the park, though, the issue with Tim was far from my mind. I wondered how many people would turn up, and if I would recognise any of them. Most of all, I wondered if talking about it to people who had been there would be a help or a hindrance. Would it help me to start to heal, or would it just take me further back into the day that I'd been trying to put behind me?

I knew the people I was looking for immediately when I saw them. I didn't recognise them as such, but I had no doubt that it was them. It was just two women, a curvy blonde and a slim brunette, both a bit older than me. They were chatting amiably, but with that slight wariness that comes from people who don't know each other well. I walked up to them with a false confidence I'd learned to hone over the years.

"I think you're the ones I'm looking for," I said with a big, bright smile that didn't quite match the emotions I held on the inside. "I'm Rosie Blake, and I'm a survivor." I forced a laugh that came out a little too loudly.

The two women smiled back at me, looking slightly uncertain. "Yes, that's us," the blonde woman said. She held out a hand. "I'm Paula Warner."

I shook it. "Nice to meet you, Paula." I glanced at the other woman, who introduced herself as Fiona Tucker and said how nice it was to meet me. She was clearly shy, but both women seemed friendly enough.

I sat down on the picnic blanket and pulled out the finger sandwiches I had made for the occasion. "Do you know if anyone else is coming?"

Paula started to shake her head, but as if on cue, a fourth person turned up. She was clearly younger than us, and so pale she made my own fair skin look positively tanned.

"Um, hi," the girl said. "Is this the Alpine group?"

Paula and I nodded, but I noticed Fiona's face had turned pale as she stared at the young girl, who didn't seem to notice. She smiled and sat down. Paula and I introduced ourselves, and the girl said "oh, I'm Destiny Johnson."

Destiny then glanced over at Fiona, who still hadn't said a word. "Sorry, I didn't catch your name," Destiny started, then paused. "Oh, I know you."

Fiona nodded, mutely.

"You're the one who told him to shoot you instead," Destiny said, realisation dawning on her face.

Fiona looked like she was about to cry. "I'm so sorry," was all she said.

Chapter 49 – Paula

Paula had recognised Fiona the instant she saw her. She remembered the day of the shooting, and how she'd thought Fiona's words were akin to suicide. It wasn't her place to pry, but she had wondered then what was going on in the other woman's life to make her stand up and make that statement. In the time since the shooting she had forgotten all about that woman, and all the other people there, but now they were face-to-face she found herself wondering about it again. Fiona looked like a perfectly ordinary woman, young and healthy. Had it just been bravery that made her stand up and offer her own life, or was there more to it? And why was she apologising now?

"Sorry?" Destiny echoed, staring back at Fiona. "Why are you sorry?"

Fiona looked down at the ground. "Well, he wasn't aiming the gun at anyone until then. When I told him to shoot me, he pointed it at you. And he…" She paused, remembering. Paula remembered, too. After he pointed the gun at the red-haired girl, he had shot the man with her.

"Oh my God," Paula said, stunned. "Your boyfriend died."

If possible, Destiny turned even paler. She nodded. "Well, he wasn't really my boyfriend, but yeah. It was our first date."

The three women all let out a sympathetic groan. In reality, losing someone you'd started to build a life with would be the more serious loss, but there was something about the optimism that came with a first date that made the loss seem even more devastating. It was, Paula thought, the loss of potential that hit so hard.

"Anyway," Destiny said, addressing Fiona again, "it definitely wasn't *your* fault. I mean, you were trying to help! He was a madman with a gun. I don't think anyone could have predicted what he was going to do. Please don't feel guilty."

Fiona smiled back at her, her relief obvious. Paula thought the other woman might burst into tears at any moment, so she swiftly attempted to move the conversation on. Strangely she felt a certain responsibility for how successful the day was, since she was the one who had planned it. "I guess we all have a story to tell," she said. "You don't have to share, but if you want to, this might be a good opportunity."

The other women all nodded, but no one volunteered to go first, so Paula kept talking. "I was there with my son, Oliver... Ollie," she said. "He was sick, and we'd just run in to get something from my workplace. I work at the cinema above the coffee shop," she added. "It was a five-minute trip, that was all. On the way out, I told Ollie he could have a milkshake. I thought it would be something nice for him." Her voice caught on the words. Even though she couldn't have possibly known what was coming, she knew she would always regret the decision to stop for that drink. Who knew something so simple and everyday could lead to such life-changing consequences? She had realised, through her therapy appointments with Harold, that that was the worst part of the shooting as far as she was concerned. It meant that she second-guessed every decision she made now. Stopping to pick up a few groceries after work could cause a delay that led to her being in a car accident, or the delay could in fact save her life from an out-of-control truck. When you didn't know what consequences your actions could lead to, you ended up overthinking every move. She didn't know if these thoughts would make sense to anyone but her. Briefly she considered mentioning them to the other women, to see if they could relate. She decided to stick to the facts instead.

"He got shot," Paula went on, the words still feeling unreal to herself. The other women were nodding along. Of course, they might not have recognised her on sight, but everyone remembered the little boy getting shot near the counter. "He's okay, thank God. It damaged his shoulder, but he should be totally fine in the future. We're both going to therapy, but he hasn't really been the same since. I mean, physically, he's fine. But emotionally..." Her voice trailed off.

There was a momentary, respectful silence after she'd finished speaking, and then Fiona spoke up.

"Well, my story's pretty simple, really. I went to the coffee shop and ordered my lunch, and next thing, in came the gunman. Like Destiny already said, I offered for him to shoot me instead."

"Why?" Paula hadn't planned to ask, but the word escaped her lips before she knew it was coming.

Fiona sighed. "My husband passed away recently – only about a month before the shooting, actually. So it was very recent. I was in a pretty bad place, and I thought if someone had to die..." She stopped, glancing over at Destiny.

"I'm so sorry," Rosie murmured.

Fiona smiled weakly. "It's okay. I'm doing a little better these days. Time heals, and all that." Abruptly, she stopped speaking.

Paula looked around the circle. "Destiny, Rosie, do you want to share? It's fine if you don't." She didn't want to appear pushy. The group seemed to be getting along well, but they were still all so new to each other, and it wasn't as though this were an official therapy session. She hoped that after they'd all shared their stories, they could move on to a slightly lighter discussion.

Destiny nodded. "There's not much I haven't already said, but sure. Luke and I were friends for a while. He finally asked me out, and we went to the coffee shop. Then the gunman went to shoot me, and Luke stepped out in front of me. He saved my life, but he died."

Paula noticed Rosie was surreptitiously wiping away a tear. "That's so awful," Paula said, reaching a sympathetic hand out to Destiny. "I'm sorry to hear it."

Destiny nodded, smiling bravely. She appeared close to tears as well.

"So that's everyone but me, then," said Rosie with a hollow laugh. "Well, I went to lunch with my twin sister, Betty."

Paula knew how this was going to end before the other woman continued. She knew the names of the two victims from the news reports she'd pored over in the days after the shooting, before Alfie made her go cold turkey on the media. And she remembered the lookalike twins from the coffee shop – she'd always been fascinated by identical twins.

"I was going to tell her about my pregnancy," Rosie went on, putting a protective hand over her bump. "But I didn't quite get there. The gunman came in, and it was all over. He shot Betty, and she... she didn't make it."

Paula noticed they all referred to him as the gunman, rather than using his name. It had been in all the news reports, but she had always refused to acknowledge it, let alone say it out loud. She didn't want to humanise him. It seemed the other survivors here had the same response.

There was a long, loaded silence after the four women finished sharing their stories. Eventually, Paula cleared her throat. "So basically, we've all been through a lot," she said. She opened up the cooler beside her. "We all deserve a cupcake."

Chapter 50 – Fiona

When Destiny told her not to feel guilty, it was like a weight had been lifted off Fiona's shoulders. True, Angela had told her much the same thing, but Angela was her lifelong friend, and was bound to be biased. Not to mention, she hadn't even been there. But Destiny was directly impacted by what had happened, and still said it wasn't Fiona's fault. True forgiveness, Fiona knew, had to come from within. But Destiny's kind words certainly helped.

The rest of the picnic had been a lot more light-hearted than the start. After they all finished sharing their stories it was as if the mere mention of the shooting had been banned, by mutual unspoken agreement. Fiona knew that they should probably return to the topic to truly help with their healing process, but for now, it was nice to simply enjoy the other women's company. She had worried they wouldn't have anything to talk about once the discussion of their shared trauma was done, but if anything, that was when the conversation truly seemed to take off.

They chatted about their lives in general – their family situations, their hobbies, what they did for work. Paula asked questions about Rosie's pregnancy, and Rosie talked with Destiny about the study she was doing. "My aunt's a journalist and loves it," Rosie told her. "It's a bit tricky to get a job, I guess, but I think you'll really enjoy the work. You're obviously passionate about it." Destiny had nodded, smiling with a shy sort of pride.

"I do love it," she said. "And I want to freelance, for a while at least, so I guess that will help since I'm not really looking for a full-time job anyway."

Then, as Fiona had known it would, the conversation turned to her. "I'm so sorry about your husband," Paula said. "Was it sudden?"

Fiona nodded. "Car accident," she said simply. It was going to take a long time for it to feel real, but the words weren't quite as gut-wrenching as they had been over the previous few months.

Paula winced sympathetically. "Do you have any kids?"

"We never wanted them." Fiona pulled out her phone. "I have a new baby now, though. His name is Burleigh," she said, showing the other women photos. They all cooed and exclaimed over the dog's pictures and Fiona smiled. She felt like she was part of a group of old friends, rather than being with women she had just met for the first time. It was a nice feeling. Although she had a few close friends, she hadn't been part of an actual *group* since high school. She and Angela were the only ones who had stayed friends since their school days, and she and Adam normally caught up alone, or with Julian – and Jacob, until recently, of course. Fiona wasn't sure if she would ever even see these women again, but for now, it was enough.

After nearly two hours together, Paula looked at her watch and sighed. "I have to pick my son up," she said, standing. "I'm sorry to cut this short. I'm really enjoying myself." She sounded sincere, and Fiona was surprised by the pang of disappointment she felt as the other woman prepared to leave.

Paula said goodbye to them, and then paused. "Would you like to do this again sometime?" she asked, sounding a little shy. "I'm sure everyone's busy, but I do think it's helped, and I thought it might be nice –"

Rosie cut her off, seemingly realising she was floundering. "I think that would be great," she said, smiling at the rest of the group. Destiny immediately nodded her agreement, and Fiona found herself quickly agreeing, too.

"Fabulous!" Paula exclaimed, the confidence coming back to her voice. "Well, it might be easiest if I take everyone's numbers and set up a group chat?" She entered their details into her phone, one at a time, and smiled. "I'd really better go, but I'll be in touch."

Fiona smiled back. "I'm looking forward to it!" she said, and she was pleased to realise that she really was.

Chapter 51 – Destiny

Destiny had been surprised by how much she genuinely enjoyed the survivors' meeting – although, she reflected, they really did need a better group name. The other women had all seemed nice, even though they were a bit older than she was, and it was just so good to be with people who really got what she was going through. Destiny was pleased when Paula messaged again the next day, just to check in with everyone's details. Rosie was the first to reply, and soon they had a fully-fledged group chat happening. There was no talk just yet about when to meet up in person again, but it was nice to just have regular messages coming in again.

The uni group used to have a group chat, but that had now stopped, obviously. Without Luke things never would have been the same, but at least they could have kept up their friendship if Ed hadn't said what he'd said. Destiny had forgiven him, but she hadn't forgotten. She could let go of what he'd said, but she didn't really want to hang out with him and Courtney on a regular basis. Maybe it was embarrassment on their part, or maybe Ed hadn't really put things behind him the way he said he had, but they didn't seem overly eager to spend time with her, either.

For now, Gemma was enough. And Nate, of course. They'd always got on, but she'd never really stopped to appreciate what a great mate he was. He'd been checking in on her fairly often, sometimes thoughtful messages, but more often just with stupid memes to make her smile.

She and Gemma had always been close, but the incident seemed to have bonded them further. They started hanging out more regularly, seeing each other at least once a week outside of uni. Destiny was starting to think of her as her link to the outside world. Things had improved for her recently, but she was still avoiding the uni classes that Courtney and Ed attended, and her social circle had definitely shrunk. Meeting up with the other women from Alpine had been great, but as well as they'd all got along, they all knew they had only met because of the shooting. With Gemma, things felt normal. They talked about the movies they'd watched lately, their part-time jobs, and how much they were struggling with their latest assignment.

"Things are going so well with Kyle," Gemma gushed to her, one lazy Wednesday when they were hanging out by Destiny's pool.

Destiny smiled, happy for her friend. Gemma and Kyle had only been going out for a few weeks, but Gemma seemed completely besotted. Destiny had never seen her like this before.

"That's great," she said, sincerely. "You guys need a couple name. Kemma? Kymma? Gel?"

Gemma grimaced. "Keep working on that," she laughed. "Anyway, I'm not sure we're quite at the couple name stage yet. I just gave him head for the first time the other night."

Destiny laughed. Gemma had always been a little too comfortable sharing details of her sex life. "That's great to know, thanks."

"So, what about you?" Gemma asked, and Destiny shook her head.

"No, I haven't given Kyle head."

"Funny. You know what I mean. When do you think you'll date again?"

"Date? Seriously?" Destiny gave a hollow laugh. "People have become nuns from less traumatic first dates."

"Mmmm, but you're not exactly the nun type," Gemma replied, as though giving it serious consideration. "Let's face it, you're going to date again eventually. I'm just asking *when*. We could get you on Tinder, if you want?"

"Gemma!" cried Destiny, frustrated. "I don't want to date again. I seriously don't know if I'll *ever* want to date again, and I definitely don't want to get on bloody Tinder right now."

Gemma held up her hands. "Okay, okay. I surrender."

They were quiet for a moment, and Destiny rolled onto her belly, tracing one finger in the water. Perhaps it was the fact that she was no longer facing her friend that gave her the courage to say, "I'm not kidding, you know. I really *don't* know if I'll ever meet anyone again."

She could almost hear Gemma rolling her eyes. "You're young and gorgeous, hon. The guys will come and beat your door down sooner or later. Trust me, you'll meet someone."

"No, seriously." Destiny glanced over at her friend now. "I really do think Luke was the one for me. I'm not interested in anyone if I can't have him." She knew it sounded a little dramatic, like an old love song or something, but she didn't really care. It was the truth.

"I know someone who'll be sorry to hear that," Gemma replied with a little laugh, and Destiny frowned. "What? Who?"

"Oh, nothing," Gemma said, waving her hand in the air. "You're probably right. There's no one else for you."

Destiny frowned, but Gemma refused to elaborate. It didn't matter, anyway. Even if there was someone out there who thought they liked her, Destiny didn't feel the same way. It would never be the same.

Chapter 52 – Rosie

I enjoyed myself at the picnic, not least of all because it took my mind off things with Tim. Not much did that nowadays. I knew one way or another, I would have to make a decision about my future with him. Did I want to stay with him for all the good parts of our relationship, or was his betrayal with Betty too much of a burden for any relationship to bear? Every so often, I wondered if I was being too harsh on him, but my blinding rage was still there, and it didn't seem to be in any hurry to go away.

Surprisingly, Tim and I hadn't actually fought since that first night when he'd told me about Betty. Sure, I'd made a couple of snide remarks in his direction, and he'd been on the receiving end of plenty of silent treatment from me, but I hadn't actually raged at him, screamed at him, told him all the things I was thinking.

The night after the picnic, I did exactly that.

I wasn't sure if the two were related. Maybe meeting new people, sharing some of my story about Betty, reopened some old wounds, or even gave me the little confidence boost I needed to make myself heard. Or maybe it would have happened regardless. Either way, it felt good, I had to admit.

"Do you know the part that's the worst of all of this?" was how I opened the conversation. Tim looked a little taken aback for a moment, possibly because I'd barely spoken to him for over a month, and partly because he was just sitting there reading an online newspaper when I started in on him.

He didn't respond, but I didn't need him to. I was going to make myself heard, one way or another. "You *know* I've always felt second best to Betty," I said. "And the second you got the chance, you ran to her. So how am I supposed to feel like anything other than a consolation prize, then?"

Out of everything, this was the thing that stung the most. It wasn't just that my partner had cheated on me, and it wasn't just that he'd done it with someone so close to me. It was that this one act confirmed every fear I'd ever held about myself. How could you believe you measured up, when your own partner chose to sleep with the person you'd always believed was a better version of yourself? And to make what should be the most heartbreaking event of my life even worse, I'd now lost Betty. I couldn't fight with her about this. I couldn't tell her she'd broken my heart. She couldn't promise to make it up to me over and over, and we couldn't reconnect and cement the twin bond we'd always had. I felt lost, and empty.

Tim's eyes filled with sympathy. "Oh, babe. You know you've never been second place in my eyes. You can't really think that way."

"Can't I?" I shot back. "I've always thought Betty was smarter, prettier, funnier, more popular than me. Isn't this just proof of that? My own boyfriend couldn't wait to shag her and pin it on 'alcohol.'" My voice was filled with sarcasm, showing him just how lame I thought the alcohol excuse was.

"God dammit," Tim muttered, shaking his head. "You're the smartest, prettiest, funniest, best person I know, and you should know that by now. There's no part of me that ever compared you to Betty. In fact…" He stopped.

"No, go on," I said. "You might as well say it. I don't think you can make things much worse here." It was true, I realised. There was still a large part of me that didn't think this relationship was at all worth saving. If not for the baby, I thought, I'd already be gone.

I think Tim recognised on my face how serious I was about this. I think he realised it was now or never. He knew he had to put it all on the line.

"It wasn't really the alcohol," he sighed. That wasn't a surprise, but I felt my body tense in anticipation. What was he about to say it actually was, then? Did I want to hear it, or was some amount of ignorance better?

"When I met you," he went on, "I thought you were incredible. And I still do," he rushed to add. "But when I found out you had a twin… I mean, any red-blooded man would fantasise about that. I think it's like textbook male fantasy, right there."

I stared at him. This was his grand idea for how to salvage our relationship? To tell me about his perverted twin fantasy? He was even more deluded than I'd thought.

Tim seemed to realise he had said the wrong thing. "I don't mean I used to sit around drooling over her," he said quickly. "I just mean… there was a part of me that was curious. And when we were there, alone, things just happened. It was a curiosity thing, but it didn't compare to what we have, babe. Not at all."

I sighed heavily. I didn't know what I had been expecting, but there was a small part of me that hoped he would be able to explain the whole thing away in some way that made me feel better about everything. This explanation certainly wasn't it. I wasn't sure anything would have been good enough.

"I don't know what you want me to say to that," I said finally.

He shook his head. "I know what I did was unforgiveable. And I know you might leave me, and I probably deserve that. But baby, I want you to stay. There's not one part of me that did what I did because I wanted Betty over you. I did it…" Tim paused. "I didn't sleep with Betty because I thought you didn't measure up. I guess I slept with Betty because she reminded me of you, and I wondered what it would be like. Things were getting so serious with us, and it kind of felt like going back to the beginning of our relationship, when everything was so simple." He sighed. "I know that's no excuse. You deserve so much better. But it was the biggest mistake of my life, and I'll do whatever I need to do to make it up to you. Please don't let us go because of this. I'd never forgive myself."

I looked at him wordlessly for a moment. He wasn't wrong about things getting serious between us, and how different it made our relationship feel. After all, I'd even told Betty on the day of the shooting about how I thought there was a proposal coming. As much as I'd been happy with the state of our relationship, there was a part of me – a part I had never admitted to before – that missed the time when everything was simple, when Tim and I were just starting out and not thinking so much about the future. When a dinner out just meant enjoying the food and company, and not wondering whether *this* was the night I'd find a ring in the bottom of my champagne glass. I'd never admitted to it because it felt childish, but it was true. Life was so complicated sometimes.

Despite that, I hadn't gone and had sex with someone else because I couldn't handle the way things were going with Tim, but he admitted himself that he'd made a mistake. Did I really want to throw everything away because of one night? We'd been so happy together for four years now.

I'd met Tim less than six months after my mum had died. Her death was expected, but that didn't necessarily make it any easier for me to deal with. I was still grieving over her and never would have expected to meet anyone while I was feeling so low. I'd felt the spark with Tim immediately, and he had made me feel like myself again for the first time since Mum had died. That was how I knew he was something special. Wasn't that all worth more than what had happened with Betty?

Betty. Sometimes I wondered if I was more broken-hearted about Tim's fling because it was with my twin, and especially because she had died. It would have been much simpler if it was some random girl at work. Wouldn't it? I had no idea, but I knew I needed to try to move on. I couldn't lose both Betty and Tim at the same time, after all. I didn't know how I'd survive without either of them, let alone both.

"Okay," I said finally.

"Okay?" he repeated, as if hardly daring to believe it.

"Okay, I'll try. No promises," I added sternly, as Tim's face lit up. "But I'm willing to give it a go."

Tim smiled at me as if all his Christmases had come at once. "That's all I ask," he said. "You won't regret this."

I let Tim hug me. I hoped he was right.

Chapter 53 – Paula

Paula had been thrilled about the success of her first picnic with the other Alpine survivors.

Unfortunately, it seemed to be the only thing in her life that was a success at the moment.

She still blamed herself for putting Ollie in harm's way the day of the shooting, even though she knew there was nothing she could have done. She couldn't have known something like that was going to happen in a quiet Brisbane suburb on an ordinary Tuesday morning. It wouldn't be good parenting to shield her son from the world, afraid to ever go anywhere or do anything. And yet, she still put the blame entirely on herself.

"You know the shooter is the only one to blame, don't you?" Alfie asked one night, not long after the shooting. "You did nothing wrong. You tried to protect Ollie as best you could."

Paula shrugged, unable to meet his eyes. "I don't know. I'm the one who left my wallet at work. I'm the one who took him to the coffee shop in the first place. He didn't ask to be there."

Alfie looked slightly exasperated. "But you didn't know there was going to be some nutcase with a gun! What else could you have done? We can't keep our kids in bubble wrap for the rest of their lives."

She knew his words were true, but that didn't change the way that she felt. Perhaps if Oliver hadn't been shot, she would have been able to justify things to herself. She knew deep down that they were lucky Ollie's injuries hadn't been worse. Being shot in the shoulder was horrific, but it was something they could move past. Either one of them could have been permanently wounded or even killed in the shooting. She should be grateful things hadn't gone worse than they had.

But it was very hard to be grateful when it felt like your world was falling down around you.

And then there was her daughter. Jasmine was continuing to act out, causing screaming fights and hanging out with a bad crowd. Paula and Alfie's relationship wasn't much better. The only bright spot in her life right now was Ollie. Sweet, caring Ollie, who wanted to cuddle with her even more than he had before the shooting had changed their lives. She wanted to hold him forever.

"You're babying him," Alfie said one night, after she'd put their son to bed.

Paula glared at her husband. "You'd baby him, too, if you'd seen what he'd seen. You have no idea, Alfie."

"You're right, I don't, because you won't let me in," he argued. "You act like this whole thing is some sacred experience you and Ollie share. I swear you love it."

"Ugh! You are insufferable!" Paula cried. "You think I'm enjoying this? I'd take it back in an instant if I could, and you know it! I'd do anything for Ollie not to have gone through that!"

"Yeah, but you can't, so you're shutting us out. It's become you and Ollie against the world. I know it, and Jasmine knows it."

Paula's mouth opened and then closed. Alfie was wildly off base on thinking she was somehow pleased to share this experience with Ollie, but he might have had a point there. She had shut her husband out in the last couple of months, telling herself that he couldn't possibly understand what she'd been through, so why bother trying? She hadn't thought she was doing the same with Jasmine, but she had to admit there might be some truth to those words, too.

"I suppose I might be," she eventually said, in a small voice. Paula had always hated to admit she was wrong, especially about something like this. She'd been through something unimaginable, true. But it was easy to step into the role of playing the victim.

To his credit, Alfie didn't look at all happy at his wife admitting to being in the wrong. He opened up his arms for a hug instead, and she stepped into them. "I wish I could have traded places with you," he said. "I'd have loved for you and Ollie not to have had to go through that. But I can't change things now, so all we can do is move forward."

She smiled a little, in his arms. The part about moving forward sounded very much like something the therapist had said in one of their group sessions, and she knew Alfie had been paying attention. He was right, too. She was lucky to have someone like Alfie around. She needed to stop taking that for granted.

Chapter 54 – Fiona

Fiona partially credited the survivors' group meeting with the fact that she was feeling strong enough to return to work. She would have had to go in regardless – Fiona knew she'd tested every last piece of her boss' patience – but she actually felt like she could be successful, rather than dreading going back.

And for the first week, it was smooth sailing.

The regulars she worked with at the aged care home seemed happy to see her, and her workmates were all supportive. No one really mentioned Jacob's death or the shooting directly, but Fiona could tell they were all thinking about it, and were treating her slightly more gently as a result. She would have liked things to feel a little more normal, but she couldn't deny it was nice to have people looking out for her.

Then a week later, there was Jim.

Jim was one of her favourites at the aged care home. He'd been living there for four years and had regular visits from his adult children, whom Fiona had also developed a relationship with over the years. Jim was in his eighties, but his mind was as sharp and quick as it must have been when he was a much younger man. Fiona always loved visiting him, sharing jokes and stories. His physical body wasn't in the same shape as his mind, but his sense of humour made him seem younger than his years.

"Good morning, Jim!" Fiona sang out, entering his room. "What adventures will this fine Thursday bring?" It was her standard greeting to him, and had been for the last couple of years. Jim normally responded with a line about how he was going to go hot air ballooning, or how he would pick berries in the forest later, or perhaps go swimming with sharks.

Today, he didn't respond at all.

"Jim?" Fiona asked, her voice rising. She stared at the man, who was lying lifelessly in his bed. "Jim!" She reached out an arm and jabbed frantically at the call button beside the man's bed.

A nurse came in and rushed to the man's bedside. "Fiona, what happened?" she asked, feeling Jim's wrist for a pulse.

Fiona shook her head wordlessly, staring at Jim as he lay still in his bed. She couldn't answer. All she could see was another person she hadn't been able to help.

"IT'S PART OF THE JOB, you know," Adam said gently, later that day. The two were having a much-needed coffee break in the aged care facility's small staff break room. "He's not the first patient to die on us, and he certainly won't be the last."

Fiona nodded numbly. She knew her friend's words were true, but that didn't mean she accepted them.

"There was literally nothing you could have done," Adam went on. "He was gone before you even entered the room."

That was true, too, but again, the words simply washed over Fiona. Adam might as well have been speaking Greek for all the good his well-intentioned words were doing her.

It certainly wasn't the first time Fiona had had to face death. It was part of the job, and she'd known that when she signed up for it. It had never really bothered her before. She had always known she couldn't cheat death, or help others escape it. All she could do was make her patients as comfortable and happy as possible in the time they spent with her, and she did a good job of it. Death had always been simply a small part of life to her, an ending, but not the most important thing to happen to a person.

But now, everything was different.

This just felt like salt in the wound. One more thing she was responsible for.

It were as if poor Jim's whole life was centred around her and around this moment, and she hated that feeling, but she couldn't stop. It seemed like death was the only thing that mattered.

Maybe she was wrong to think she could go back to work, after all. Maybe home, with the covers over her head, was the safest place for her. Not just for her but for everyone else, too.

And so, Fiona went home.

Chapter 55 – Destiny

Destiny was at uni when Paula messaged the survivors' group, suggesting another meet up. Destiny surprised herself when she was the first to reply, responding enthusiastically in the affirmative. She had sort of assumed she'd be one-and-done with the survivor group meetings, but she was actually looking forward to seeing the other women again. It felt a bit like therapy, but she liked the fact that it wasn't so formal. And besides, the other women were all really good company. She particularly felt drawn to Rosie, although she didn't know why. It wasn't as if their lives were at all similar, but they seemed to get on well.

They arranged the meeting at a Mexican restaurant this time. It felt, in a small way, like healing. A Mexican restaurant was absolutely nothing like a coffee shop in a shopping centre, but it was more like it than a picnic in an open park, and Destiny knew that baby steps were the only way forward. It wasn't like they were all suddenly going to arrange to go back to the scene of the crime and share coffee together in the place where their lives had all been shattered, but meeting at a Mexican restaurant made an assumption of the survivors that life was continuing.

This time there was less notice for the meet up, and it felt more like a casual gathering of friends than anything organised and structured, like their first meeting had been. They arranged the lunch date for two days away, and Destiny put less effort into her appearance this time. Weirdly, it already felt like she'd known the others for years – there was a real familiarity even though they'd only met once before. Maybe trauma did that, bonded you to people. Well, she'd rather do without the bonding if it meant having to go through trauma, but it was a nice side effect.

Destiny was the last to arrive at the meeting. She smiled at the other women as she walked in. "Sorry I'm late," she said. "Have you ordered anything yet?"

"Just drinks," Paula replied. "We're all getting our margarita on! Well, except for this one," she added, gesturing towards Rosie and her swollen belly.

Rosie smiled warmly at Destiny as she sat down. "You'll join me in a sparkling water, right, Destiny?"

"Sorry, but you're on your own," Destiny laughed. "And call me Desi, guys. All my friends do." Of course, her friendship group was smaller now than it had been before, but she tried not to dwell on that.

"Desi it is," Paula said. "How has everyone been since we last saw each other?"

Destiny chatted away about her uni classes and how she'd taken up tai chi on the weekends. "It's been a great help," she gushed. "I feel like a normal person there again, at least for a little while."

"That's great!" Paula replied. "I've been doing pretty well, too. I don't think I told you guys last time that I've been taking things out on my hubby. Anyway, we had a bit of a fight and he called me on some of my BS, and things have been better since then. I think I've been way to focussed on being a mum and not so much on being a wife, so I'm going to try to make my relationship with him more of a priority."

Rosie spoke up next. "I've been okay. My partner and I are going through some things, too," she said, looking at Paula. "But we also had a fight, and I think that's actually helped a little. I'm trying to move on." She laughed. "Maybe we all just need to go and fight with someone and get our aggression out."

Destiny noticed that Fiona had been more quiet than normal during the discussion. As if reading her mind, Paula said "What about you, Fiona? Are you okay?"

Tears sprung to Fiona's eyes, and she wiped them away with the back of her hand. "I'm sorry," she whispered. "It's just been a really crappy time, and I thought things were getting better, but..."

Haltingly, Fiona filled the other women in on the patient she'd lost that week. The women all gasped in sympathy. "I couldn't do what you do," Rosie said, reaching out and putting her hand on Fiona's. "My sister was a nurse, and I think it takes a really special kind of person to work with sick people. It sounds like the patients there are lucky to have you."

"You know it's not your fault, though, don't you?" Destiny asked, frowning. "I mean, the guy was old. It's horrible and everything, but you can't stop death."

Fiona smiled a little. "If I didn't know it before," she said drily, "the world certainly seems happy to teach me that lesson right now."

The group fell silent. Destiny remembered how Fiona had told them at their first meeting about her husband dying. It had to have been a rough year for her. No wonder she was taking this so badly.

After a while, Rosie cleared her throat and broke the silence. "Well, on a slightly different but still traumatic topic," she laughed, "it's mythirtieth in three weeks."

"Rosie!" Destiny exclaimed. "We have to have a party for you!" Under normal circumstances it would have seemed like a strange thing to suggest to a virtual stranger but somehow, in this case, it felt natural.

"No, thanks," Rosie replied. "It's going to be such a weird day. I had been looking forward to it for a while, but now... well, I don't think I'll be having much of a birthday. It won't be my day, it'll just be the first milestone of many that Betty didn't get to see, and the first one I have to do alone." She looked like she might be about to cry, too.

Destiny knew that if all the other women started crying, she would too, and that was the last thing she wanted. "Well, I think that sucks," she said, trying to keep the tone light. "Can't we do something for you? Please? It might actually help."

Fiona and Paula nodded their agreement, and eventually Rosie laughed. "I guess we could have a small celebration, just us girls," she said. "I can save the miserable stuff for my family."

"Fabulous!" Paula exclaimed. "That'll be fun. What date is your actual birthday?"

"Thirteenth of June," Rosie replied, and Destiny entered the date into her phone. "We won't monopolise you on the actual day," Paula promised, "but we'll plan something for close by. We won't be too over the top, don't worry."

"Why don't I believe you?" Rosie asked, and the four women laughed together.

Chapter 56 – Rosie

My twenty-week scan was coming up, and Tim and I had agreed to find out the baby's sex. Well, it was more like I'd *told* him we were finding out the sex, and Tim had gone along with it. Things had been getting marginally better in our house since our frank discussion the week before, but they were far from normal between us. I felt like Tim was walking on eggshells around me, trying not to upset me further. I should have felt guilty about that but to be honest, I kind of liked it. I told myself I wasn't being malicious, it was just human nature at play.

We had a family barbecue planned for the weekend after the scan, since Dad and I were making an effort to see Jeffrey and the kids as much as possible. I told Tim we would hold off and tell the family the sex then. I was excited to see their reactions in person.

I felt strangely nervous the day of the scan. I didn't actually care one way or another what I had, as long as the baby was healthy, but it was still a nerve-wracking experience. Of course there was also the off chance that something might be wrong with the baby, but I felt pretty confident. Perhaps it was the naivete of the first-time mum, but I felt like I was far enough into my pregnancy that I would have noticed if anything felt too different.

Tim held my hand at the appointment, just as he'd done at the first scan. It was as if the baby scans were our best bonding time. Well, that and when we were around my family, but those times were mainly because I was playing happy families for Dad's sake, rather than because I actually wanted Tim's company.

"Everything looks good," the sonographer said as she moved the ultrasound wand over my belly. "Would you like to find out the sex?"

We both nodded. I'd thought maybe we'd be able to tell immediately like some people said they could, but looking at the grainy image on the screen, I didn't have a clue.

"It's a girl," the sonographer said triumphantly, and Tim and I smiled happily at each other. He'd told me in the lead up to the scan that he didn't have a preference either, but hearing the sex just made the whole thing more real. It was as if the thing inside me had gone from an abstract idea to an actual baby.

That weekend at the family barbecue, Dad seemed to feel much the same. He whooped when I said it was a girl, and threw his arms around me. It was the happiest I'd seen him since Betty died. In some ways, it was probably the happiest I'd seen him since Mum died.

"Congratulations," he said, looking misty-eyed. "I loved having two girls to spoil. I can't wait to meet this one. And it makes two grandsons and two granddaughters," he added, the pride evident in his voice. No matter what else was going on in my life right now, I felt thrilled that I was able to make him so happy.

"I'm so happy it's a girl," Poppy chirped, wrapping her arms around my growing belly. I laughed and hugged her back. "I'm sure you'll be an amazing big cousin," I told her, and she beamed with pride.

Later, I offered to help Jeffrey tidy up. When we were in the kitchen, he said "So you're pretty happy about the baby?"

"Definitely," I replied, putting a protective arm around my belly. "It's good to have something to look forward to."

A strange look came over Jeffrey's face then, and he was silent for a minute before he spoke again. "Do you know?"

My heart nearly stopped. "Do I know... what?"

He gave a short bark of a laugh. "If you know, then you know what I mean."

Shit. I had just assumed Betty hadn't told Jeffrey anything. He had seemed so... well, not normal exactly, with everything going on. But his grief didn't seem complicated like mine was. He was every part the bereaved husband. Then again, I probably seemed like any other bereaved sister to the outside world.

"About Tim and Betty?" I asked, not sure what I'd say on the off chance I was reading him wrong. I was relieved when he nodded.

"I didn't know you knew," I said quietly, and he replied, "She told me a week before she died."

"You didn't seem like you knew." It wasn't the sentiment I was trying to express, but I was finding it hard to form words.

"Neither do you," he pointed out. "You and Tim seem perfectly happy."

I pondered how to answer that. My first instinct was to reply "It's a lie", but that wasn't entirely true anymore, either. I'd made the decision to try to move on, and that's what I'd started doing, even though I knew it would take a lot more time. In the end I simply said, "A lot goes on behind closed doors."

He nodded. "I get that. When did you find out?"

I laughed bitterly. "About five minutes before she died," I said, and his face dropped. "Jeez, that's rough. I'm sorry, Rosie."

I shrugged. "I'm glad she told me, at least. It would have been a lot harder hearing it from Tim after she died. And I got to tell her it was okay."

"You forgave her?" Jeffrey asked, shocked.

"Forgive is a strong word... but I let her make her peace with it, and I'm glad I did. She was so terrified when the gunman came in." I closed my eyes, picturing Betty's tear-streaked face, and the feeling of her hand squeezing mine as we both wondered if we were going to die. "It was horrible. I was glad to at least be able to ease her mind a bit."

Jeffrey shook his head slowly. "It's a lot to deal with, though, isn't it? I had a week to come to terms with it. Maybe that's harder, I don't know. I was..." He started to choke up. "I was barely speaking to her the day she went to meet up with you."

"Oh, Jeffrey," I sighed, reaching a consoling arm out to him. No one could blame him for his reaction, but he must have been second guessing everything after she died. In a way, the way I had found out was almost kinder than his experience.

"She said she was going to tell you," Jeffrey said, "but I didn't know if she managed to or not before..."

Jeffrey's voice trailed off, and we were both quiet again for a moment, absorbed in our own thoughts.

"I'm glad she told you," he said. I nodded. When all was said and done, I was, too.

"The truth is," I said after a moment, "I've been angry at Tim, not really her, but I think that was just because I couldn't stand to be angry at her when she was already gone. But deep down..." I couldn't say it, but I felt it. Deep down there was a fury raging in my chest, and it was directed at my sister. A partner cheating was a horrific betrayal, but I had never thought my own sister would do something like that. Especially not when we'd always been so close. When it really came down to it, the bigger betrayal was from her, and I couldn't deny that forever. It wasn't healthy for me, or for my relationship with Tim.

Jeffrey sighed. "I know. I've been angry at her, too. Even after she died, I mean. I just kept thinking how much easier it would have been to mourn her if all of this hadn't happened." He paused, looking surprised at his own words. "I don't mean I'm *not* mourning her," he added quickly. "It's just so damn complicated now."

I nodded. "I know. I'm angry, and I miss her, and I love her, and I hate her."

The truth of my words rang out in the silence that followed. I'd gone to a couple of counselling appointments after the shooting, but maybe it was just too raw for me. I hadn't really felt like I was getting anywhere, so I hadn't gone back for more appointments. Speaking to Jeffrey, now, in his kitchen, felt so much more cathartic than talking to a professional. It was true. I did love and hate her, in equal measures. I was so angry at what she'd done, but I would give anything to get her back. I could have screamed at her or even slapped her in the face for what she'd done. Then I would have got over it, and we would have rebuilt our bond. But I didn't have that chance, and I never would.

"I guess I'm kind of the opposite to you, though," I added. "I think it's been easier for me to focus on their... fling, rather than on her death. I know that sounds crazy, but Betty dying is such a horrific thing to have to go through. If I put all my energy into hating them for what they did, then I don't have to feel that pain as much as I would otherwise."

He shook his head. "That doesn't sound crazy."

We were both silent again for a minute more, each processing our thoughts.

"Will you stay with him?" Jeffrey asked, nodding towards the living room, where Tim was.

I sighed. "That's the million-dollar question. I don't know... I mean, if not for the baby, I think I would have left already. And I'm definitely not going to stay with him long-term just for the sake of the baby. That's not good for anyone. But then I think... maybe what we have is more important. Maybe we'll get through it." I paused, trying to put it into words. "I managed to forgive Betty, even though I think I'm still angrier at her than I'm letting myself process at the moment. How can you be angry at your dead sister? So every so often I think, can't I forgive Tim, too?" I looked at my brother-in-law. "If she'd lived, would you have forgiven her?"

Jeffrey looked like he was giving my question some serious thought. "I don't know. I mean, I was so angry. *So* angry. But then... it's Betty, you know? She's..."

"Intoxicating," I finished for him. It took me a moment to realise that we were talking about her in the present tense.

"And it was one mistake," Jeffrey went on. "I mean, they fucked up royally, but it doesn't replace an entire lifetime. They're still the same people they always were. I don't think I ever could have left her. We both loved Betty for years."

"Forever," I said.

That was undeniably true. Did one mistake make an entire lifetime of love and happiness just vanish? Would I sacrifice the next few decades with Tim because of what he had done with my sister?

But on the other hand, could I ever let it go? *Really* let it go, where I stopped feeling the undercurrent of resentment? Stopped picturing the two of them together and feeling sick about it? Stopped feeling like Tim owed me a debt he could never repay?

That was what I had to figure out.

Chapter 57 – Paula

Over the next few days, Jasmine grew even more withdrawn.

Paula had no idea what had caused the growing rift. Since Alfie's comment about how it seemed like Paula and Ollie against the world, she'd been making an increased effort to reach out to her daughter. Rather than making things better, it felt like every time she reached for Jasmine, her daughter took a step back. Paula was starting to wonder if things were ever going to change. She felt a pang as she thought back to her sweet, ballet-dancing daughter from not that long ago. The year Jasmine turned twelve, it was as if that girl disappeared overnight. Paula had heard plenty of horror stories about life with teenagers, but she hadn't expected her daughter to morph into a whole new person, or for it to happen so suddenly. Since then, it had felt like Paula had been trying to catch up with a daughter who seemed to have no problems leaving her behind.

Finally, she decided she needed to approach things head-on. Wasn't her therapist always telling her to talk things through? And things had started to improve between her and Alfie since he had spoken to her about his feelings. Maybe things would get better with Jasmine, too.

Paula knocked on her daughter's door, surprised at how nervous she felt. Raising children could break your heart in a hundred new ways every day.

"Yeah?" Jasmine mumbled through the door, which Paula took as an invitation to enter.

Jasmine's room was messy, like most teenagers'. There were clothes strewn everywhere, and band posters of angry-looking people Paula had never heard of. She still thought of herself as relatively in touch with things, but it only took entering the bedroom of a fifteen-year-old to make her feel ancient.

"Hey, honey," Paula said gently, approaching her daughter. Jasmine was on her bed, her legs crossed, mobile on her thigh. "What are you doing?"

Jasmine shrugged.

Paula had always hated her children shrugging in response to a question, but she decided to let this one go. Pick your battles, and all that. "Sweetie, I know things have been tough for you lately," she said. "I feel like you've been pushing me away. Is it anything to do with the shooting? I know Ollie has been getting more attention than you lately..."

Jasmine sneered. "I don't need attention."

"Well, what is it?" Then Paula remembered the way Harold spoke to her. "Is there anything you'd like to talk about?" That was better. It was more of an invitation than an intrusion.

Jasmine shrugged again, looking down. Then, to Paula's shock, she started to tear up.

"Oh, honey!" Paula was taken aback. Jasmine had never been much of a crier, and Paula certainly hadn't said anything to provoke that reaction. A feeling of dread formed in her stomach. Something was really wrong here. "What is it? Please, tell me."

Jasmine started crying in earnest, and mumbled something that Paula couldn't hear. Her hair formed a protective curtain around her face.

Paula reached forward and moved the hair away from her daughter's cheeks. "I missed that, baby girl."

"You'll hate me," Jasmine repeated, her voice slightly higher now, and verging on hysterical.

"I could never hate you!" Paula rushed to reassure her. "Nothing you do could make me hate you. Just please, tell me what it is."

Jasmine was silent for a long time, and Paula had to almost physically bite her tongue to keep herself from saying more. Whatever it was that was upsetting Jasmine so much, rushing her wasn't going to help. It was probably a minute until Jasmine spoke again, but the wait felt a lot longer. It was agonising.

Not that things got any better when Jasmine did finally speak.

"I'm pregnant," she whispered, staring at the ground.

Chapter 58 – Fiona

Her patient, Jim, had died on a Wednesday, so Fiona arranged to have the next two days off before returning to work the following Monday. It wasn't long enough to get her head around things, but she felt like nothing ever would be. Besides, she was glad to have had the meeting with the other survivors. Destiny was right; you couldn't stop death. No matter how hard Fiona tried, she was going to lose patients. It was always going to be rough, but she hadn't even been in the same room as Jim when he died. She couldn't possibly blame herself for it.

It didn't exactly help the way she was feeling, but it was enough to get her out of bed, and that was all that really mattered. The rest would come in time.

"So good to see you," Adam exclaimed when she walked into work on the Monday. "We just got you back and you left again. I was starting to think I'd have to find a new work wife."

"Not that bitch Colleen," Fiona joked back. Colleen was a stern woman in her sixties who worked at the front desk. "I'd never let that happen. I'm back for good."

Adam smiled and gave her a quick hug before continuing on his way. "And thank goodness for that. We'll catch up properly later," he called after him.

Taking Angela's advice, Fiona had stuck to the rule of going out socially once a week. It was a bit harder when she was tired from work, but it also seemed more important. Otherwise, her life started to revolve around work, and she knew that wasn't much healthier than staying in bed. This week's dinner was with Adam and Julian the following night. They'd invited her over to their place. "Bring Burleigh," Adam had added when they'd made the plan. Julian hadn't yet met the dog, and Fiona was excited to get a chance to show him off again.

Fiona turned up at Adam's place on the Tuesday night, Burleigh in her arms. Adam opened the door and grinned at the sight of the dog. "Oh Fi, he's just so adorable! Let me have him," he exclaimed, reaching out for Burleigh, who leapt happily into Adam's arms. Fiona loved how much of a people person – people dog? – Burleigh was. She'd heard about dogs who didn't want to be with anyone but their owner, or those you couldn't trust not to bite people, but Burleigh was always friendly and loving. Fiona wondered how she'd gone so long without ever owning a pet. It gave her a whole new lease on life.

"Hey, Fiona," Julian said, kissing her on the cheek as she walked into the kitchen. "And this must be your new man," he added, gesturing to Burleigh. A few weeks ago, the mention of a 'new man' would have instantly made her think of Jacob, but now she just smiled, taking the comment in the easy-going way she knew it was intended.

"This is him," she said, laughing as Julian got down on the floor to greet Burleigh, who jumped all over him.

"So," Adam said as they sat down to dinner, "how's life going for you? How did your meeting with the other tragics go?"

Fiona shot her friend a mock glare. She knew Adam was keeping it light, and to be honest, she was sick of thinking of them as the 'survivors'. Tragics wasn't much better, but the fact that he was willing to joke about it indicated he thought she was doing better. Between Jacob's death and the shooting, everyone had been walking on eggshells around her for so long, and she was tired of it. "Yeah, it was good. We've met up twice now, actually. We saw each other last week and we're planning a thirtieth for one of the women."

"Really?" Adam laughed. "That's a bit quick. Are they your besties now?"

"Not besties," she said, "but it's amazing how quickly we all bonded. I guess a lunatic pointing a gun at your heads will do that to people." Fiona, too, was trying to keep things light. The shooting was far from a joking manner, but as far as coping mechanisms went, humour wasn't a bad one.

"That's great," Julian said sincerely. He had always been kind and considerate towards her. "Something good had to come out of all this."

Fiona nodded, smiling. She hadn't thought of it that way, but Julian was right. As traumatic as the shooting was, at least it had led to one good thing. She hadn't had a group of friends since high school, and definitely not one as varied as this. The mum in her forties, the young widow, the pregnant woman and a uni student barely into her twenties. It was an unexpected group, but somehow it worked.

"Anyway, enough about me and my horrific life," Fiona joked. "What about you guys? How are things in Chez Jam?" It was a nickname she and Adam had given the house a few years ago, standing for Julian and Adam Morgan. Julian's own family had largely disowned him after finding out he was gay, so he had taken on Adam's surname when they got married.

The two looked at each other. "Actually," Adam said, "we're both taking some long service leave and going travelling for six months." Julian was a high school teacher. "We're going to Europe," Adam continued, and Fiona gasped with envy.

"That sounds amazing!" she exclaimed. "But what am I going to do at work without you? Will I have to find a new work husband?"

"You'll be fine, but I'd better not come back to find you've cheated on me," Adam quipped. "We're not leaving 'til January, so you've got some time to get used to the idea. We thought we'd time it so Julian was leaving at the start of the new school year. Plus, it gives us time to save." He grimaced and gestured to his slightly overweight frame. "I'm going to have to sell my body on the streets to make it work financially."

"Oh God," Julian teased. "We'll have to stay in hostels."

Adam slapped Julian playfully, and Fiona laughed. She missed this part of her relationship with Jacob. The simple, everyday back-and-forth banter that she'd only really ever had with him.

"Anyway," Adam went on, "I know you've always wanted to go to Italy, and we're spending a few weeks there. Rome, Florence and Venice. We were wondering if you'd like to join us."

"Seriously?" Fiona squealed, looking between the two of them. Then she paused, suddenly disappointed. "Oh, I'll never get the leave though, after all the time I've had off, and especially with you not there, Adam."

"Well, see how you go but it is still more than six months away," Adam pointed out. "Gives you enough time to save *and* enough time to work up some time off, if you're keen."

Fiona considered it. It was true; she and Jacob had always planned a trip to Italy but had never made it there. And it would be so amazing to have something to look forward to, for the first time in recent memory. If she saved hard enough she could potentially afford to even take some unpaid leave, if it came to that. She'd never spent much on clothes or food, and it wasn't as if she was spending a fortune at the pub every week like so many people seemed to do. Besides, Jacob's life insurance money had come through, which gave her an extra feeling of security. It wasn't a huge fortune by any means, but it helped, and she'd felt too guilty to even think about spending it so far. Maybe this would give her a reason to spend it that she knew Jacob would have approved of.

"I'll definitely think about it," she said, smiling at her friends.

Chapter 59 – Destiny

Destiny had always loved party planning, so it seemed only natural for her to take charge of the organisation of Rosie's thirtieth birthday celebrations. Destiny had organised every detail of her own eighteenth and twenty-first parties, as well as arranging the high tea they threw for her mum when she turned fifty a couple of years earlier. This was a lot more low-key than those had been, of course, but it was still fun to have something to occupy her mind other than constant thoughts of Luke or of the shooting.

She set up a new group chat with Paula and Fiona, leaving Rosie out of it. Together they set a date and decided the venue would be Fiona's house. "I've got enough space, and I live alone," the other woman wrote. "I've got a pretty big backyard too, if we want to do it there."

"Partners?" Destiny wrote, and Fiona replied "I don't mind. It would just be Tim and Paula's husband anyway."

"Alfie wouldn't come," Paula messaged. "Classically anti-social."

"Unless you have someone you'd like to bring, Desi?" Fiona wrote back, and Destiny replied with just a laughing emoji. No, there was no one for her.

"Just us four, then," Fiona said. "Rosie wanted simple, anyway."

Destiny smiled as she put her phone away. They had settled on a lunchtime gathering, and Fiona had suggested they shouldn't have any "30" signs or balloons. Destiny agreed; the focus should be on a nice gathering for the four of them, with the added bonus of gifts for Rosie. It felt cruel to draw too much attention to the fact that Rosie was turning thirty and her sister never would. It would be a tough time for her but Rosie deserved to be celebrated, too.

After the party planning was done Destiny returned to her study, but the words swam in front of her eyes. It had been harder and harder to concentrate since everything had happened. She was relieved when her phone lit up with a message again. She picked it up, expecting to see a message about the party from one of the girls, but it was Nate. "I'm bored. Want to get a pizza?"

Destiny smiled to herself as she quickly responded. "Name a time and place and I'm there!" She hadn't really been studying for long enough to warrant a break, but that was entirely beside the point.

They met half an hour later, at a small pizza restaurant not far from Destiny's place. She smiled when she saw Nate, and he gave her a quick hug in greeting.

"How have you been?" Nate asked once they were sitting down together. "I've missed seeing you around at uni."

Destiny sighed. "I've been okay. I've just been skipping out on most of my classes, unless I have to go. I mean, I'm still studying, but I just don't want to be there right now."

"Because of Ed?" Nate asked, a concerned look on his face. When she nodded, he said "I thought things were better between you guys."

"I mean, he said sorry, as you know, and I said I understood... and I do. Well, kind of. But there's a difference between understanding and wanting to be in the same room as him."

"It must be tough," Nate said sympathetically. "But Ed really does regret what he said. We had a chat about it. And you can't just throw everything away because of one jackass."

"I'm still studying," Destiny repeated. "I'll still pass, I'm sure."

"Yeah, but think of what you're missing out on. You can't just stay home all day," Nate argued. "You're not getting to see your friends because of him. And you *know* you learn better face-to-face. You're the one who told me that."

It was true. Honestly, it had been a struggle to keep up with all her uni requirements without attending classes. A journalism degree was done mostly on assignments rather than exams, and they were all submitted online anyway, so the practical side of things was easy. But Destiny knew she wasn't taking in as much as she would have been if she was there, listening to her lecturer rather than doing her readings and watching the occasional lecture online. And Nate was right, she did miss seeing more of her friends. The longer she was spending at home, the harder she was finding it on the days when she did have to go out to the university campus in person. It wasn't healthy. Destiny thought of her vow to live her life to the fullest in Luke's honour, and she had to admit she wasn't doing it.

"You're right," Destiny sighed. "I'll come back to classes."

Nate grinned. "Tough love did the trick," he said lightly, lifting his water glass in a mock 'cheers' and looking pretty pleased with himself.

Suddenly there was a bang, shocking her with how loud it was. Destiny froze, then began shaking all over. It was happening again. She never should have left the house.

"Destiny?" It was Nate's voice, sounding like it was coming from underwater. She looked up and was taken aback to see him still sitting in his chair, staring at her. He looked concerned, but it didn't seem as though he was terrified.

She looked around and saw everyone else in the pizza place was still sitting at their tables as if nothing had happened. Then she saw a little boy crying over near the counter. Had he been hurt? She thought of Ollie the day of the shooting.

"It was a balloon," Nate said quietly, his eyes still fixed on her. "Are you okay?"

Destiny took a deep, shuddering breath. That was why the boy was crying. He hadn't seen a crazed gunman. He hadn't been shot. His balloon had popped. The rest of the world was continuing on like nothing had happened, but Destiny was back in that coffee shop in that shopping centre.

"Did it..." Nate paused, as though trying to find the right words. "Did it take you back?"

She nodded wordlessly.

"I can't imagine what you've been going through," he said sympathetically. "I haven't asked much about it because I wasn't sure if you were ready to talk, but you can tell me anything. You know that, right?"

Destiny nodded again. She did know that he would always be there to listen, but she wasn't sure if she was able to talk about it just yet.

"I guess I've been focussing on Luke's death," she said after a long pause. "Like, I haven't really given much thought to the actual shooting because what happened to him was so horrific." She didn't even know if she was making sense, but Nate was nodding.

"I guess it also felt a little... I don't know, selfish? Self-indulgent?" she went on. "Talking about myself when Luke died that day. I mean, what I went through was nothing, really."

"It wasn't nothing," Nate protested. "Even if you hadn't gone through what you did with Luke, a shooting is still a pretty bloody traumatic thing to have happen! Anyone would struggle after their life was threatened. Absolutely no one would think you were selfish if you needed to talk about it."

She knew he was right, but that didn't make it any easier.

"Have you had therapy or anything?"

Destiny shook her head. "Mum wanted me to, but I don't know. I don't think I've ever really been interested in that sort of thing. I mean, I have nothing against it," she added quickly. "One of my friends from school went to therapy after her dad died, and I know it helped her a lot. I just don't think talking over my problems is going to help. It's not going to bring Luke back." She felt dangerously on the verge of tears now and she tried to laugh. She didn't want to fall apart in front of Nate, at this cheerful pizza place. She could see the sadness in his eyes, though. She wasn't fooling anyone.

"I'd do anything to change this for you," Nate said softly, and she smiled.

"I know you would. I'm lucky to have you guys," she said, assuming he would know she meant him and Gemma. "But there's nothing anyone can do, so in the meantime, I guess we have pizza."

"I guess we do."

As if on cue, the waitress came to take their orders. Once she'd left Destiny, determined to change the subject to something a bit lighter, started filling Nate in on her meetings with the other girls. "I thought it was going to be a bit lame," she said, "but it's been amazing, actually. We don't talk much about the shooting, so it's not all depressing, but they really get what I'm going through, which is nice. Aside from you and Gemma, they're the only people I've seen much of lately who I'm not related to."

"They sound great," Nate said, smiling. "Are you going to see them again?"

Destiny nodded, telling him briefly about the thirtieth birthday lunch she was planning. "It's been so much fun, planning it," she gushed. "It's only really small and simple, but it's something I'm looking forward to. And I'm going to make it special for Rosie. Her favourite colour's purple, so I'm going to arrange all these purple decorations and everything. It should be fun."

"Want me to get some flowers for the day?" Nate offered. His older sister was a florist, so Destiny knew it wouldn't be too hard for him to arrange it with her, but Destiny was touched by the offer. "That would be awesome," she said, smiling at him. "I think she'd really like that. Thank you!" He'd obviously seen how much her new friendships meant to her, to even suggest becoming involved with it.

Their pizzas arrived then and the two dug in, sharing a happy silence as they ate.

Chapter 60 – Paula

"What did you just say?" Paula asked, staring at her daughter. She felt as though the wind had been knocked out of her. She must have misheard. Surely it couldn't be what she thought.

"I'm pregnant," Jasmine repeated with a sniffle, and Paula sat down on the bed beside her, dazed.

"How..." A million questions ran through Paula's head. She hadn't even known Jasmine was dating anyone. She'd had no idea she was having sex. She was still so young! "How far along are you?" she asked finally. It wasn't really the most important question, but it seemed like the easiest.

"Not long," Jasmine said with a shrug. "Like eight or nine weeks."

Paula felt her shoulders sag. "When did you find out?"

"Three weeks ago," Jasmine replied in a small voice. "I've been wanting to tell you, but I was... I guess I was hoping it would go away."

Paula felt a pinch of pain at the idea of her daughter dealing with this alone. The last few weeks must have been hell for her. "Who's the father?"

"Brad," Jasmine muttered. He was a friend of hers, but Paula had never really approved of him. He had always seemed like a bad influence, and this didn't exactly do a lot to change her mind. Paula hadn't known their relationship had progressed beyond friendship. "I didn't know you two were dating," she said, and Jasmine started crying harder.

"We're not," she wailed. "Not really. We just... he broke up with his girlfriend, and he said he wanted to be friends with benefits. I was just... curious, I guess. It was so dumb."

"Oh, Jasmine," Paula sighed. "Didn't you use anything?"

"A condom, but it broke. I thought it would be okay. I didn't want to face going to the doctor."

Paula recalled being that age, and the mortification that came with talking about sex. She hadn't slept with her first boyfriend until she was eighteen, but she could imagine she would have just hoped everything would be okay rather than going to a doctor about it, too. "Oh, sweetie," she murmured, grabbing her daughter and pulling her in for a hug. "It will be okay. I'll look after you."

Her daughter wrapped her own arms around Paula in return. It was a terrible circumstance, but it was so nice to have her daughter express some physical affection for her again. It had been so long.

Paula didn't ask whether Brad was aware of his impending fatherhood, or what her daughter wanted to do about the unplanned pregnancy. While theoretically pro-choice, she wasn't sure how she felt about Jasmine potentially having an abortion. On the other hand, she wasn't sure any of them were ready to have a baby in the house, either. There was always the option of adoption, but that had its own difficulties. How would Jasmine fare knowing she had a child out there in the world, living with strangers? How would Paula and Alfie feel about not knowing their own grandchild?

Whatever the answer, it was too complicated right now. Paula just wanted to stay here and hug her daughter.

Jasmine had been fearing her mother's disappointment, but Paula knew her own reaction was mild compared to what Alfie's would be. He and Jazzy had always been pretty close, but she knew he struggled to see her as a young woman rather than a little girl. Even when she got her period at twelve he'd had trouble dealing with it, and that had been a natural part of growing up. Teenaged pregnancy was something different altogether. Alfie was a good man, but he was undeniably old-fashioned about some things. Paula dreaded telling him this, but she knew it had to fall to her. Jasmine couldn't be there when Alfie found out the news.

Chapter 61 – Rosie

I woke up the day of my thirtieth birthday celebration feeling surprisingly excited. My actual birthday was still a few days away, but I was probably looking forward to my celebration with the girls more than the birthday itself. I was sure my family would make my actual birthday special, but we'd all have mixed feelings about the celebration. This felt a lot more simple and straightforward.

I turned up at Fiona's house at eleven as instructed and was greeted by all three women calling out "Happy birthday!" I smiled as they all hugged me in greeting. It was the first time any of us had hugged, but it felt natural.

We walked onto Fiona's back patio together. I had told them not to go to any great effort, but when I arrived, I saw a beautifully decorated table with balloons, flowers and candles adorning it, and a lilac tablecloth. We had agreed on simple chicken and salad for lunch, but I was surprised to see a large plate of nibbles already out. "You guys!" I exclaimed, feeling my eyes well up. "This is amazing."

"Uh-oh, here come the pregnancy hormones," Paula laughed. "It was so much fun to organise. Of course, Destiny did most of the work," she added, and I gave Desi's arm a little squeeze of thanks.

"It was nothing," Destiny said modestly. "I had fun choosing the tablecloth and plates sand stuff, and my friend Nate organised the flowers and balloon bouquet."

The three of us looked at each other knowingly.

"What?" Destiny asked, all innocence.

I laughed. "Oh, honey, your friend Nate has a big crush on you."

"No!" Destiny protested, but I noticed a bit of colour rising in her cheeks. "His sister's a florist. It was no biggie."

"Florist sister or not," Fiona said firmly, "he's, what, your age?"

"Twenty-one," Destiny murmured. "So, a little younger."

"Yeah, no twenty-one-year-old guy in the world has ever gone out and arranged flowers and balloons for some woman he's never met just because it's convenient for him to do so."

Destiny continued to protest, while the rest of us laughed. "Ah, young love," I teased.

"Speaking of which," Paula said, "how did you meet your man?"

I smiled, thinking of the early days with Tim. "It was through a mutual friend," I said. "It wasn't a set-up or anything, but we went out as a big group for her birthday. Tim was working with her at the time, so he came along. We just really hit it off, and he asked me that night if he could get my number." It was a simple story, but it had always made me melt to think about. It had just seemed so right, straight away. I'd been a year out of my previous relationship, which had been all kinds of difficult by the end. With Tim, everything felt easy.

It was the first time I'd had to tell that story since Tim had told me he'd cheated, and telling it now didn't fill me with quite the same feeling that it used to. Like everything else in our relationship, it seemed tainted now.

The other women's cooing over my story brought me out of my own head, which I was grateful for. I was so sick of going over this. It was nice to concentrate on my new friends' company instead.

The rest of the day passed happily, with a lot of laughter and easy conversation. The others all bought me presents, even though I'd told them not to, and I was touched by their thoughtfulness. For people I had known such a short time, they really seemed to understand me.

Chapter 62 – Fiona

Fiona hummed to herself as she drove home from Rosie's birthday gathering. She couldn't remember the last time she'd enjoyed herself so much.

At that moment Angela called, the sound of the shrill ring through her Bluetooth making Fiona jump. She clicked on the 'answer' button on her steering wheel, still on a high from the day so far. "Hey, Ange," she chirped.

"You sound happy!" her friend laughed. "Good day, then?" Fiona had filled her in on her plans, and Angela had seemed happy that she was branching out a bit more.

"Yeah, it was great," Fiona replied. "They're really nice company, and Rosie seemed to appreciate it all. Oh, and I haven't told you yet about what Adam and Julian asked me."

"Threesome?" Angela quipped, and Fiona laughed.

"Nothing quite that scandalous. No, they're going to Europe in the new year and they suggested I come and join them for the Italy part of their trip."

"No way!" Angela exclaimed. "Would you?"

"Honestly, I'm thinking about it. I've always wanted to go, as you know, and it seems like as good a chance as any. Now that Jacob's gone, I don't know who else I'd go with, and I don't think I'm ready to go alone." She knew that Angela had done some solo overseas travel before she was married and had loved it, but Fiona had done so little travel that she wasn't prepared to branch out independently. Besides, Angela had always had the bigger personality than Fiona.

"No, that sounds great! You should definitely go," Angela enthused. "I can help you come up with a budget, if you want?" *Ever the accountant,* Fiona thought fondly, smiling to herself.

"Maybe I'll take you up on that," Fiona said. "I've got Jacob's money, but I don't want to blow it all, so I want to do as much out of savings as I can. But I'm just not sure how Jennifer would take it," she added, referring to her boss.

Angela made a *pfft* sound down the phone. "Jenny can deal with it," she said. Absolutely no one called Jennifer Jenny, but Angela liked to do so, sarcastically, when talking about her. "It's not 'til next year, after all, and it's not like you took time off this year so you could just loaf about. I think she has to be a little bit understanding about it all."

Fiona nodded, even though her friend couldn't see her. Maybe Angela was right. Seemingly sensing that Fiona was coming around, Angela added "Of all people, you know how short life can be. You might as well live it."

Fiona was silent for a moment, the simple truth of Angela's words ringing in her ears. She'd been avoiding life for so many months now, but maybe that needed to stop. "What about Burleigh?" she asked.

"I'll look after him. The kids'll love it," Angela said breezily. "I think you're just about out of excuses now, aren't you?"

Fiona laughed in response. "I guess I am."

"So you're doing it?" Angela squealed.

Fiona smiled more widely this time, starting to feel excitement bubbling up inside her. "I think I am. I'm going to Italy!"

Chapter 63 – Destiny

Destiny had tried to dismiss what her friends had said about Nate the moment they'd said it, but she couldn't deny that their words kept circling around in her brain. Could it be true that Nate liked her in that way? He'd definitely been attentive towards her, but that didn't necessarily mean anything. He'd always been a great guy. He was just being a supportive friend while she was going through a bad situation. He would do the same for anyone.

She thought of what Gemma had said the previous week, and decided to go home via her friend's house. Maybe Gemma could give her some clarity.

"Desi!" Gemma exclaimed as she opened the door. "What are you doing here? You look amazing! You're all fancy!"

Destiny smiled. "I just came from Rosie's thirtieth that I was telling you about. Can I come in?"

"Of course," Gemma said, opening the door wider. "I thought you might have ditched me for the old aged crew."

"Never," Destiny replied, giving Gemma a quick squeeze. "They're nice, though. I think you'd like them."

The two got settled on the couch, with Gemma opening a packet of chocolate biscuits she had brought in from the kitchen. They put them on the couch beside them and Destiny pulled one leg up on the couch as she turned her body to face her friend.

"Last time I saw you," she said, "you made some crack about someone being interested in me?"

"Did I?" Gemma asked, all mock-innocence. "I must have forgotten."

"Who were you talking about?" Destiny was trying to sound more casual than she felt, but she knew she was failing.

"It doesn't matter," Gemma replied breezily. "I was probably totally off base. Besides, you said you weren't interested in dating, anyway." Destiny could tell the other girl was enjoying dragging this out, teasing her.

"Seriously!" Destiny said. "The others today said something... weird."

"Oh, did they? And what might that have been?"

"Nate arranged a flower and balloon bouquet for Rosie's birthday, and they said they think he's interested in me."

Gemma snorted out a laugh. "Well, they sound like regular detectives, then! I'm glad they could see what's perfectly clear to everyone except you."

Destiny's heart sank. "So you really think Nate likes me?"

"It's obvious," Gemma replied, far more casually than Destiny felt the conversation warranted.

"Ugh! This is awful!" Destiny exclaimed, and she saw surprise register on Gemma's face. "Really? You don't like him back?"

"Of course not!" Destiny cried. "I'm still getting over Luke. I'm not interested in Nate as anything more than a friend. Don't you see how *complicated* this makes everything?"

Gemma shrugged. "If you're really not interested, you're not interested. It's not so complicated."

"But I don't want to lose him as a friend."

"I'm sure you won't. He's a good guy. He'll just be happy to be around you, even as a friend. It's not like he's tried anything, so he doesn't even know that you know."

Destiny was struggling to put her feelings into words. "Well, I guess the crush could go away," she finally said, lamely. It wasn't what she wanted to say, but it was the easiest thing she could think of.

"Not likely," Gemma laughed. "He's *always* liked you. Like, probably even before *Luke* did. I don't think it's going away anytime soon."

"No!" Destiny exclaimed. She was willing to believe Nate might have a little thing for her, but she couldn't picture it being any serious. If it had really been going on for that long...

"Seriously," her friend replied. "He just saw your googly eyes towards Luke and decided to... give up, I guess. Poor guy."

Destiny shook her head, trying to process this. She thought of the day she'd met Nate. She'd literally bumped into him at one of the uni cafés, and he'd grinned at her and asked, "Had a few too many?" She'd thought he was cute straight away, but she wasn't *into* him exactly. She'd just always seen him as a buddy. They'd got chatting, and he'd invited her to a party he was going to that night. She'd gone along since she had nothing better to do, and she'd dragged Gemma along with her. Luke was at the party and the moment she'd locked eyes on him, it was all over. He'd taken her breath away and it had taken her a while to recover her composure. From then, it had been hard to imagine being with anyone else. She had only had eyes for Luke.

Oh, God. Maybe Gemma had a point, after all.

That night was the start of the forming of their group of six, with Courtney and Ed connecting with the rest of them a year later, through Nate. Now Destiny was seeing it all in a new light. Maybe Nate had never really intended to be part of a friendship group with her, after all? Maybe his feelings had been different all along. Maybe they'd just fallen into the friend zone because as a group, they had all got along so well, and it just seemed to make sense.

Regardless, there was no way she could act on it now, even if she returned Nate's feelings – which she didn't. She could just imagine Ed's response to that, his sneer. "Really working your way through the group, aren't you, Desi? Will it be me next, or will you switch over to one of the girls?" Gemma seemed supportive enough of the idea, but she knew Courtney would also think that Destiny was taking Nate on just because she couldn't have Luke. He would always be seen as second choice, and Nate deserved better than that. People would think she'd let Luke die for her, and then just moved on to his good friend. People would say his sacrifice wasn't worth it, and they'd probably be right.

She shuddered to think about it. No, it was way too complicated, just as she'd said. Besides, she'd sworn off men entirely, so it really didn't matter.

Chapter 64 – Paula

As Paula had expected, Alfie exploded when he heard the news. She had deliberately told him when Jasmine was at her after-school job and Ollie was at a mate's place, knowing he wouldn't be able to keep his reaction calm and rational. Alfie had never been violent, but his face turned red and he stormed away, hands in fists.

After a few minutes, he had finally calmed down enough to talk about it. "What's she going to do?" he demanded.

Paula shook her head. "I'm not sure. I only just found out myself last week, and I haven't asked her what she plans. My priority right now is her mental health."

"Well, she can't keep it," Alfie retorted, and Paula stared at him, feeling her mouth fall open in shock. "Are you serious?" she exclaimed. "It's Jasmine's baby, and it's her choice. When it comes down to it, we'll support her whatever she decides."

"It's not her choice. For God's sake, Paula, she's a child."

"She's clearly not that much of a child!" Paula replied hotly. "I know this isn't ideal for anyone, but we can't make her have an abortion. If it's not what she wants, she'll never forgive us." She sounded surer than she felt. Her own feelings about what to do were still so up in the air, but she wasn't about to say that to Alfie.

"She could adopt it out," he replied. "We can't afford this baby, Paula."

Paula knew he had a point there. The reason for the larger age gap between her two children was that they were trying to make themselves more financially independent before having Oliver. They had only partially succeeded. Paula herself had wanted a third child, but she'd known it would be more of a financial strain than they could bear. A few years on things were somewhat better than they had been, but they weren't exactly rolling in cash. It wouldn't be easy for them to help support another child, but she was determined not to let money be the deciding factor here. After all, if she herself had fallen pregnant again, they would have made it work. There was no way she ever would have aborted a baby, or given it up. If it came down to it, they would do the same thing here. Make it work.

"Well, if this is going to be your attitude, I don't want you talking to her about it," Paula snapped. "Just go on acting like you don't know anything. I'll talk to her and hopefully find out what she wants to do."

Alfie shook his head. "You do whatever you want, but you know I'm right."

THAT NIGHT, WHEN JASMINE got home, Paula waited until Alfie was in the shower and then went to talk to her daughter in her bedroom. Despite the circumstances, she was pleased that Jazzy let her in more willingly than she had done the week before. Maybe, just maybe, this whole thing would break down some of her daughter's walls.

"Hi, sweetie," Paula said softly, closing the door behind her. "How are you doing?"

Jasmine looked at her. "Have you spoken to Dad?"

"No, not yet. He wasn't in the right mood." It wasn't entirely a lie. Alfie was certainly not in the right mood for any of this.

It was the first time Paula and Jasmine had talked about the baby since Jasmine had confided in her a week earlier. Paula had deliberately steered clear of the topic, trying to give Jasmine some space. Now, she wondered if her silence made it seem like she was the one who didn't want to face it. "Have you thought about your plans?" she asked.

"With the baby?" Jasmine asked, as if her mother might be suggesting she star in the school concert. When her mother nodded, she replied, "Not really. I mean, I haven't even told Brad about it yet. I haven't told anyone... except you. It just doesn't feel real." She looked like she was about to start crying again.

"I'm here for you, no matter what," Paula told her. "If you keep it, you know you and the baby both have a home here. If you decide you can't keep it, I'll support you through that, too."

"I was thinking of maybe adopting it out," Jasmine murmured. "But I know that'll be really hard. I looked it up and it said a lot of people regret doing it. So I don't know. But I don't really think I could go through with an abortion. I think I'd feel too guilty."

Paula's heart ached for her daughter. She wished she could just turn back the clock and go back to a simpler time.

"I'm not going to lie to you, baby. Whatever you choose, it's going to be a hard road. But we're here for you."

She got up to leave, and as she got to the door, she heard Jasmine say, "Dad knows, doesn't he?"

Paula turned and looked at her daughter. She'd always been perceptive, and Paula decided there was no point lying to her any further. "Yes, he does."

Jasmine nodded. "I thought so," she said in a small voice, and then she curled up on her bed.

Chapter 65 – Rosie

The night of my birthday celebration with the girls Tim met me in the entry of the house and I perched on one of our wooden stools, chatting away about the day. I filled him in on the food we'd eaten, the gifts I'd received and the beautiful decorations. It was only after I'd drawn breath that I realised it was the most I'd spoken to him since I'd confronted him about Betty.

Tim was smiling when I got to the end of my monologue, perhaps noticing the same thing. "It sounds great," he said, his tone sincere. "I'm glad you have friends like that."

I nodded. I was, too. It sounded cliched, but Betty had always been my best friend, as complicated as our relationship could sometimes be. Between her and Tim, I felt like I had all the company I needed. I'd never really had many close female friends. I realised now that I hadn't known what I was missing.

"I have a surprise for you," he said, reaching out for my hand. I took it, only slightly hesitantly, and let him lead me into the living room.

I gasped when I saw what was waiting for me: Two beautiful black leather recliners and a two-seater recliner couch. "Tim!" I exclaimed. "This must have cost a fortune."

He shrugged, smiling. "I got a good deal, and I figured it was time for a change," he said lightly. He didn't refer to the obvious issue with the previous couch, and I didn't either. I went over and sat in the chair, which was deliciously comfortable. The leather was so soft and buttery.

"But that's not all," Tim added. "You have to get up for the next part."

I groaned. "Can't you bring it to me?" I asked, reclining the chair back. I had no intention of going anywhere soon.

Tim shook his head, still smiling. "Sorry. You have to come with me for this one. I promise it'll be worth it."

I sighed and begrudgingly got up. I finally followed him upstairs, wondering what he had planned.

If the chairs downstairs had taken my breath away, they were nothing compared to what awaited me in our spare room. Tim and I had painted the walls a soft lilac the week earlier, but the room had been completely empty. It was now filled with a gorgeous, old-fashioned looking cot, a small wooden chest of drawers and – my favourite touch – a wooden rocking chair in the corner with a pink cushion and a blush pink throw rug on top.

"This is amazing!" I cried, looking around the room. It was really starting to look like a home for our baby. "I can't believe you did all of this in one day."

He grinned. "I put the order in last week, but I made sure to have it arrive the day of your party. I wanted to surprise you."

"It's beautiful," I said honestly. I was impressed by Tim's thoughtfulness. We hadn't discussed what we wanted the baby's room to look like – beyond the lilac walls, of course – but he'd nailed it. The classic, retro touches were exactly my style, and not Tim's at all. He had done it all for me. I walked over and gave him a hug, feeling the weight of my belly nestled in between us. "Thank you."

He bent down and kissed the top of my head. "Anytime," he said, resting one hand on my stomach.

I'd been trying to convince myself for months now, but for the first time since the shooting, I really believed we stood a chance.

Chapter 66 – Fiona

It felt almost rebellious to Fiona when she and Paula started private messaging, away from the group of four.

Naturally there was nothing in the messages that the other two couldn't have seen, but Fiona had felt an instant affinity with Paula. They were closer in age than the others – Paula had mentioned she was forty-two, and Fiona was thirty-seven – and although Paula had kids and Fiona didn't, they seemed to have a lot in common. Sometimes you just clicked with someone.

She was in the middle of a texting session with Paula the Saturday following Rosie's birthday celebration when a message from Angela came through. "Exercised today?" it asked.

Fiona groaned. She had taken on three of Fiona's four steps – everything except the shopping part – but the exercise part hadn't yet proven to be as successful as the socialising or the dog ownership, even though it was the step she'd been the most open to. She found herself dreading it every day. "Yep," she wrote back, and had barely pressed send before Angela's reply came through. "Liar."

She should have known there was no fooling Angela. They'd been friends for too long. "Going now," she replied, and she got up and put her exercise gear on.

As she was getting ready to go out for a jog, another message from Paula came through. Fiona read it, then replied impulsively. "I'm going for a jog. Care to join me?"

The reply came through quickly. "If it becomes a walk instead of a jog, I'm in. Meet at the fountain at the park?"

Fiona laughed, reading it. A walk suited her even better than a jog. "Meet you in 15," she wrote back, and made her way out the door. She took Burleigh with her, figuring Paula wouldn't mind.

She arrived at the fountain before Paula, so took some time to stretch out her legs and admire the surroundings. Burleigh clearly admired the surroundings as well, leaving a souvenir for Fiona to clean up. She was throwing the bag into the bin when Paula arrived. The other woman laughed and handed her hand sanitiser over to Fiona without a word. Fiona laughed too, taking it. She needed to remember to start bringing that on walks with her.

"Hey, Burleigh," Paula cooed, bending over and rubbing Burleigh's ears. "Oh, and hi there, Burleigh's owner."

Fiona laughed it off. She was getting used to the dog receiving greetings before she did. "I'm glad you could join me," she said.

"I'm glad you asked!" Paula replied. "I think I definitely needed to get out of the house."

"I thought you might be busy with the kids," Fiona said, but Paula waved her off. "I've left Jazzy in charge of Ollie. The beauty of having a larger age gap," she said as the two women started walking.

"Yeah, that's handy. Although it does prolong the torture," Fiona said, and then grimaced. "Sorry – I do like kids, I just can't imagine having some of my own. I'm sure it's not really torture!"

"Nah, you nailed it," Paula joked. They fell into a companionable silence, and after a while Paula said "Actually, I do have something to tell you."

"Oh?" Fiona looked at her new friend, surprised. There was a serious tone to her voice that Fiona hadn't heard before.

"Promise you won't tell anyone," Paula said. "I haven't told anyone aside from Alfie, and Jasmine would kill me."

"What's wrong?"

Paula took a deep breath, then said "Jasmine's pregnant."

Fiona's eyes bulged in surprise. "Oh. That's... she's... sixteen?"

"Fifteen," Paula replied. "It's such a mess."

"Does she know what she wants to do?"

Paula shook her head. "She said she's thinking of giving it up for adoption, but I'm not sure if she's really ready for all of that."

"How far along is she?"

"Not very, thank God. She's got some time to plan. We've got her twelve-week scan coming up on Thursday."

"That has to be tough," Fiona replied sympathetically. "Let me know if there's anything I can do." It felt like such a useless platitude, but she didn't know what else to say. She would have loved to solve this problem for her friend, but there wasn't much anyone could do about it.

"The little rat bastard whose baby it is doesn't even know," Paula continued. "She hasn't told him. They're not really together, you see. One of these damned friends with benefits things they all have nowadays."

Fiona winced. Teenaged pregnancy was always going to be tough, but at least a supportive partner would have eased some of the burden. "Maybe he'll be more helpful than you expect?" she suggested.

Paula shrugged, clearly doubtful. "Maybe. Anyway, thanks for letting me vent. It's nice to talk about it to someone." Not for the first time, Fiona recognised that Paula's social circle seemed as small as her own. It was lucky they had found each other.

"I actually do feel better," Fiona said at the end of their walk. "I wasn't sold on the whole exercising thing, but this was nice."

"Same," Paula said, smiling. "Maybe the key is to go with a friend."

Fiona nodded. "We could make it a regular thing?" she asked, feeling oddly nervous. Starting up a new friendship was so much like starting up a romantic relationship. There was almost as much second-guessing and self-doubt involved.

"Absolutely! Life's a bit crazy right now, though, so we might have to stick to just once a week."

Fiona nodded. "It's a date!" she said, and she went home with a smile on her face.

Chapter 67 – Destiny

With only three months of uni left until graduation, Destiny was counting down. She'd always enjoyed her classes but with the finish line in sight, she just wanted to get it all over and done with. Her mother walked in as she was crossing the day off the calendar.

"Don't wish your life away," Janet reminded her. It was something she'd always said, but it took on a new meaning now, and both women winced as the words hit the air. "You know what I mean," Janet muttered.

Destiny laughed, putting the cap back on her pen. "Yeah, yeah. I'm not wishing my life away, but I *am* wishing uni away. I'll be out in the real world soon." Despite the optimism of her words, she felt a slight tickle of anxiety in her belly as she said it. While freelancing had been her plan for years now, it somehow didn't seem like it was enough. The only thing that had got her through these last few months was keeping busy with study, her friends and her part-time job. She wasn't sure if spending time cooped away in her bedroom with only her laptop for company was the best idea for her.

Her mum seemed to sense her hesitation. "Are you still planning on doing freelance work?"

Destiny shrugged, sharing some of her misgivings with her mother. "I'm definitely not saying never, but I don't know. Maybe I could step up my hours at the store, and then just do freelancing in my spare time."

Janet frowned. "I'm not saying that's an issue, but you didn't go to uni to just write in your spare time, remember. Why don't you see about doing some work experience at a newspaper? It doesn't hurt to leave your options open."

Destiny nodded. She hated that the shooting was derailing her long-held plans, but she knew looking after her mental health was the most important thing. Freelancing could always wait a few years.

The first paper she contacted said they already had their fill of work experience students in the short term, but the second paper, in Ipswich, said they'd be happy to take her on the following week. She hadn't expected anything so soon, and it was a bit of a drive, but she knew better than to turn the offer down. Fortunately she only had one shift at the clothing store, which she was easily able to swap. Before Destiny knew it, she was arriving at the paper for her first day of work experience.

She'd put on her most professional outfit, a slim-fitting black dress, and used a straightener to tame her unruly red hair. She knew she looked more confident than she felt, but that was okay for now. Fake it til you make it, and all that.

The first couple of days were mostly spent sitting at her desk, trying to look busy as she watched people bustle around her, but on the third day the staff photographer must have taken pity on her. He asked if she would like to join him in conducting a vox pop, asking people on the street their opinion on the fact that the local library was being torn down. It wasn't exactly front-page material, but Destiny was thrilled to finally have something substantial to do, and she enjoyed chatting with the people on the street and writing down their responses to the simple question. The photographer must have given her some good feedback, because the next day the editor asked if she would like to interview a local couple who were celebrating their sixtieth wedding anniversary. It was just a human-interest piece that would be buried fairly deeply in the paper, but Destiny was thrilled to have been given her first article. She went to their house and spoke to the sweet older couple, then spent the afternoon writing and checking over her piece before sending it off for editing. It appeared in the paper the next day. She bought a copy at the newsagency on her way home, excited to have it for her slowly growing portfolio which, until now, had consisted only of articles written for the university newspaper. Seeing her name in print in a proper paper was as exciting as she'd always hoped.

On her fifth and final day at the newspaper, the editor walked out into the newsroom. "Destiny, could I see you?" he asked, turning and walking away without waiting for a response.

Destiny's heart leapt anxiously, like she was a kid who'd been called into the Principal's office. She followed the editor, Michael, wondering what he might be about to say. She didn't think she'd done anything wrong, but she wasn't sure.

"You've been a great asset to us this week," Michael said without any preamble. "Your writing is pretty good, but it's your people skills that have really stood out to us. Congratulations on your good work."

"Thank you," she said breathlessly. This hadn't been what she'd expected at all.

"We have an internship programme and we're hiring for next year. I'd like you to put your name into the ring for it. If you're keen."

"Oh!" This really took her by surprise. "That's a tremendous honour, thank you," she said formally. "I'm definitely interested. What would I have to do to apply?"

"The information is on our website. No promises, naturally, but we're looking for two interns, and you've certainly impressed us. It's worth your while to at least apply."

Destiny was flattered. She hadn't expected anything to come from this week aside from something to put on her resume. A possible job had been the last thing on her mind. "Thank you," she said again. "I'll have a look online and I'll definitely apply."

When she walked out, she was smiling.

Chapter 68 – Rosie

My actual birthday was a strange and somewhat sombre affair. I woke up in the morning with an odd sensation in my belly, and then I realised. It was my birthday. The first birthday that wouldn't be spent with Betty. The first birthday that Betty wouldn't get to celebrate. I'd love to say I was excited. Instead I wanted to cry, but I didn't feel I had the energy to even do that. All I felt was numb. Numb and tired.

"Happy birthday," Tim exclaimed, coming into the bedroom with a cup of tea and a piece of fruit toast. I had always loved it when he woke me up that way, but I couldn't muster much enthusiasm today. I smiled at him, though, as I took the mug off him. It was going to be a tough enough day without acting like a bitch to him.

"Thank you," I whispered, putting the mug on my bedside table and biting into my fruit toast. "I can't believe I'm really thirty." It wasn't really true – thirty didn't seem that foreign a concept to me. There were things I couldn't believe about the day, but that wasn't one of them. It just seemed like an easier thing to say than any of the other things I was feeling.

"I'll bet," Tim laughed. He was thirty-two, so we'd celebrated his milestone together a couple of years ago. "Anyway," he continued, "the plan is for midday at your Dad's place. Did you want to do anything before then?"

I looked at my bedside clock – 9:26am. Even though Saturdays were busy at work I had taken the day off, more out of concern for Dad's emotions on this day than some desire to be there to celebrate my birthday. "Nah," I said. "I'm happy to just sit with a book for an hour or so."

Tim smiled. "I'll leave you to it, then," he said, and went into the en-suite for a shower. I was glad he was giving me the space I needed.

I didn't read a book, though. I opened my phone and scrolled through the Facebook album Betty had made five years earlier, for our twenty-fifth. Although it wasn't really the milestone celebration Betty had insisted it was, she had been determined to make it a special day. She had included a photo from each of our birthdays, as well as a picture of the two of us with our parents the day we were born. I smiled, looking through it, and before I knew it, I had started to cry.

After my discussion with Jeffrey, I'd realised that what I had said to him was true. I had been focussing on Betty and Tim having sex because it was easier than feeling the full force of my emotions about Betty's death. It wasn't fair to anyone, least of all me. I needed to let myself feel the pain of losing my sister. Betty deserved that much. When it came down to it, she was truly my other half. And regardless of what had happened between us, it just wasn't fair that she wasn't here with me for this day. Before I could second guess myself, I had changed my profile pic to one of the two of us on our tenth birthdays, all rosy cheeks and happy smiles. I wrote a quick status update. "Happy Heavenly birthday to Elizabeth Mary Blake. Wish we could be together to celebrate!"

I put the phone away before I could read the notifications that came through. Between my own milestone birthday and the loss I'd suffered I knew the post would attract plenty of attention, but I didn't want to see any of it. I was emotional enough without seeing the well-meaning messages of my friends and family.

Dad had invited Jeffrey and the kids over for lunch as well – the joys of a Saturday birthday. When I arrived they were all there already, and everyone greeted me with big, enthusiastic hugs and kisses. I could tell instantly that Jeffrey had been crying. It was nice that he'd come along to celebrate my birthday, but I knew that Betty wasn't far from his thoughts. The three kids, luckily, seemed fairly oblivious to the significance of the day. I didn't need to see their emotions on display while I battled with my own.

You wouldn't have known anything was wrong with Dad, either, to look at him. I did, but only because I knew him so well. He was trying his best to acting like it was just another nice, normal, happy family day, so I gave him the respect of not mentioning Betty. I knew of families who had birthday cakes or balloons, or empty chairs, for loved ones who had passed away, but that hadn't even been something we'd discussed. It was all too raw, still.

After lunch, Dad brought out some brightly-wrapped presents. I opened the first one and gasped when I saw Mum's beautiful drop pearl earrings, which I had always loved so much. "Oh, Dad," I cried, welling up again. I couldn't stop myself lately. "They're absolutely beautiful." I gave him a big hug.

He smiled, seeming touched by my joy at the gift. "I'm glad you like them," he said, a little stiffly. "They're your special present, but I have a couple of other things for you as well."

As it turned out Dad had outdone himself this year, buying me two of the new novels I'd wanted, a soft leather notebook, a pair of noise-cancelling headphones (to listen to my audiobooks while the baby slept, he told me), and a beautifully soft blue scarf. Dad had always struggled to buy gifts for me since Mum had died. She'd always taken on the lion's share of the shopping, but he'd done so well this time. I wondered if shopping for me had helped to take his mind off things with Betty. I hoped it had.

"I'm waiting for home, but I think you might have outdone me there, Phil," Tim playfully sulked. I looked at him in surprise. "I thought the new furniture was my gift?" I asked, but Tim waved me off. "That's for the baby," he said. "Today is about you."

"We have a gift for you, too," Jeffrey said, clearing his throat. He handed me a card, which I was unsurprised to find had money inside. I hadn't really expected Jeffrey to get me anything, but money was definitely the easiest option from a brother-in-law. I smiled and thanked him and the kids, but was surprised when he also handed over a gift wrapped in plain blue paper. I could tell it was a book.

"What's this?" I asked, ripping the wrapping off. My breath caught in my throat as I opened it.

"It's a diary. It's... Betty's diary," he said.

I shook my head in disbelief, looking at the book in my hands. "I didn't even know Betty kept a diary." I knew she had in high school, of course, we both had, but I'd assumed she'd stopped in her adult years, like I had.

"Well, she did. She always has, actually, but this one she only started two years ago."

I flipped through the pages, feeling myself choke up at the sight of Betty's handwriting. It wasn't messy, exactly, but she wrote too fast, as if trying to get her ideas down in time before she forgot them. Her handwriting was as familiar to me as my own.

"I thought you might like to read it, later on," Jeffrey said. "Alone." He caught my eye meaningfully, and I suddenly realised what the true meaning of this gift was. Clearly, Betty talked about what had happened with Tim in the pages of it.

I suppose it would have been a natural reaction to not want to see, to not want to expose myself to any of it. But that wasn't how I felt. I couldn't wait to get home and start reading.

Chapter 69 – Paula

Paula could barely calm her nerves on the morning of the scan. Seeing the baby on the screen would make all of this so much more real. She wondered if they were really prepared for it. Jasmine's skinny frame was far from showing any signs of the pregnancy yet, and she hadn't been sick or had any other symptoms. It was easy to pretend as if it wasn't real. Seeing the ultrasound on the screen would be undeniable proof.

Alfie still hadn't spoken to Jasmine about the pregnancy, and Jasmine hadn't raised it with him, either. Paula hadn't even told him that Jasmine knew that he was aware of it.

They had made a Thursday appointment for the scan, so Paula had swapped her shift at the cinema. She called in and told the school that Jasmine would be away for 'personal' reasons. It was the understatement of the century. She wondered how the school would react about this. Jasmine being caught smoking in the toilets had been a huge issue for both Paula and the school, but in comparison to this it seemed laughably small.

Jasmine had always had big ambitions. As a child she had wanted to be an actress, then a singer. As she'd matured she'd decided she wanted to be a marine biologist, and that had remained her obsession for the past few years. She was razor sharp and, before her recent behaviour issues, had always been a good student.

Paula herself had never really had big ambitions for her life. She'd never really had anything she wanted to do. Her marks had always been fine, average, but good enough. If she'd tried a little harder at school she probably could have received higher marks, but she'd never had the drive. She was realistic enough to know that working in a cinema wasn't considered a smashing success for most people; that she wouldn't wow her old classmates with it at a high school re-union. But it had always been enough for her because she'd never been one of those people who wanted her life to revolve around her work.

Honestly, Paula's main dream in life had always been to be a mother, and now she felt as though she was failing at that.

When the appointment started, Paula asked Jasmine if she was sure she wanted her mother in there with her. "Of course," Jasmine replied, looking at her with big eyes. "I can't do this alone." In that moment she was her little girl again, but not in the easy, uncomplicated way Paula had hoped she would be for so long.

When the scan started, Jasmine reached for Paula's hand and grasped it tightly. Paula held it firmly back, trying to show her daughter through touch that she would never let her go. She remembered her own scans with Jasmine and Ollie. She remembered how she had never wanted to leave their sides when they were babies, to the extent that she even watched them as they slept. She wished this scan was a happy occasion for Jasmine, the way it had been when Paula herself was pregnant.

They gasped in unison when they heard the heartbeat, when the abstract form of the baby appeared on the screen. Paula felt herself nearly tearing up, which surprised her. Right here and now, this baby didn't feel like the burden she'd thought it was. It seemed like a miracle. She thought of Jasmine's comment from the week before, about how people often regretted giving children up for adoption. Paula had thought adopting it out was a feasible option for them, but now she wasn't so sure.

"Would you like to know the sex?" the sonographer asked, and Paula looked at her in surprise. "You can tell already?" She hadn't expected that for at least one more scan.

"Not always, but it's pretty clear to me here."

Paula and Jasmine looked at each other, and Jasmine nodded. "Yeah, I think I'd like to know." Since everything with the baby was still so up in the air, they hadn't discussed what they thought the sex of the baby might be. Paula was unsure that finding out the sex was the right move, but she kept quiet. It was Jasmine's decision.

"It's a boy," the sonographer replied, and Paula lent down and gave her daughter a quick hug. Jasmine looked even closer to tears now.

It was a boy. It was a real baby. This had gone from being an abstract decision to an emotional one, very quickly. Paula had no idea what they were going to do.

Chapter 70 – Fiona

Fiona was in the shower when she felt the lump in her breast.

She had been checking her breasts semi-regularly since she was twenty, a habit her mum had instilled in her when she was younger. Fiona knew she didn't do it as often as she probably should, but when she remembered she tried to check them in the shower, just to be safe. Her aunt had died of breast cancer, so she knew as well as anyone that you couldn't be too careful.

She had never expected to actually feel something.

It can't be, she thought, when she ran her finger over it. *You're imagining things.*

She checked again. She wasn't imagining it. The lump was definitely there.

Fiona tried to keep her thoughts rational. After all, a lump could be many things, couldn't it? She wasn't even forty yet. It was probably nothing at all.

But her brain screamed the opposite at her. She'd been trying to give up on life for so long now, ever since Jacob had died. Was it any wonder that life should throw a hurdle like this at her, now? Wasn't it just what she deserved?

When Fiona got out of the shower, she wrapped a towel around her body and sat on the bed without actually drying off. The first person she called was Angela. Her voice wavering, she told her friend about the lump.

She knew Angela well enough to hear the concern in her voice, although her friend tried to hide it. "It's probably nothing, but you should go to the doctor," Angela said. "You won't rest easy until you find out what it is."

"You're right," Fiona sighed. "I'm just not sure I'm ready for this."

"Do you want me to come with you?"

Fiona smiled, grateful once again for Angela's friendship. "Thanks, but I'm okay. I'll see when I can get an appointment."

"Alright, but remember, I'm just a phone call away," Angela replied. Fiona knew that was true. Angela would drop anything to help her out.

When she'd hung up, Fiona looked up the number of her doctor and dialled, her hands shaking. "Oh, hi, it's Fiona Tucker," she told the receptionist. "I've just discovered a lump in my breast. Is It Dr Ramsay I see about that?" It had just occurred to her that she had no idea what the protocol was with this sort of thing. Did she need to go straight to a specialist, or would her GP do?

"Yes, I can get you in with Dr Ramsay tomorrow," the receptionist replied, as if this were just an everyday call. For her, it probably was. "The first available appointment is 10:15. What time suits you?"

Fiona mulled it over. She would love to get in as quickly as possible, but results weren't going to be immediate, anyway, and she didn't want to arrange another day off work. She booked the appointment in for 5:30, the last available appointment of the day, which would give her time to make a quick getaway from work and arrive in time.

Fiona made chicken and veggies for herself for dinner and settled down in front of a television show that she paid no attention to. She already knew she wouldn't manage to get much sleep tonight.

Chapter 71 – Destiny

It only took four days after Destiny's internship application to get called in for an interview. One day after that, Michael called and offered her the job.

Destiny was over the moon when she got the call. The only job she'd ever been offered before was the one at the clothing store and the aunt of one of her friends from high school owned it, so it wasn't the same. This felt like something she'd really earned on her own, and she couldn't be more proud of herself. How many other people would be able to attend graduation with a job already lined up?

She called Gemma immediately to tell her the good news.

"That's awesome!" Gemma exclaimed. "We have to celebrate! Let's go out for drinkies."

"I'm in," Destiny laughed.

"Cool. I'm guessing you don't want Court and Ed there, but I'll invite Nate?"

It was a definite question, rather than a statement. In the past, the assumption would have been that all six of them would meet up. Ugh. Why did things have to become so complicated?

Destiny paused, thinking it over. If what Gemma said was true, and Nate was into her, then she didn't want to lead him on. At the same time, though, he was a good friend, and she didn't want to lose him. She'd lost enough friends already this year.

"Yeah, okay," she said finally. "Let's do it."

After telling Gemma and her mum, Destiny was surprised to realise that she wanted to tell Rosie, Paula and Fiona next. She couldn't describe the bond between them, but it was real.

"Great news!" she wrote in their group message thread. "I got an internship for next year! Start full-time in January." She tried to make it sound as modest as she could, thinking the women, being older, probably didn't think it was such a big deal. She couldn't have been more wrong.

"Desi, I'm so proud of you!" Paula quickly replied, and Rosie's message came in next. "That's awesome work. Any chance we could go to your graduation? Is that weird? I'd love to celebrate your hard work! I never went to uni and I think it's such a great achievement!"

The message took Destiny by surprise, but it gave her a warm feeling. It was nice to have people who had your back. She did some quick maths. She got four tickets included with her grad, and she had planned on taking her mum and her brother Ben, but wasn't sure who else. Gemma and Nate, of course, would already be there for their own graduation, and she was sure none of her high school friends would really be excited by the idea of coming to a formal ceremony. She didn't think it would be a big drama to arrange to buy a fifth ticket.

"Of course," she wrote back, "if you all want to. Might be a bit boring for you, but I'd love to have you there! It's the 29th of August." The group of six had deliberately done some subjects over the summer semester the year before so they would graduate mid-year. Luke had suggested it to get them out into the working world sooner. Destiny had mainly just gone along with the idea so she wouldn't fall behind her friends, but now she was glad they'd made the decision. She was so excited to be finishing.

The three other women all replied in the affirmative, and just like that, it was arranged.

Chapter 72 – Paula

It took a while, but finally, Alfie calmed down about the pregnancy. Paula was thrilled to have her husband back, but more importantly, she knew Jasmine needed her dad's support.

Alfie still didn't directly address Jasmine about the baby, but when Paula and Jasmine talked about it in front of him, he didn't feign oblivion. It was small steps, but at least now they were going in the right direction.

"You need to tell Brad," Paula told Jasmine one afternoon. Jasmine was fifteen weeks along, and her belly was still relatively small, but the difference was noticeable on her thin frame. Besides, it was the right thing to do. Brad might not have been Paula's idea of a dream candidate for the father of her grandchild, but he deserved to at last know about the baby. Who knows, she thought sardonically. He might even surprise them.

Her hopes weren't high.

"I know," Jasmine sighed, sticking out her lower lip and suddenly looking a lot younger than her years. "It's just hard to say it."

Paula didn't doubt that. It was her daughter's sixteenth birthday the following week. She should be going to the shops with her friends and sleeping in on the weekends, not making life-altering decisions. It just didn't seem fair.

The following day, Jasmine came home from school in a terrible mood. Paula stayed out of her way, accustomed to teenaged angst. She just assumed this was evidence that Jazzy had broken the news to Brad and it hadn't gone well. She figured her daughter would come and talk to her when she was ready.

When Jasmine finally did come to her, it wasn't what she expected.

"I'm guessing you told Brad?" Paula asked.

"No," Jasmine snapped, looking away. "I told Charlotte."

Charlotte was her best friend. The two had been close for three years, but Paula's heart sank. Charlotte was a nice enough girl, but she was also a notorious gossip. Paula had a feeling she knew how this story was going to go.

"And now *everyone* knows," Jasmine wailed, confirming Paula's worst fears. "Brad, my teachers, everyone. I thought I could trust her to keep her mouth shut about something like this!"

Paula sighed. It was a rough lesson to learn, but sometimes even the closest of friends couldn't hold on to gossip as juicy as this. Her heart went out to her daughter. If only Jasmine had told her she was planning to tell her friend, she could have warned her against it, but it was too late now.

"I can't believe she did it," Jasmine raged. "I thought I could, like, start with her and work my way up, you know? I thought it would be easier to tell Charlotte. But it wasn't. I wish I hadn't said anything. I wish I'd never been born!"

It wasn't the first time Jasmine had expressed a sentiment like that, but in the past Paula had always put it down to adolescent melodrama. Now, though, Jasmine had real problems. Grown-up problems. It couldn't be easy, having the entire school know something like that. As far as Paula knew, there hadn't been a pregnant student at the school in the time Jasmine had been there. And she was only in Year Ten. It would be a scandal, not to mention the greatest source of gossip the kids at the school had had for a while. Paula would have to make an appointment to talk to the principal about it.

"And Brad?" Paula ventured once Jasmine had quietened a little. "How did he take it?"

Jasmine shrugged, a hollow expression on her face. "He didn't even talk to me about it. He told Charlotte that I'm a slut and it could be anyone's." She broke down into earnest tears at that point.

Paula's whole body filled with rage. How dare that little son of a bitch say something like that about her daughter?

"I've only ever been with him," Jasmine wailed. "It's not true. It's definitely his baby."

"Sweetie, sweetie. Even if he weren't the only one, he'd be totally out of line calling you that horrible word." Paula pulled Jasmine in, and the younger girl cried on her shoulder. "I could kill him for what he said about you."

Jasmine pulled back, wiping the tears from her eyes. "I made a decision, though."

"You did?" Paula worked on making her face neutral. Whatever the choice was, there was a long, hard road ahead. She needed to be supportive of her daughter, despite whatever her own feelings might have been. Right then and there she wasn't sure, anyway, what she would choose if given the option. None of the choices seemed particularly appealing.

At the scan she'd started to feel far more positive about the baby, but that wouldn't make life easy if they decided to keep him.

"I'm going to give it up," Jasmine whispered, fresh tears filling in her eyes. "I just want everything to be normal again."

Paula nodded. "It's your decision, honey, and I'm here for you." She leant in and hugged her daughter, grateful that Jasmine couldn't see the tears that were forming in her own eyes. She, too, wanted desperately for everything to be normal again, but she knew that nothing would ever be the same.

Chapter 73 – Rosie

I waited until Tim went out for his daily walk that evening before I opened Betty's diary. I wasn't sure what emotions the diary entry would dredge up, but I knew that this was something I needed to be alone for.

I opened it up and saw that the entries had started when Poppy was a toddler. They mainly talked about how tired Betty was, how hard it was balancing work with three kids. Sometimes I forgot how young Betty was when she had children. It wouldn't have been easy. But right now, I couldn't focus on that. I flipped towards the back, finding the most recent few entries. My breath caught in my throat when I found the one I was looking for. I huddled into my chair and started to read.

I can't really even put this down in writing. I'm the worst sister in the world. I did something unforgiveable, and I don't know if Rosie will ever speak to me again.

The thing is, I've always been a little jealous of Rosie. I know that's awful – she's my sister and I should be nothing but happy for her! But she seems to content within herself – so confident – and she's got this great relationship with Tim. They're so passionate about each other. Meanwhile, I'm with a man who doesn't ever touch me. I'm in a job I don't even want anymore. Rosie has always seemed to just be happy with her life in a way I never have been. I've always been... I don't know.... restless? I know I shouldn't have done it, but when Tim and I were alone, something just came over me. Came over us, I suppose. I think I wanted to feel the way she feels. It didn't work, of course. I just feel worse about myself now. But, for one brief moment there, he really wanted me. I was the twin who had it all... for a change.

That was where the diary entry stopped. I stared at it, my hands shaking. I wanted to throw up. Was this some kind of a joke? Had Betty really felt that way? She'd never expressed anything like it to me before. But then, had she had any idea I was jealous of her? It wasn't exactly the sort of thing you sat down and told someone. Still, why would someone like Betty – the twin who had it all – ever be jealous of me?

Trembling, I turned the page.

I told Jeffrey today. It was just eating me up inside. He screamed at me, which I deserved. He threw a plate at the wall, which I never thought he'd do! I felt terrible, but at the same time, I can't believe he still feels so passionately about me. I can't believe I made such a calm guy totally lose control.

I have to tell Rosie next, and I really don't know how. Am I even strong enough? But I can't risk her hearing it from anyone else, especially now Jeffrey knows. I can't guarantee he won't tell her out of revenge.

I don't want to lose Jeffrey but if that's his choice, I will have to live with it. But I can't lose Ro. I don't know what I'm going to do. I've made a mess of everything.

That was her final diary entry.

If things had gone differently, she'd have probably updated after our meeting, written about how I had taken things, how she felt about it.

But now there was nothing. It all felt like a cruel prank. Thanks to a man with a gun, there were no more insights into Betty's mind. Never again would she write her feelings down in this beautiful journal.

Chapter 74 – Fiona

Dr Ramsay was calm and professional when Fiona arrived for her appointment, and for a moment, Fiona could pretend this wasn't a potentially life-altering event. "What can I help you with today, Fiona?" she asked smoothly.

Fiona took a deep breath. "I found a lump in my breast," she said, the words still feeling strange as she said them.

The doctor nodded, still maddeningly calm. "Okay. At your age, results are likely to be benign. Often we find it's a cyst, but obviously we need to proceed with some tests to make sure. So this is a new lump?"

Fiona nodded. She felt herself go into a kind of trance as the doctor continued her examination. She answered all the questions, but it felt like she was floating above, watching the scene, rather than really being there.

The doctor ended the appointment by giving her a referral for a mammogram. For this appointment, Fiona *was* willing to take a day off work. She didn't want to wait any longer than absolutely necessary.

It was a three day wait before she could get in for her mammogram, and it was the longest three days of Fiona's life. She couldn't believe that someone who had stood up in front of a crazed gunman and instructed him to shoot her was now so frightened about some potentially deadly test results. That was something to be said for the survival instinct, that was for sure.

The day of her mammogram, Fiona experienced the same eerie, out of body feeling she had had at the GP. There was no doubt in her mind that the results would be cancer. She had never had a mammogram before, since they only offered them as a routine thing from the age of forty, and she felt anxious as she waited for the radiographer to see her. She thought about the term 'routine testing', and wondered if it would ever actually feel routine. Did people really get used to this kind of thing, or was everyone in the waiting room with her a bundle of nerves as well?

When the radiographer called her in Fiona undressed for the mammogram, feeling miserable. She had just decided she was willing to embrace life again, and now it seemed like the choice was going to be taken away from her.

Chapter 75 – Destiny

In the lead-up to drinks with Gemma and Nate Destiny started to panic, picturing the three of them sitting around, the absences around them so obvious. On a whim she messaged Lucy and Frankie, two girls she had become close to over the years from one of her lectures, and asked if they would join them for the small celebration. Destiny told herself it was because it would be more fun with a few more people, but in reality she knew she was looking for a buffer between her and Nate.

It shouldn't be awkward, she told herself. Nate didn't even know that she knew. It shouldn't be any different from any other evening out.

But still...

Destiny's brother gave Gemma and Destiny a lift to the bar in the Valley, where they were the first to arrive. Gemma quickly went to grab their favourite corner booth. They used to go there all the time, but the last time they'd been there had been for Luke's birthday. Destiny had nearly suggested meeting at a different bar when she'd thought about that, but she'd dismissed the idea. If she tried too hard to avoid places that reminded her of Luke, she'd never go anywhere again.

Lucy and Frankie arrived next, giving Destiny a hug as they arrived. "Congrats on the job!" Lucy enthused, hoisting her petite frame onto the soft seat of the booth. "I'm so jealous."

"Ugh. Me, too!" Frankie cried, taking a seat next to Lucy. "I've been searching through the job ads and there's *nothing*. Only graphic design jobs to be seen," she sighed dramatically. "Us poor journalists aren't wanted anymore."

"I'm not even looking," Gemma said, waving her hand dismissively. "The right thing'll come along sometime."

Destiny grinned. Gemma had always had a blasé approach to life, and Destiny was pleased about her casual approach to this. She was so happy about her own job offer, and she didn't want to feel guilty because her friend hadn't found anything yet. "You guys haven't even graduated yet," she pointed out with a small laugh. "I definitely wasn't planning on looking for anything for ages. This just kind of... happened."

"Oh, my dream job just sort of *happened*," Frankie said in a falsetto, making them all laugh.

"I didn't mean it like that!" Destiny protested. "I'm thrilled about this. But I'll be working my butt off for not much money, so you know, maybe there's something better out there for you guys."

She was playing it cool, but the truth was, Destiny couldn't have been more thrilled about the job offer. It was so weird, considering how she'd just wanted to freelance such a short time ago! The job was something real and concrete that she could hold on to, something that would occupy her time. It was exactly what she needed right now.

"I'll get our first round," Gemma said, taking orders and heading to the bar.

It was while she was gone that Nate arrived, so it was only natural that he slotted in next to Desi, where Gemma had been sitting a moment earlier. "Hey," he said, reaching in for their usual hug hello but surprising Destiny by giving her a quick kiss on the cheek as well. "Congratulations, working girl."

"Doesn't that make me sound like a prostitute or something?" Destiny laughed, hoping the heat she could feel rising to her cheeks wasn't visible in the dim bar. She didn't want Nate's quick, friendly kiss to have affected her, but she knew it had, more than she wanted to admit. She wondered if it still would have if she hadn't had the conversation with Gemma about Nate's feelings. She'd been oblivious for so long.

"Ah," Lucy said, mock-knowingly. "Maybe *that's* how she's really making her money."

Gemma returned with the drinks then, wiggling her eyebrows at Destiny behind Nate's back when she saw him sitting there. Destiny tried to conceal her impatient sigh. Gemma was a good friend, but she wasn't exactly known for her subtlety. Destiny hoped she wouldn't say anything embarrassing.

"Sorry, Nate," Gemma said, handing the drinks out. "I would have got you something if I'd known you were here."

Nate shrugged. "You're fine, I can go up. Anyone want anything else? Chips or anything?" he asked, standing up.

Frankie nodded. "Always chips."

Destiny was surprised to realise she felt a little disappointed after he went up to the bar and Gemma slid into the spot beside her again.

"Oh, would you like me to leave this spot open?" Gemma joked, as if reading Destiny's mind. Desi reached out and slapped her lightly with the back of her hand.

"Oh?" Lucy asked, always quick to catch on. "Is there something going on that we should know about?"

"No!" Destiny said quickly, shaking her head. "Gemma's just being an idiot."

Gemma smirked, but thankfully said nothing.

"You could do a lot worse than Nate," Lucy said, watching his back as he stood at the bar. "He's a good guy, and he's *hot*."

"Lucy," Frankie said reproachfully. "I don't think Destiny's really looking for anyone right now."

Lucy looked a little chastened by her friend's words. The two girls had been at Luke's funeral, so they knew what Destiny had been going through. Destiny suddenly felt sick to her stomach. The funeral somehow felt like it was years ago, and only a few days previously, at the same time. In reality, it had been just under five months since the shooting. Only five months. It was such a short amount of time.

Frankie was right. What sort of person would possibly be looking for someone else after such a short length of time?

Nate returned with his drink then, and the group of five toasted to Destiny's new job. Destiny smiled at her friends. She still felt guilty about what she'd been thinking about Nate, but she told herself to put it out of her mind. This night was about the future, she reminded herself. She could have just one night where she didn't have to feel guilty about Luke.

And so, she slammed down her drink as though her life depended on it.

Chapter 76 – Paula

Rosie instigated the next group meeting. Paula had become their unofficial 'co-ordinator', but she was always happy when someone else suggested a gathering. It meant that the others were just as eager to meet as she was. When she was the one making group plans, Paula had always worried that people didn't really want to spend time with her. That had been basically confirmed by the amount of friends who had completely disappeared from her life over the years, once she stopped making the effort.

Paula wasn't planning to say anything about the baby, but once they'd met and gone through the small talk, Fiona asked how she was going. Fiona knew, of course, but Paula knew she could trust her new friend with her secret. Still, something about the way Rosie and Destiny smiled at her when she started talking made her want to confide in them. Besides, her whole life had been revolving around it lately.

"I have some news," she said with a shaky laugh after she'd finished talking about how Ollie was going at school, how his night terrors seemed to have stopped for now, thank God. "I'm going to be a grandmother."

The other two looked at her in shock – probably not least of all because, Paula realised with a pang of guilt, she'd barely talked about having an older child. She'd mentioned Jasmine, of course, but her conversation had been dominated by talk of Oliver. That was probably natural, given what he'd been through and the reason they were all meeting, but it still didn't exactly qualify her for mother of the year status.

"My daughter Jasmine is having a baby," she added. She hadn't said the words out loud like that much before, and they still felt alien to her. She thought they probably always would.

"Oh, wow!" Rosie exclaimed, in that cautious manner that people used when they were unsure what their reaction should be. "Congratulations! How do you feel about that?"

"Taken aback," Paula laughed, deciding to be honest. She knew she could be with these women. "I didn't expect my teenager to be having a baby, that's for sure! But she's four months along now. I've had time to come to terms with it." She was surprised to realise that was true. The baby news, so shocking when Jasmine had told her, was now a part of their life. It always amazed Paula how easily people adapted to a new set of circumstances. She and Ollie had lived through a shooting and now her baby was having a baby, and both, somehow, had become a normal part of her everyday life. Well, 'normal' might be a strong word, but they had certainly adjusted more than she ever would have expected.

"Anyway, at this stage she's giving the baby up for adoption," she said. "Who knows what will happen when she actually gives birth and the hormones have kicked in?" She always added that as an addendum when she said Jasmine was giving the baby up – even whenever she thought it. She wasn't going to let herself be taken by surprise if Jazzy changed her mind when she saw her baby boy. Paula herself knew how strong and instant the maternal pull was, and having done plenty of research on adoption since she'd found out about the pregnancy, she also knew how common it was for birth mothers to change their minds. Still, she hoped for Jasmine's sake that she would indeed be able to give the baby up. It wouldn't be easy for any of them, but the idea of raising the baby between herself and Jasmine was a much harder one to comprehend. Paula was realistic enough to know that it would be Jasmine and Paula doing the lion's share of the work. Brad clearly wasn't going to be any help, and Alfie hadn't been overly involved when their own children were babies, so he was unlikely to suddenly become a hands-on grandpa. And it was unrealistic to expect Jasmine could manage it all alone, especially at her age. No, Paula would become at least a part-time mum of an infant again if Jasmine were to keep the baby. She'd resigned herself to the possibility, and took pains not to let it influence how she spoke to Jazzy about the pregnancy. This wasn't a time to be selfish. Jasmine's wellbeing had to be the priority, not Paula's, especially while Paula herself was still so conflicted about it all.

Sometimes motherhood just felt like one long self-sacrifice.

"Well, if she needs anyone to talk to, feel free to pass on my details," Rosie said, putting her hand over her own bump. "I know I'm older than she is, but I can relate to the unplanned pregnancy thing, at least. The uncertainty. If there's anything she's scared about, she can ask me."

Paula was surprised and touched by her friend's suggestion. "Thank you," she said. "I just might take you up on that." Jasmine was fairly wary around anyone older than about twenty, assuming they didn't understand what life was like for a teenager, as if they'd never been one themselves.

Still, Rosie had a calm sort of self-confidence which put the people around her at ease. Maybe Jasmine would relate to her more than she thought.

Destiny had been silent, but finally she spoke up. "We're all here for you," she said, giving Paula's arm a quick squeeze and smiling at her. Paula smiled back. Destiny was a lot closer to Jasmine's age than her own, but she seemed so much more mature. Of course there was a world of difference between fifteen and twenty-two, but it was more than that. Having not known her before the shooting Paula could only assume, but she guessed the traumatic experience had resulted in Destiny growing up pretty quickly.

"Anyway," Paula said, eager to change the subject. "Desi, tell us more about this job?"

The four women chatted for hours, like old friends.

Chapter 77 – Rosie

The catch-up with the other women took my mind off it for a while, but in truth, I didn't know how to feel for a long time after I read Betty's diary. I couldn't process the feelings I had, which seemed to be a mixture of grief, rage and sheer confusion. Why had Betty talked about being jealous of me, when she so obviously had no reason to be? A part of me had hoped that reading her diary would help me to understand why she'd slept with Tim, but now I was more confused than ever. It felt like an elaborate practical joke. I couldn't imagine my fabulous sister really being jealous of me, but I also couldn't think of a reason why she'd have lied to herself.

There was only one person to ask.

"Hey, Dad," I called out as I let myself into the family home. "You here?"

Dad walked into the entry and I greeted him with a hug. "How are you?" I asked him. Dad knew that when I asked him that now I was genuinely asking about his wellbeing, rather than just offering the typical cursory greeting. It had been the case since Mum first got sick, and it was even more so now. I was always going to worry about my old man. In turn, he was always going to worry about me.

"I'm okay," he said, leading me into the kitchen and pouring me an iced tea without my needing to ask. "How are you feeling? You look well."

I smiled and thanked him, but couldn't help but think of how often I'd been told I looked well or healthy lately. It seemed to be polite code for *gigantic,* which was also true. I was starting to wonder if there were twins in there myself, I was getting so big! Still, I'd never been happier with my appearance in the mirror. I'd always thought people were talking rubbish when they said pregnant women glowed, but then I'd seen Betty glowing when she was pregnant. To my surprise, I seemed to have a bit of the same light around me now.

"Actually, I had something to ask you," I said in an even tone. I hadn't planned to get straight into it, but my heart was racing and I just wanted to get it over with. "You know I got Betty's latest diary for my birthday?"

Dad nodded.

I started to second-guess myself here. Dad didn't know about Tim and Betty, obviously, so I'd been planning to just frame it as a general question about her apparent envy towards me, but I didn't want to do it in such a way to make Dad worry that Betty had been unhappy. As far as I knew, she'd always been a pretty content person, but the diary entry had made me wonder. Dad had been through enough lately, and I didn't want him to start wondering about Betty's state of mind the way I had been.

I couldn't completely back out now, though, so I decided to keep it as vague as possible. "She said something that made me wonder... I mean, you know I always felt a little jealous of Betty."

Dad nodded again. That was no secret.

"She said something that made me feel like she might have been a little bit jealous of me, too," I said, my words coming out in a rush.

Dad was silent for a moment, taking this in, before he responded. Finally, he simply said, "she was."

I gaped at him. "What? She said that?" Here was confirmation of what I'd read, and I still couldn't wrap my head around it.

Dad shook his head. "She never said anything to me, but I could tell. I always thought it couldn't be easy, growing up a twin. Especially not an identical one. Your mother and I never compared you," he was quick to add. "You know we always thought you could be anything you wanted, as long as you were good people. And you were both *such* good people. Well, you still are, of course."

I felt my eyes begin to well up. Dad looked like he was on the verge of tears as well. "But you always compared yourselves," he went on. "Everything you achieved, you thought Betty had achieved more. And despite everything Betty did in her lifetime, she always felt like you were doing better." He paused. "She didn't have to tell me. Neither did you. A dad knows his own children."

Now it was my turn for a contemplative silence. I turned Dad's words over in my head. "She was so amazing," I said finally. "I can't really think of anything I did that was better than what she did."

Dad laughed. "And she would be sitting here saying the same thing about you," he said. "Don't get me wrong, Betty achieved a lot, but you always seemed to have this lightness about you. You always seemed more content. She was always quicker to judge herself."

That, I could see. Betty had always been a perfectionist, and it was probably that, more than natural aptitude, that had led to her impressive academic achievements at school and university. She'd always been driven. Was it so hard to imagine that behind that drive and perfectionism there was an element of never being satisfied?

"Thank you for telling me all of this," I said. "I wish I'd known sooner." I wondered how different things would have been if only Betty and I had been a little more honest about our feelings all along. We'd always been close, but maybe this would have helped bond us even further. Or at least maybe we both would have felt better about ourselves.

Dad smiled and nodded wordlessly. He'd never been one for opening up, so this was a departure for him. I was pleased he'd decided to do it.

I cleared my throat, wanting to rid the air of the sombre mood. "Movie time?" I asked, and before long we were in the living room, watching a mindless comedy. It was exactly that we needed.

Chapter 78 – Fiona

The lump was benign.

Fiona was so shocked, she almost couldn't comprehend the words. She was okay? How was that possible? She'd been so sure she was sick. She'd talked herself into believing it. It was wonderful news, of course, but news that she simply couldn't process. Maybe it was a false negative? Maybe she needed another test, a second or third opinion?

"You absolutely don't need another test," Angela informed her, sounding slightly frustrated when Fiona called her about the results. "You need to appreciate the fact that you're well and healthy. If the results were positive, would you have asked for a second or third opinion about that?"

Fiona knew her friend had a point. If she'd been told it was cancer, she would have been devastated, naturally, but she would have accepted the news immediately. There was no reason why she couldn't accept a good result just as easily.

"Do you want to know what I think this is?" Angela asked, and Fiona laughed.

"Do I have a choice?"

"I think," Angela went on, ignoring her words entirely, "that you gave up on living a while ago, and this is the universe's way of telling you that it hasn't given up on you."

Fiona considered this. They were strangely New Age words coming from Angela, and her first instinct was to dismiss them immediately. Surely the universe had better things to do than to give her a lump in her breast to teach her a lesson about living! But then, maybe Angela had a point. Fiona hadn't died in the car accident. She hadn't died when the shooter came into the coffee shop, even after asking him to shoot her. She didn't have cancer, so she wasn't going to die from that either, or at least not for a while. Maybe there was a reason for her to stick around after all.

"So if the universe wants me to stick around," Fiona said, "what am I supposed to do with all this extra life I've been given?"

Angela was quiet for a moment, seemingly pondering the question. "Well, you can keep on being a good friend to me and to your other friends, for starters," she said. "We don't want to lose you."

Fiona had realised that one a while ago, when she'd heard Angela's horrified reaction to the words she'd spoken to the shooter. There had to be more to life, though, she thought. Angela had plenty of other friends. Fiona knew that she was a good friend, but that wasn't enough to build an entire life around.

"Or maybe you're going to save plenty of lives at your work," Angela went on. "Lives that matter. Those are people with loved ones, who would miss them if they died."

Fiona sighed, and it was then that she realised her problem. Her work, which had always filled her with a sense of achievement, hadn't felt the same since the shooting. Well, since Jacob's death, more accurately, given that that was when her extended period of leave had started. She knew what she did was important, but lately it just felt like she was surrounded by more death. Jim's death had rattled her more than she liked to admit, even to herself.

When she expressed these feelings to Angela, her friend replied, "Maybe that's it?"

"Maybe what's it?"

"Maybe you need to try something new for a while," Angela said. "I know how amazing you are at your job, but if you're not feeling it anymore, maybe there's something else out there for you."

Fiona frowned. "No," she said. "I couldn't. This is all I know."

"O-kayyyy," Angela said, in the lilting voice she sometimes used when she thought Fiona was making a mistake. "It's your life."

Fiona hung up, feeling certain of her decision to stay where she was. She was young and she was healthy, and that was more than she'd thought that morning. Her life was good.

A WEEK LATER SHE WENT into her boss' office, knocking tentatively on the door. "Hi, Jennifer," she said. "I was wondering if I could talk to you."

Jennifer looked up from her computer. "Sure, Fiona. What's up?"

"Well, it's about next year," she said hesitantly. "I know Adam spoke to you about taking some leave for Europe, but he's asked me to join him for part of the trip. I was wondering if I could take four weeks off in January." They were only spending three weeks in Italy, but she'd decided to take an extra few days off so she wouldn't be a complete wreck when they got back.

Jennifer's lips pursed. "You've already had a fairly significant amount of time off this year," she reminded her, as if Fiona had forgotten. "It's not really ideal timing."

Fiona felt her cheeks flush. "I know I've had some compassionate leave, but this would be different," she said. "I wouldn't take any more leave next year, I can promise you that. I'm still entitled to my annual leave."

"You won't have earned four more weeks by January."

"No, but I thought I could use some sick days as well, and I'm happy to take some leave without pay if I need to." Fiona was surprised to hear a pleading note in her voice. Until now, she hadn't realised just how much she had been looking forward to the Italy trip. "I really think I need it for my mental health. I'll do overtime, whatever you need."

Jennifer was silent for a moment, and then shook her head. "I'm sorry, Fiona. I know what you've been through, but I simply can't give you any more time off. It wouldn't be a good look for everyone else. Besides, I need you while Adam is away."

Fiona closed her eyes, feeling dangerously close to tears. On the one hand, she could see it from Jennifer's point of view. Her boss had already been quite generous with leave, and hadn't blinked an eye when Fiona had walked out without any notice following Jim's death. On the other hand, Fiona had been a loyal employee there for years, and everyone always said what good work she did. Plus, anyone could see the year she'd been through had been spectacularly shitty.

She would have thought the good reputation she'd made for herself would have bought her a little bit more understanding from her boss.

Then she took a deep breath, remembering Angela's words. She managed to steel herself as she stood up and fixed her boss with a smile. "Not a problem, Jennifer. Thanks," she said, and turned and walked out of the office.

If this was one of those messages from the universe that Angela had been talking about, then the intention was clear. Fiona did need to find a job elsewhere, after all. She wouldn't quit until much closer to her trip, but there was no need to change her travel plans, either.

Now, she just had to figure out what she could do.

Chapter 79 – Paula

Apart of Paula had felt like her issues with Jasmine had started as some sort of karmic payback for focussing too much of her attention on Oliver. Now, as a sick joke, it was Ollie who needed her, as if she'd been spending too much time and energy thinking about Jasmine. Did parents of more than one child ever feel like they'd got the balance right? Paula wondered. Or was it all just some eternal game of catch-up?

Ollie's problems had started a little more subtly than Jasmine's, which was fitting. Ollie had always been the quieter and less dynamic of the two of them. He'd been the easy child, so it only made sense that even his meltdown started so quietly, and with so little fuss, that Paula hadn't initially realised there was anything wrong with him.

Embarrassingly it was Harold, her therapist, who alerted her to it. "I'm sure you've noticed young Oliver has had a bit of a backslide," he said to her at their private appointment.

Paula paused, wondering if she should feign awareness, before deciding to admit to her ignorance. It would do Ollie no good to pretend. "Backslide?"

"Well, yes. He seems to be struggling again with dealing with his emotions about the shooting."

Paula could have kicked herself. After the first traumatic weeks following the shooting, Ollie seemed to be doing so well that she hadn't even considered he might be struggling with it still. Of course he was. Being witness to a shooting wasn't something you'd easily forget. Not to mention, Ollie had been shot himself. If anything, it was a miracle that he hadn't started showing signs of trauma earlier. Paula had been pleased at how well he'd settled back into school, thrilled when his nightmares stopped. It hadn't really served her to dig any more deeply into that and wonder if he had some problems he couldn't put into words, but it made sense. She herself was barely coping since the shooting, so it was ridiculous to expect that her child would be doing any better. She had always known that Ollie internalised things.

"I guess I've been so worried about Jasmine, I didn't really realise," Paula finally admitted, feeling like a failure as a mother.

Harold nodded. She had filled him in on Jasmine's pregnancy at her previous appointment. "I know things must not be easy at the moment," he said. "The shooting alone is cause enough for years of trauma, let alone what you've been facing with your daughter at the same time. I just hope you're taking care of yourself."

Paula shrugged. "That's why I'm here."

"Yes, but you spend most of your time talking about your children or your husband," Harold pointed out. "I wonder if you may be focussing on them to the detriment of your own mental health and wellbeing. Maybe it would be helpful for you to take a brief trip away on your own?"

"Oh, I couldn't," Paula protested. Travelling alone had never been her thing. She wasn't very well travelled at all, in fact. Why would she travel and have nothing to show for it afterwards when she could be putting that money towards something tangible, like the mortgage?

"It's something to consider," Harold said, and he left it at that. The fact that he wasn't pushy was one of the things Paula appreciated most about him.

Over the next week, Paula put in a greater effort with her son. She made his favourite snacks for school, including the zucchini and cheese muffins that he adored but that she hated making because they seemed to take so long. She took him to the park to play several times throughout the week, and even spent far too much money on the new video game he wanted. She didn't want to spoil him, but he'd been through a lot. Maybe a little spoiling was exactly what she needed.

"What's this for?" Ollie exclaimed in surprise when she handed him the video game.

Paula smiled. "Do you like it?"

"Yeah, but... is it a birthday present?" His birthday was still two months away. Oliver wasn't used to receiving extravagant gifts for no reason; neither of their kids were. It was something that had started out as a deliberate strategy, with Alfie in particular careful not to spoil them or get them accustomed to a lavish lifestyle that they couldn't keep up. Over the years, Paula had to admit, it had become more of a necessity. There simply wasn't all that much money left over by the time the bills were paid.

"No, it's just for you," she said, ruffling his hair in a way she hadn't done for years. "Just because you're so special."

Oliver apparently decided not to question his luck any further. "Cool!" he cried, running off to play it.

Paula didn't broach the subject of the shooting with him that day or ask how he was handling it. It seemed more important to just let him have fun, the way he wanted to. The way he should have been able to all along.

Chapter 80 – Rosie

I was starting to feel less like a glowing pregnant woman, and more like an elephant.

"How long are you planning on working for?" Tim asked. It was a reasonable question, given that I was 34 weeks pregnant and yet to discuss any kind of plan for maternity leave. With Tim, that is. I'd talked it over with my manager already. Not for the first time, it struck me how much of my pregnancy I was keeping from the father of the baby. Well, 'keeping from him' was probably a bit strong. It wasn't as if I'd developed some maniacal scheme to keep my maternity leave plan under wraps from Tim. We simply weren't communicating the way we normally would have been.

"Two more weeks," I replied, slipping my hand into his as we walked down a slight incline. It was more to keep myself balanced than to express my undying affection for him, but regardless of the reason, I saw him smile as I did so.

We were on our way out to a date, a term that felt ridiculously childish in the nicest possible way. While we'd always spent quality time together we'd never really had a classified 'date night' the way some couples did. The idea of it really took me back to the start of the relationship, when everything was so new and exciting.

The date had been my idea, but Tim had quickly agreed. I wanted to try to cement the relationship before the baby came along. Things had definitely been better between us over the last month or so, but we were still a long way from being back to normal. If such a thing as normal was possible for us anymore. I wasn't sure, but I was willing to try. Having a newborn would be difficult enough without everything being up in the air between us.

We'd pulled out all the stops for our date night. Tim was dressed nicely, in a long-sleeved shirt and tie. I was wearing one of the few nicer dresses that still fit me now that I was roughly the size of a beached whale, and I'd even gone to the effort of curling my hair. We were going to a fancy restaurant, the kind we usually dismissed as too pompous for us. The strangest part of all was how much I was looking forward to it.

The restaurant was within walking distance, so we'd decided to make the most of the evening and go there on foot. I obviously wasn't going to be drinking, but driving was fairly uncomfortable for me now that I was larger, and I was happy to avoid it. Besides, walking to our date somehow made the whole thing feel more like a romantic event, especially on such a beautiful, cool evening. Feeling cool was a luxury I didn't have much of anymore. It was still only the end of August, but it was starting to feel a lot more like spring than winter. Spring in Brisbane has never been all that different to summer, and now that I was pregnant I might as well have been perched on the surface of the sun half the time. The return to a cooler evening felt incredibly luxurious.

Tim helped me into my chair when we arrived at the restaurant, like we were an old-fashioned couple that was newly courting – when you ignored my swollen belly, at least. He smiled at me as we sat down.

"You do realise we haven't even discussed names yet?" he asked me.

I had realised, but it didn't mean I hadn't been thinking about them. In response to his statement, I pulled out my phone and handed him the list I'd written in the notes section. He laughed as he looked at the screen, which was filled with at least two dozen girls' names. There was one section marked 'first names', and underneath the first list was a separate list, 'middle names'.

"Why separate lists?" Tim asked. "Wouldn't you just pick two that you like and make them the first and the middle?"

I shook my head at his ignorance. "They have to *go* together, Tim. Like, if we pick a first name like Hannah, we'd want a one-syllable middle name, but if we picked Jade as the first name, we'd want two syllables for the middle name."

"Of course," he said, deadpan. "How foolish of me." He scrolled through the list and grimaced. "Not Lily. I had a girlfriend with that name in high school."

"Oh, God. You've never mentioned her," I said, snatching the phone back and wiping Lily from the list.

"Didn't last long, but she was a bit of a bitch, looking back on it. Do I get to add any names to the list?"

"Of course," I replied. "What do you want?"

Tim shrugged. "I don't actually have any ideas. I just wanted to see if I was allowed." His tone was light, but the meaning was clear.

I sighed. "I know I haven't been involving you as much as I should."

"I mean, I get it. I haven't exactly proven myself as partner of the year material," Tim replied self-consciously. "But it's still my baby, and if this is going to work then you need to let me in."

"I know. I'm working on it."

That was the reason for the date, after all. But I hadn't been partner of the year to him lately, either. I wasn't going to lose any sleep over that, given the fact that if he hadn't cheated on me we'd be in a much better place, probably even engaged by now. But I had to admit it, at least to myself. I'd barely let him touch me affectionately since the shooting. You could forget about sex – that hadn't happened since before I'd found out the truth about him and Betty. I was secretly thinking about changing that tonight, though. I wasn't sure if it was the pregnancy hormones or the fact that I was starting to get over his betrayal.

"Anyway," I said, hoping to shift the subject on to something lighter. I didn't want to talk about the baby, either. "Wait 'til you hear about Sadie," I said, naming a woman at work.

I filled him in on Sadie walking out on her husband for her new lesbian lover, Roxie. They'd moved in together after being involved for only a couple of weeks, and Sadie had quit her job at the restaurant to join Roxie at her new internet company, which Roxie had promised would be 'the new Google'. "Well," Tim said, laughing in surprise. "None of that sounds even remotely doomed to failure."

"Nope. We'll feel so silly when they're rich and famous," I joked.

My light-hearted anecdote achieved its goal of tempering the mood between us. The rest of the night was filled with laughter, good conversation and, yes, sex.

Chapter 81 – Destiny

After what felt like several years, the night of her University graduation had finally arrived. Destiny could hardly contain her excitement!

She looked at her reflection in the mirror, grinning as she smoothed down her emerald green dress. Everyone said it didn't really matter what you wore under your gown because not much showed, but that hadn't stopped her from going out and buying the outrageously overpriced, totally hot new dress. She loved it. She'd always liked the look of green with her red hair and blue eyes. She felt like a mermaid.

The graduation was being held in the concert hall in town, and she and Gemma had arranged to meet there before getting their caps and gowns. Her mum and Ben had their tickets, as did Rosie, Paula and Fiona. Everything was organised.

Destiny knew a graduation didn't really change anything. She already had a job to go into - a minor miracle in itself - and classes had finished a few weeks earlier. She had received her final grades already. Nothing would change as a result of tonight.

But *everything* would change. Destiny would have her certificate there in her hands to show that she had achieved this. She would officially be a graduate. She couldn't wait.

Of course, the idea of graduating brought a little sadness with it, Destiny reflected as she looked out the window of her Uber twenty minutes later, headed into the city. She knew she and Gemma would stay friends, but they wouldn't see each other several times a week the way they had for the last couple of years. She was less certain about her friendships with Frankie, Lucy and even Nate. Would they stay in touch after they were no longer bonded by seeing each other regularly? Of course, her relationship with Courtney and Ed was already done. Even though they'd officially made up, she would be quite happy not to have to see them again after tonight, and she was fairly sure the feeling was mutual. She knew Gemma and Nate had pretty much wiped the other two as well, so she wouldn't have to awkwardly run into them at parties or anything in the future. Maybe that was part of why she felt so excited for graduation. Not because of Ed and Courtney specifically, but just because the whole thing felt like a clean break. A fresh start. She sure as hell could use that.

It had been over six months since the shooting, a fact that still took her by surprise. It still felt like yesterday. On the other hand, she could barely remember life before the shooting. Destiny sometimes felt as if she had a permanent weight in her stomach now, a ball of grief and anger and sadness. She knew it hadn't been there before, but she could barely remember what life felt like without it. Destiny wondered from time to time if it would ever go away, or if she was stuck with it for good. It certainly hadn't seemed to get much smaller over the past six months.

Still, she was fairly lucky. Destiny hadn't been physically hurt by the shooting, and even though the loss of Luke still devastated her, she no longer held herself personally responsible for it. She had finished uni, and she had a great job waiting for her. She had good friends, a supportive family. Things could definitely be a lot worse.

Arriving at the concert hall, Destiny hopped out of the Uber and squealed when she saw Gemma striding towards her, looking even taller and more confident than usual in her killer heels. The two girls embraced and even jumped up and down a little as they did so, like clichéd movie characters. They grinned at each other as they broke apart. Destiny couldn't remember the last time she'd felt this happy.

Chapter 82 – Fiona

Not wanting to arrive at the concert hall alone for Destiny's graduation, Fiona offered to pick Paula and Rosie up. Rosie thanked her but declined, saying her partner was going to drive her, so it ended up being just Fiona and Paula in the car, and that was how the invitation happened.

Paula was chattering away in the passenger seat, talking about Ollie's "step back" and how she was worried she'd been concentrating too much on Jasmine at the expense of her son. "He's been through so much," Paula went on. "I know Jasmine's going through this really hard experience too, but I had kind of forgotten how much Ollie's been dealing with over the past six months."

Fiona could empathise. It had been hard enough looking after her own wellbeing after the shooting, without having to worry about anyone else. She couldn't imagine having to balance the needs of two children who were both going through a tough time.

"My therapist thinks I've been worrying too much about them and not enough about myself," Paula added with a laugh, as if this statement were ridiculous and not plainly true. "He even told me I should go away by myself. Imagine that! 'Sorry Alf, I'm heading to the coast!'"

"Why not?"

"Why not? I don't travel by myself. I mean, I really don't travel at all, not even much before the kids were born. It's never been my thing. Oh, don't get me wrong, I'm so jealous of your Italy trip," Paula added hastily, as if she might have offended Fiona. She hadn't – Fiona knew travelling wasn't for everyone. "But I'd rather use the money on the bills, or maybe some home renovations. You know, something that benefits all of us. Something practical."

Fiona laughed. Paula was a fun person to be around, but when she talked about money you could be forgiven for thinking she was some kind of octogenarian aunt, too anxious about finances to let her hair down. "You're allowed to do something just for you," Fiona reminded her. "If not a holiday, then maybe just a nice pedicure or something?"

Paula was silent for a moment. "I mean, maybe the trip away would be nice, but I still don't think I could go it alone."

"I'll go with you," Fiona said. She was mostly joking, but when Paula exclaimed "Would you?" it suddenly didn't seem like such a crazy idea.

"Well, where do you want to go?" Fiona asked.

"Nowhere too extravagant. I was thinking maybe a weekend at the Sunshine Coast."

"That would definitely be doable," Fiona replied, starting to feel excited despite herself. She hadn't had a beach weekend away in ages, and even though she and Paula had only known each other for a few months, they'd become so close. Angela would always be Fiona's best friend but since she had a family of her own, they didn't really travel together. Looking back on her marriage to Jacob she realised that they hadn't done enough of it either. Not that a weekend at the Sunshine Coast, only ninety minutes' drive away, even really counted as travelling, but it was something to look forward to at the very least. "It would have to be just for the weekend, though," Fiona added, filling Paula in briefly on the disastrous conversation with Jennifer about trying to get time off.

Paula pulled out her phone. "Let me look some things up right now."

"Ugh, jealous," Fiona said, glancing over at the other woman. "I wish I could read in the car. I get sick."

"Well, we don't want you doing that right now, anyway – not while you're driving!" Paula replied with a light laugh. Fiona was surprised to realise that the comment didn't transport her back to the night of Jacob's accident. A comment like that would have in the past, but now she just took it as the light-hearted remark that it was intended to be.

Paula kept searching and announcing different hotel names and prices, and by the time Fiona parked her car at the concert hall, their weekend away was booked.

Chapter 83 – Paula

Paula and Fiona met up with Rosie outside the graduation hall, excitedly filling her in on the weekend away they'd just booked. Paula felt a slight pang of guilt at not involving Rosie and Destiny, but of course, Rosie wasn't going to be going anywhere for a while and as much as they got on with Destiny, Paula couldn't imagine a weekend away with the younger girl. Luckily, Rosie seemed nothing but excited for the two of them. "I suppose my weekends away are over for a while," she sighed enviously.

Paula knew that her own weekends away might also be numbered. Jasmine was still planning on giving the baby up, but Paula hadn't forgotten the fact that the birth might change that notion completely.

The three grabbed their seats for the graduation, pleased to see that they had a fairly good view of the stage. After a while a middle-aged woman and a boy in his twenties came and sat next to them, smiling over at them.

"You must be Destiny's mum and brother," Paula said, extending a hand. Desi had told them ahead of time that the five tickets had them all seated together. "I'm Paula."

They all introduced themselves. "You must be so proud of Desi," Rosie beamed.

"Oh, we are!" Janet exclaimed. "She's the first in the family to graduate from university."

"That's wonderful," Paula said with a smile, just as the ceremony started.

There was a posthumous honour for Luke, which Paula hadn't been prepared for. She should have thought of it, of course. She found herself dabbing her eyes. When Luke's picture appeared on the screen, he received a standing ovation. Paula couldn't see Destiny up on the stage but she assumed she was tearing up, too. It was an emotional moment even for those who didn't know him, let alone someone as close to him as Desi.

When they got to the J section and "Destiny Johnson" was announced in a loud, clear voice, the three women all shouted out, drowning out Destiny's family's more polite and subdued clapping.

When the ceremony was over they all rushed to greet Destiny, who was looking happy and overwhelmed as she clutched her certificate, which she quickly handed over to her mum. "You'll look after it better than I will," Destiny laughed, hugging them all in turn.

Destiny had asked the week before if they wanted to go for a celebratory dinner with Gemma and Nate and their families. They all headed by foot to the Turkish restaurant at Southbank, chatting happily between them all.

Halfway to the restaurant Destiny left her mother's side and came back to the group of women, clutching Paula's arm like they were young girlfriends. "You guys will never believe what happened tonight," Desi said, beaming.

Chapter 84 – Destiny

Destiny had thought she couldn't be happier than she was when she arrived at graduation, but she was wrong.

"Nate!" she had squealed, opening her arms up for a hug when she saw her friend at the start of the night. "We made it!"

They were both already in their gowns and mortar boards, and Nate looked as handsome as she'd ever seen him. Handsome was such an old-fashioned word, but it seemed to fit him right now. *Hot* didn't really do it justice, although, she realised, that was true, too. She tried to ignore the butterflies she felt in her stomach. Gemma had disappeared for family photos, so the two of them were alone – well, alone, surrounded by several hundred people all milling around excitedly. Destiny had seen Ed and Courtney briefly earlier, but they had just exchanged a tight smile at one another from a distance. She didn't need the awkward interaction, and apparently neither did they.

"Your parents are here?" she went on, glancing towards the audience as though she could see them in the crowd of thousands.

Nate nodded. Destiny had never met his parents before, since they lived in Townsville and had only visited Brisbane once in the time she and Nate had been friends. "I'm looking forward to meeting them," she said. "Actually, I'm looking forward to dinner in general. I'm starving." She'd only had a ham and salad wrap for lunch, which she was regretting now. Graduation was the awkward time of 6pm and they had needed to be there a couple of hours early to get their gowns and photos done. Their dinner was booked for 8:30, and Destiny didn't want to think about how hungry she'd be by then.

"They're looking forward to meeting you, too," Nate said. He paused, then added "They've heard a lot about you."

Destiny's heart rate quickened, not for the first time around him.

At their drinks a few weeks earlier she'd indulged a bit too much, and she thought they'd had a moment together. The three other girls had been up dancing, so it was just the two of them alone in their booth. Nate had pulled out his phone to show her a funny clip he'd found online, and she'd leant in so she could hear the noise properly over the sound of the bar. In response, Nate had moved in closer to her, and she could feel the heat radiating from his body. She'd also felt the heat of Gemma's stare on them as she watched their every move from the dance floor, a triumphant look upon her face.

It was nothing you wouldn't see in a G-rated movie, for crying out loud. Definitely nothing to be getting all hot and bothered about weeks after the fact. But for whatever reason, she couldn't get it out of her mind. They'd hugged plenty of times before, so it was strange that this had affected her so much, but it just felt so... intimate. You could hug friends. Her mum even hugged virtual strangers, friends of friends when they were introduced to her. But this felt like a private moment that only they shared. Destiny couldn't explain it, and she didn't want to.

After that she'd started to keep her distance from Nate, still feeling guilty about her feelings. But tonight, Destiny was surprised to discover that she wasn't keeping her distance. She just didn't want to. Maybe it was her thought from earlier about how graduation would be a fresh start, but she just wanted to enjoy her time with Nate. It was a nice feeling.

"Everything's going to be so different after tonight," Destiny said, not replying to his comment about his parents.

"Sure is," Nate agreed. "Out there in the real world and all that."

"What are your plans?"

He shrugged. "I'm going to apply everywhere and see what I can get, but I thought I could do some freelance work in the meantime. Hell, I can even set up my own photography business if I want to." Destiny admired his confidence. He seemed completely unconcerned about leaving uni life behind, even though he didn't know what was ahead of him. She was the one who already had a job lined up, and she still felt slightly nauseous at the idea of leaving the safety net of uni.

"That's great," she said sincerely. There was a long pause, but not an uncomfortable one. Eventually she said what she'd been wondering but hadn't wanted to put into words. "Do you think we'll still see each other?"

Destiny and Gemma had had the same kinds of discussions, even though the two girlfriends were both certain they'd remain close. Still, they talked about how often they might see each other now, aware that the friendship would involve more work than it had in the past, when they naturally got to see each other in classes or working on group projects together. But with Nate the conversation felt different, and much more loaded. She wondered if it did to him as well, or if she was just imagining things. She knew the whole thing was crazy after being friends for a couple of years now!

"Absolutely!" Nate replied without hesitation. "You're one of my best friends. That's not going to change now just because I'm not sitting next to you in a lecture theatre."

Destiny smiled. It was exactly the answer she'd wanted to hear.

And then, without saying another word, he leaned in and kissed her.

She was so surprised she pulled back momentarily, but then, acting almost totally on instinct, she leant back in.

The kiss was amazing. She'd never felt chemistry like this before with anyone. Not even with Luke, although in fairness, they'd never actually kissed. Still, this was... electric.

When they finally drew back, Nate was grinning. "Holy shit," he said. "I didn't actually plan that. It just kind of happened. I'd say I'm sorry, but..."

He didn't need to finish the sentence. He'd say he was sorry, but she was clearly just as into the kiss as he was.

There was another momentary silence, more awkward this time, and then Destiny started laughing.

"What is it?" Nate asked, his deep brown eyes reflecting some anxiety now. "Was I out of line?"

She shook her head, not really sure why she was laughing, but unable to stop. "No. I was just thinking... I guess we will stay in touch, after all."

Chapter 85 – Rosie

Ahhh, young love, I thought, smiling to myself as I walked into the house. Fiona had given me a lift home in the end, so I didn't need to get Tim to collect me. Destiny and Nate were so cute together over dinner. They obviously thought they were being subtle in front of their families, but they couldn't stop grinning at each other over their meals, and I was fairly sure there might have been a bit of footsie going on under the table. It had been a nice night, and – at the risk of sounding geriatric – something about seeing the younger couple together made me feel hopeful, somehow. They were positively giddy together, and I couldn't be happier for my friend.

I walked in as far as the recliner and lowered myself down into it. I was too exhausted to get all the way to my bed. I would get up and head in, but right now I just wanted to sit for a while. Tim was already asleep, but he'd left some lights on for me.

I was thirty-five weeks pregnant, and painfully aware that the next few weeks would be the longest of my life. I'd never been so tired or so sore before. My ankles were swollen and my entire body felt puffy, but it would all be worth it, I reminded myself. I closed my eyes, feeling myself start to drift off to sleep.

The next thing I knew, it was morning. I'd slept the whole night in the armchair. I spent a few minutes gently stretching out my arms and legs, trying to recover from the awkward sleeping position.

I wasn't working until the evening, so I decided to visit Dad. I'd felt a bit like a bad daughter lately, even though I knew he understood that I wasn't really feeling up to casual pop-ins. I thought about ringing him first, but decided to just go and visit. He was likely to be home and if not, at least the drive would get me out of the house for a while.

"Dad?" I called out as I arrived at his house. I walked into the family room and stopped dead. "Oh... hi, Brenda! Sorry, I didn't know you were here."

Brenda, Dad's neighbour, was sitting at the kitchen table, a mug of tea in front of her. She smiled as she saw me. "Hi, Rosie! Oh, don't you look lovely," she said.

I'd seen Brenda at Dad's place plenty of times before, but this seemed different. There was something about the way she was sitting at the table as if she belonged there, and the way that she and Dad smiled at each other, that made me take a second look. Was I imagining things, or was something more than just neighbourly hospitality going on here?

"I don't feel too lovely," I laughed, giving Dad a quick kiss on the cheek and trying to act completely normal. I didn't want to embarrass either of them. "I feel absolutely gigantic."

"We all feel like that at the end of the pregnancy," Brenda sympathised. She had two adult children, and her own husband had died nearly a decade earlier, before she'd moved to Dad's neighbourhood. "But it's all worth it in the end."

"Well, that's what I keep trying to tell myself."

"Do you want a tea, love?" Dad asked. "Or some biscuits or something?"

"Oh, I -" I was about to make my excuses, say that I'd just popped in for a quick visit. If I wasn't imagining things, then I didn't want to intrude. But just then, Brenda swallowed the last of her tea and stood up. "I should get going, anyway. Lovely to see you, Rosie. And you, too, of course, Phil." Dad walked her to the door, while I walked – waddled, really – into the kitchen and helped myself to a couple of sugary biscuits.

When Dad walked in, I raised my eyebrows at him. "Is there anything you want to tell me?" I hadn't planned on a confrontational approach, but that's how it came out.

"Tell you?" Dad asked innocently, sitting down at the table again. "Like what sort of thing?"

I nodded my head towards the front door, gesturing towards Brenda. "You two just looked quite friendly there."

"Oh, yes. Well, you know Brenda's been checking in on me these last few months."

I laughed and put my hand on his. "Dad, if you're seeing her, it's fine by me."

"It is?"

"Of course it is! Mum's been gone for years now. I just want you to be happy." Actually, it was exactly the news I didn't know I'd needed to hear. Knowing your parent was with someone new was always going to be a little strange, but at least if Dad was seeing someone I wouldn't have to worry about him as much as I had been doing. Besides, I had always liked Brenda.

Wait 'til I tell Betty the goss!

The thought flew through my mind before I could stop it. I often had those kinds of thoughts, fleeting moments where I forgot what had happened. Moments where I thought I could just pick up my phone and tell my sister everything, the way I always had. Those moments were hard, harder even than the times of outright grief or anger. There was nothing in this world that was worse than false hope.

Still, I forced myself to stop thinking about Betty and I walked over to give my dad a quick squeeze. "I really am happy for you," I told him, smiling.

When I left Dad's about an hour later, I was still smiling. It was funny how I'd seen the start of a young romance last night with Desi and Nate, and here I was, seeing Dad and Brenda get a second chance at love. It was really awesome, sometimes, to see the circle of life in action.

Chapter 86 – Paula

It was a strange concept for Paula, at forty-two, to suddenly find herself spending her downtime researching the adoption process, but that was her reality now.

She'd always thought work, keeping the house in a somewhat respectable state and driving her children to and from their various sporting commitments were enough to keep her busy. Now there were counselling appointments for her youngest child, and obstetricians for her eldest one. If you'd told her a year ago that this would be her life now, she'd have laughed. It would have been far too unbelievable.

And yet, life had a way of surprising you.

The most surprising parts of all were that there were upsides to it all.

If given half the chance, Paula would, naturally, have made sure none of this ever happened. She would have taken Jasmine to the doctor and put her on the Pill, no longer unwilling to face the concept of her child being sexually active. She would have kept Ollie at home that Tuesday morning, the two of them safe on the couch, instead of facing down a madman and his gun.

But she couldn't go back, so she might as well make the best of the way things were.

The largest and most obvious difference was with Jasmine. From the surly teenager she had been, she'd suddenly become willing to be her mother's girl again. The new Jasmine offered hugs without needing to be prompted and sat down beside her mum after school to fill her in on her day, instead of disappearing to her bedroom. Every so often Paula idly wondered if this side of her daughter would remain when all of this was over, but she pushed the thought away. If Paula had learnt anything over the last six months, it was to live in the moment, and she was trying to do exactly that.

Besides, Paula knew as well as anyone that this would never really be 'over'. Whatever happened with the baby, he would be a part of Jasmine's life forever. Even if he was living with new parents, it wouldn't be as if this had never happened. Paula knew there could be depression in Jasmine's future, and she could live to regret her decision. Jasmine might spend the rest of her life wondering what was happening with the baby boy out there in the world. Or they could arrange an open adoption, which could ease the burden of not knowing but might be even harder for Jazzy, in a way. Looking in on the boy's life from the periphery couldn't be easy, either.

Paula's research had told her that there was post adoption support available, which was a blessing. She had never looked into it before but she was sure that fifty years ago, families would have just been expected to surrender their child with little regard for the birth parents' wellbeing. Interestingly, though, she noticed it was a lot easier to find information about how to adopt a child, rather than adopting one *out*, which she found interesting. Most of the information was geared towards prospective parents, rather than the birth parents wanting to find a suitable home for their baby. Were there so few voluntary adoptions in Australia these days that the information just wasn't needed anymore? She felt a pang for all the prospective adoptive parents out there, waiting for something that might never happen. She imagined a hopeful couple out there right now who might one day end up raising Paula's grandchild as their own.

After researching for a while, she finally found an online information brochure. She knew she could have seen her doctor about it or asked the obstetrician for more information, but she wanted to get things clear in her mind before she asked someone else for guidance. Asking for help had never really been one of her strengths.

In everything she read online, there was a big push towards family members caring for your child, which filled Paula with even more guilt. Was she being selfish in not giving much consideration to this option? After all, she'd always wanted a third child. But she pushed the thought away. Yes, she'd always wanted another, but not at the age of forty-three, as she would be by the time the baby was here. And not with the added complication of the child being her grandson. She'd had enough friction with her own mother when she'd given birth to Jasmine and Oliver about some of the parenting decisions she'd made, and her mum had been interstate! She couldn't imagine the negative impact it would have on Jasmine for the two of them to be essentially co-parenting Jasmine's baby. Alfie wouldn't be keen for that option, either. Paula knew that without having to ask him.

The process she'd found online documented it all in a clear, clinical way. Firstly Jasmine would need to undergo pre-consent counselling, where the Child Safety Officer would explain the process and the possible effects of adoption, to help Jasmine make the best decision for both herself and the baby. Paula hoped those two things would be one and the same. If they clashed, who would Jasmine choose to favour in the process? Herself, or the baby?

Suddenly, Paula hit the information section about the father of the baby. Somehow, she'd almost forgotten he existed. Of course, Brad seemed perfectly happy to act that way, too. The web site mentioned that refusing to disclose information about the father could jeopardise or delay the adoption process. Both parents had to give consent to the adoption. Paula sighed to herself. Brad couldn't stay irrelevant forever, then, as much as she would like him to. The information said he could apply for parental responsibility, but at least Paula wasn't concerned about that. Brad certainly wasn't lining up to be a dad.

Paula went on to read that if the parents were less than eighteen years old themselves they were still able to consent to giving their child up for adoption, but they would need an additional assessment. Her heart sank as she read the next line, which stated that this was a necessary step because consenting to adoption had lifelong implications. Paula had known that was true, obviously, but every time she read information like that, it just hammered home the point further. Whatever happened here, there was no happy ending. Jasmine would be dealing with this for the rest of her life.

Chapter 87 – Fiona

Finally, it was the weekend of her trip away with Paula. She had arranged for Katie's teenaged son, Sebastian, to move into her house and look after Burleigh for the weekend. It was only next door, after all, so Katie wasn't too concerned about Sebastian being there alone. Fiona knew some people left their dogs alone with someone just checking in on them, but there was no way she could have done that. Burleigh needed someone to cuddle up next to at night, not just someone to throw him a tennis ball and give him some food.

Paula had suggested picking Fiona straight up from her workplace at Auchenflower. It only saved them about fifteen minutes of travel time compared to meeting at Fiona's place but somehow, it seemed more exciting that way. Adam gave Fiona a lift to work that morning and she'd kept her packed bags in the office of the aged care home. She spent the day watching the clock, counting down the time until she saw Paula and they got on their way.

When it finally hit 5:30, Fiona was out of there on the dot. She waved excitedly when Paula's car pulled up a few minutes later. Paula got out to help her put her bags in the boot, and soon they were coast-bound.

"It's been so long since I've been away," Fiona chirped excitedly. "I couldn't decide what to read, so I've brought two books along. I'm hoping for plenty of reading time by the pool."

Paula smiled. "Sounds good to me! We're getting fish and chips on the beach for lunch one day, right? That's what I'm most excited about!"

"Absolutely! That sounds heavenly."

They continued chatting amicably throughout the drive, but then Paula surprised Fiona by saying "Tell me about your husband."

Fiona was touched by the request. It didn't seem like much, but so many people seemed afraid to mention Jacob in front of her, as though she would collapse in a heap. She understood where they were coming from, but the emotions that Jacob's name stirred up were still better than acting as though he had never existed.

"He was so kind," she said. "He could talk to anyone, and he usually did! He was always making new friends everywhere he went."

Paula smiled. "It sounds like he was a great guy."

Fiona nodded. "He was. He was always funny, and he really looked after me, you know? If we were on the couch and I said I wanted a drink, he'd always leap up to get it for me. If I ever needed him to drop everything and come and pick me up from somewhere, he would." She paused, thinking about it. To be honest, that was what she missed the most about Jacob. She missed his smile and his warmth, but the one thing she felt the loss of overwhelmingly was how safe he made her feel. With him, she never felt like she was alone in the world.

It was nonsensical, but part of her felt like if he'd still been alive, the shooting never would have happened. At the very least, his support afterwards would have helped her get back on her feet.

Of course, if he'd been in the world, she would have been at work that fateful Tuesday and not at the shopping centre.

But she was there, and he wasn't, and she couldn't change that. No matter how hard she wished she could.

"I wish I could have met him," Paula said now, and Fiona smiled. "Me too," she said simply. She knew Jacob and Paula would have got on well.

"I hope this isn't out of line," Paula said after a brief pause. "But... do you ever think about getting out there and dating again?"

Fiona sighed. "I do sometimes," she admitted. "But I pretty much just start feeling guilty every time I think about it. Jacob hasn't even been gone a year. I know some people move on a lot faster than that, but I can't picture being with anyone else. I was only twenty-five when I met Jacob. I've never had to do Internet dating or anything. I wouldn't know where to start!"

"You'd be fine, I'm sure. You're a gorgeous, *young* woman," Paula said seriously. "I think you forget that sometimes."

Fiona had to admit that was true. Sometimes she felt closer to fifty than her actual age of thirty-seven. Between being widowed and going through the shooting, it was as though she'd aged by decades in less than twelve months.

"Anyway," Fiona said, "Jacob was a perfect fit for me. Why bother going out and finding someone else who wouldn't be nearly as good of a match? If you've been having filet mignon for twenty years, it's hard to go back to hamburgers."

"How do you know this new guy wouldn't be a good match?" Paula asked reasonably.

"I mean, they might be a *good* match. But Jacob was like..." She paused, trying to think. "He was like a comfortable pair of slippers and my sexiest dress, all in one. He made me feel completely warm and at home, but he also made me feel like the most exciting person in the world. Not many people can do that."

"No," Paula agreed with a smile. "Not many can. And even with everything that's happened, I've got to say, I'm a little jealous of what you had! I love Alfie, but I wouldn't describe him like that. We've got the comfortable and old part down, at least." She paused. "But I wouldn't trade him for anything. I don't know how I would have got through the last few months without him. So maybe you can't find what you and Jacob had again, but maybe you can find something better than..."

"Better than what I have now," Fiona said, filling in the blanks for her friend.

"Well, yeah. I mean, I'm not trying to diminish your life. You have your friends, and Burleigh, and your work. You have a whole lot! But I'd love you to find an amazing partner again."

Fiona smiled. It was nice to have someone looking out for her.

"Maybe you're right," she said after a while. "But I don't think I'm ready just yet."

"And that's perfectly fine! Maybe you won't be ready for six months or five years. That part is up to you. I just don't want to see you writing off the possibility entirely."

"No," she said. "One day, I want to find someone again."

It was a small admission, but for Fiona, it was enormous. It was the first time she'd let herself admit it, even to herself.

Then she cleared her throat and leant over to turn the radio up. She didn't want to be rude, but it was time to change the topic to something less serious. Paula got the hint, and soon the two were singing along together.

With the Friday afternoon traffic, it took nearly two hours to get to the Maroochydore hotel where they were spending their weekend. It was dark by the time they arrived but Fiona snapped photos from their balcony regardless, looking forward to seeing the view with some sunlight the next day.

They decided to start the morning early, so they could see the sunrise and go for a walk along the beach. For now, though, the two new friends sat down in front of the television together, ordered some Indian takeaway and opened a bottle of wine. It was the most relaxing night Fiona had had in a long time.

The rest of the weekend passed in a similar fashion. The two women went swimming, read their books by the water and went for pedicures together. On their last afternoon, they went for high tea at a nearby coffee shop.

"This has been so great," Paula said enthusiastically as they devoured their finger sandwiches and mini quiche. "Thanks for coming away with me."

"You're definitely welcome!" Fiona laughed. "I'm more than happy to do this sort of thing much more often."

"We should," Paula said. "We could make it an annual thing, invite Rosie and Destiny next time. The baby would be old enough by then."

"Oh, that sounds amazing! Count me in."

They hadn't even been friends for six months at that point, which would have normally been far too early to start talking about annual weekends away, but in their case it felt natural. After what they had all been through together, they were bonded for life.

Chapter 88 – Destiny

Following their kiss at graduation, Destiny and Nate had their first official date. It made her think back to how nervous she had been the morning of her previous date, with Luke that fateful day. In a weird contrast, she wasn't nervous at all as she waited for Nate to come and collect her at her house. Maybe it was a bad sign; maybe Nate didn't get her as nervously excited as Luke did. Or maybe it was a good sign; she already felt so comfortable around him that she didn't need to be nervous.

Or maybe she didn't have to compare them at all.

Seeing Luke's image the night of graduation, not long after her first kiss with Nate, had been truly surreal. She had known that he was going to be honoured, and that his parents were coming along for the night. She had known it would be difficult. She hadn't expected, though, to have such a warm feeling come over her when she saw his image. For the first time since his death the thought of Luke filled her with love and warmth, rather than guilt or grief. She grew misty-eyed at the standing ovation the audience gave him, her tears a mixture of happiness and sadness. She saw Nate looking at her sympathetically from his spot in the line where they were already standing in alphabetical order. She wished he were beside her so she could take his hand. She loved that she could openly grieve for Luke in front of him, without Nate feeling threatened by it.

When Nate pulled up in his second-hand red Mazda, she ran out to the car, grinning widely. "Hey, you," she said, smiling over at him as she hopped in the passenger seat. Nate responded by reaching over and giving her a quick kiss. She shouldn't have been surprised, given graduation, but she was. Compared to the passionate kiss at graduation this one felt so casual, like something an established couple would do when they saw each other. She loved it.

"Ready for the beach?" Nate asked, putting the car into drive and heading down the road.

They'd decided on a day trip to the Gold Coast. It had been Nate's suggestion and her instant response had been to feel nervous about him seeing her in her swimmers so early on. What if he thought she was too pale, too freckly, too skinny? Still, it wasn't like her normal clothes were overly modest, so he probably had a pretty good idea of exactly how pale, freckly and skinny she was, and he liked her anyway. Besides, Destiny had seen her own mum struggle with wearing bathing suits in public for the exact opposite reason – she thought she was too large to be seen in so little covering. Destiny had always vowed never to be like that. She would rather live her life than hide away, especially now!

"Can't wait," Desi said now, in answer to Nate's question. "Do you go to the beach often?" She didn't mean it to come out sounding like the cheesy pick-up line it did.

Nate didn't seem to pick up on it. "Oh, I practically live there," he said. She had known that, of course, from his discussions about the beach in the past. Maybe she was more nervous than she'd thought, after all. "I've been surfing since I was a kid. You?" he added.

"Yeah, I try to get there a fair bit. Not as often as I should, really." It was only a fifty-minute trip to the Gold Coast, so she didn't know why she didn't go down to the south coast more often. "But I don't surf. I'll cheer you on for that part." She liked the fact that he'd suggested a beach date, when that was something that was such an important part of his life. It felt like he was opening up to her.

They kept talking easily enough about their lives, and the rest of Nate's parents' visit. They had gone back to Townsville two days earlier. "I didn't tell them about today," Nate added. "I thought I'd see how things go first. But they're coming back next month for a show at Southbank anyway, so I thought maybe we could all have dinner then."

"Definitely!" Destiny smiled. It was a positive sign that he was asking her already, rather than waiting until the end of the date. She had liked Nate's parents instantly, although meeting them not long after her first kiss with their son had been a little surreal. His dad was your typical Aussie bloke and his mum an elegant Sudanese woman. Both had been friendly and welcoming, and Destiny couldn't shake the feeling that perhaps they knew there was something more than friendship going on.

They were pulling onto the highway when she asked him "What would you do if you won a million dollars?"

She'd been trying to think of something interesting to say, and had settled on a hypothetical. It wasn't the most scintillating question in the world, but she'd always thought hypotheticals revealed a lot about a person. Not to mention, it was hard to keep her train of thought around him. She couldn't wait to get out of the car so she could start kissing him again. It was so weird to think like that about Nate. Nate!

Nate frowned, seeming to give the question serious consideration, which pleased Destiny. Not everyone gave hypotheticals their due respect. "I think I'd probably travel the world for a year, just take time off and not have to worry about money." He paused. "Not that I actually have a job to take time off from. But yeah, I think a big world trip for a year and a new car, and then I'd be all sensible and invest. What would you do?"

"Mine's a bit more boring than yours. I'd probably save some straight off the bat, so I could keep getting interest." The truth was, she'd thought about this before. Having grown up without a lot of money, she'd often played around with the idea. She laughed a little at herself, inwardly, wondering if there was any less seductive dating technique than talking about compounding interest. "I'd give some to charity. Then I'd buy a house for Mum and put the rest towards one for me. A million doesn't go as far as it used to."

"I hope you don't only want me for my riches," Nate joked.

Destiny laughed. "Your money? No. I want you for your hot bod."

She'd said it as a joke, but she was acutely aware of wanting to get his shirt off him as soon as possible. The beach trip really was very convenient, after all.

"Ah, I see," he said, mock-seriously. "You're just using me."

"Yep. You okay with that?"

Nate pretended to think it over. "I think I can live with it."

"That's good. I have high hopes – I've never been with a younger man, you know," she teased, referring to the six-month gap between them. She didn't mean it to be as sexual as it came out sounding. It wasn't as though she hadn't thought about what sex with Nate would be like, of course. She had thought of little else since their kiss at graduation. Her small amount of experience in the bedroom with previous boyfriends had been nothing to write home about. She knew she was getting ahead of herself, but she had a feeling it would be entirely different with Nate.

"Oh, you'll love it," Nate replied blithely. "We're full of... stamina. Or something."

Now Destiny wondered if *he'd* intended that to sound as sexual as it had. She thought of the phrase Gemma loved to quote: *You're only as old as the man you feel.* Desi glanced down at her lap, feeling her cheeks warming up as if Nate could read her thoughts.

She was still feeling flustered when they pulled up at the beach a few minutes later and started unloading the car. Fortunately, the rest of the date passed much more comfortably. The two chatted the day away, stopping only for some brief make-out sessions on the sand. At one point they waded in the water together, hand-in-hand, with Destiny holding her shoes in her other hand. It felt so romantic, like something out of an old movie. By the time they packed up to leave the beach, she was flushed with excitement for the future. It was something she had thought she might never feel again. The excitement brought with it a spark of fear – she knew now how easy it was to lose everything. But she also knew it was worth the risk to get to feel like this.

Her phone went off on the way home. Destiny glanced down at it and smiled when she saw the message.

"What's up?" Nate asked, glancing over at her.

"It's my friend Rosie, the one you met at grad," Destiny replied. "She's had her baby."

Chapter 89 – Rosie

Labour wasn't what I would call a fun way to spend an afternoon, but it wasn't as horrendous as I'd been led to believe by books and movies, either.

There was pain. I pushed. There was more pain, and it momentarily felt like more than I could stand. I gave birth to my baby girl. And then there wasn't any pain anymore, just bliss. For the first time, I could understand why people went back for more than one child. The sight of them really did erase all of the labour pains, pretty much immediately. Mum had always said that, but I'd never believed her. Of course, Mum had been lucky enough to have twins and get it all done in the one go.

"She's beautiful," Tim laughed, tearing up for the second time this year. I smiled at him. The big softie.

At that moment, I couldn't believe I'd ever thought we wouldn't work out. Maybe it was just the hormones coursing through my body, but I'd never been happier. I felt like the luckiest person alive.

I knew that later there would be some pain associated with Betty not being there to give me support or to share in this moment with me, but not now. Now, I was just simply happy, in a way I hadn't been since before the shooting.

"So," Tim said later, when we were alone, "we should probably tell the family about her soon. Might be nice to have a name for her when we do."

I grinned, looking the baby over. We never had settled on a name, and some of the ones I'd considered didn't seem right now that the baby was actually here. I was silent for a moment as I mulled it over.

Then it came to me, as though the answer had been there all along. "The middle name needs to be Hope," I said definitively. "That's the only thing that's got me through this year. And the first name... how do you feel about Eliza?" It hadn't been one of the names on our list.

"Eliza?" he asked with a little frown. Then, his face clearing, "you mean –"

Yes. Eliza, after Elizabeth. It was similar enough to Betty, and clearly a tribute to her, but it was still different enough that little Eliza wouldn't be bound to her late aunt for her whole life. It was different enough that she could still stand on her own two feet.

It was all I had ever wanted for myself, too.

"Is it too strange?" I asked. I didn't finish my sentence, but the context was clear. Was it too strange, considering everything that had happened? I didn't think it was. If Tim had come out declaring he wanted the baby to be named after Betty then that would have been a different story, but she was still my twin sister, first and foremost. A twin sister who wasn't perfect, and had made a devastating mistake, but a twin sister I loved and missed.

Tim shook his head wordlessly. He was staring at our daughter as if she was the only other person in the world. I knew the feeling. It was incredible to think that this tiny little person, who took up such a small place in the world, could fill my heart with so much love.

Chapter 90 – Paula

It was strange timing to receive the text about Rosie's newborn, Eliza, while Paula was taking her own daughter to her pre-adoption counselling appointment. She had driven Jasmine there, but waited outside during the consultation. She needed Jasmine to be free to open up, to express every possible emotion she was experiencing, rather than holding back for her mother's sake. When she saw the text, she was particularly pleased it hadn't come through while she was driving, when Jasmine would often check her phone for her. Paula was thrilled for Rosie, of course. This was such a special time for her and her family. But Jasmine didn't need to see a photo of the sweet, pink-faced newborn nestled in her mother's arms.

Paula took Jazzy for ice cream after the appointment. It reminded her of when she'd taken her daughter out of school early for various check-ups and appointments over the years. It broke her heart.

"How did it go?" Paula ventured over their ice creams. They'd driven there in silence, Paula not wanting to pressure her daughter. But now, the silence was becoming fraught with tension. Paula needed to know what was happening.

Jasmine took a deep breath in. "It was okay. She said she's happy that I've considered the 'legal and emotional ramifications.'" She made air quotes as she said this part. "But... oh, Mum, I just wish it was easier than this."

Paula reached a hand out, sympathetically. "I know, baby. I do, too. But we have to deal with what we've got."

Jasmine nodded. "I know. It was just... so stupid. I'm never having sex again."

Paula laughed, despite herself. "Well, I'm not sure you really mean that one. We'll just make sure to get you on the Pill first. And try to pick someone better than Brad next time." They both made a face at the same time, making each other laugh.

"So, what's next?" Paula asked.

"I've got another appointment, to make sure I have time to think it over. I told them I've already thought it over, but I still have to have it. Anyway, then I need to see a psychiatrist because I'm a minor or whatever."

Paula smiled. Her daughter had been forced to grow up so quickly over the last few months. It was a relief to still hear her use childish phrases sometimes.

"Then I can't consent to the adoption until thirty days after the baby's born, to make sure I'm really ready."

Paula was familiar with that from what she'd read online. There was also a thirty-day revocation period in which the birth parent could withdraw consent. She remembered thinking *like a cooling-off period* when she'd read the thirty-day policy. In fact, the whole consent procedure was very much like setting up a bank account, buying a car or any other legal exchange. It needed to be witnessed by an authorised person who had to see two forms of ID and check that they had the necessary documents. All this to determine the course of a child's life.

"Oh," Jasmine added, "and I can get a say in what sort of parents I want to adopt the baby."

Paula had read that, too. She'd seen so many American movies and TV shows that dealt with adoption that she was used to seeing birth parents wander into people's homes and determining them worthy of raising their child, but she knew it was different in Australia. You could specify whether you wanted married or de facto parents, same or opposite sex couples, or people from a particular religion, but you couldn't open a book and say *yep, that's them. Those gorgeous Hollywood stars. They're the ones!*

"So," Paula said as lightly as she could, "there's a bit to go through still, but we'll do it together. You know Dad and I are in your corner."

Jasmine nodded. "Yeah. Thanks, Mum."

The two finished up their ice creams and headed home.

Chapter 91 – Fiona

Fiona was the one who arranged heading over to Rosie's to meet little Eliza, a week after she was born. They had decided not to bombard her in the hospital, although Fiona had sent flowers. For their visit, Fiona was bringing home-made scones, Paula had agreed to make sandwiches and Destiny was buying a cake from a local bakery. They all assured Rosie that they couldn't care less if the house looked like a bomb had gone off in it. The only thing she needed to do was provide some tea.

Fiona was the first to arrive and she literally cooed when she saw little Eliza, swaddled in a soft lilac blanket. She was just adorable. Although Fiona had never wanted kids of her own, she'd always been a sucker for babies. Babies she could cuddle and give back, of course.

"She's just perfect," she told Rosie honestly, in that strange whisper-voice people used when talking around newborn babies. "How's motherhood treating you?"

Rosie smiled. "Well, I'm exhausted, but it has been so amazing. So far. We only stayed one night in the hospital, so I've had some time to adjust to life at home with her. Tim's still on paternity leave," she added, "but he's gone to do some groceries. He's been so anxious about leaving us! I told him this would be a good time, while I've got some company." She paused. "Would you like to hold the baby?"

When Paula and Destiny arrived, separately but at nearly the same time, Fiona was clutching little Eliza in her arms. She smiled at the other women as they came in. "You can try, but I'm not giving her up."

Paula laughed. "You've got exactly five more minutes with her and then she's mine," she warned, walking over to hug Rosie before heading into the kitchen to start setting up her sandwiches.

Destiny smiled as she sat down on the couch next to Rosie. "Are you loving it?" she asked. "Having a baby, I mean."

"I am," Rosie replied. "I never really thought I'd have kids, but here I am! Of course, my dad's besotted. It's been so nice seeing him so happy. I think he would have moved in with us by now, except he's started seeing someone."

"Oh?" Fiona asked.

Rosie nodded. "His neighbour, Brenda. She's a lovely lady, about his age. She's widowed, too. I don't know if he'll ever get remarried or anything, but it's so nice that he has someone looking out for him. Stops me worrying about him quite so much."

"And are you exhausted?" Destiny asked, and Rosie laughed.

"Do I look it?"

"Nah," Destiny replied after scrutinising Rosie's face. "I just know I would be."

"Well, you've got a while to worry about that," Fiona said. She paused, remembering the date Destiny had told them about a week ago. "Unless you have something to tell us?"

"No!" Destiny laughed, starting to redden. "Definitely not."

"Don't talk about Desi's date until I'm back in there," Paula yelled from the kitchen.

"There's nothing really to tell," Destiny said a couple of minutes later when they were all together. She picked at an egg sandwich while Paula managed to pull the baby away from Fiona. "I mean, it was great! He's such a good guy," she added enthusiastically, and Fiona hid a smile. It was obvious that Destiny was trying to downplay how much Nate actually meant to her. "But it's early days yet. We've only been out twice. And I'm still not sure I should even be dating him, after everything with Luke."

The three other women all protested at once. "You deserve to be happy," Paula said, and Fiona added "Denying yourself love doesn't help anyone. Believe me."

The weight of her words settled over them for a minute. Fiona had finally come to realise they were true. She had spent so long shutting herself away from the world, unable to deal with her own guilt and grief over losing Jacob. She hadn't realised it at the time, but a part of her had felt like she didn't deserve to keep living her life if Jacob couldn't live his. It seemed crazy that it had taken a literal siege and a breast cancer scare to welcome her back into the land of the living, but there you had it. The world worked in mysterious ways.

"How long until you start your new job, Desi?" Rosie asked, leaning back in her chair. She seemed to be enjoying the opportunity to have her hands free while the baby was passed around between her friends.

"I don't start until January," Destiny replied, "so I have some free time between now and then. I'm just going to keep working at the store until then."

"Speaking of jobs," Fiona said, "I'm going to leave mine." She filled them in on Jennifer's refusal to give her time off for her travels, and how Fiona had been struggling with her work lately. "Ever since Jacob died, I just don't think it's the same for me anymore. It's a shame, because I've always loved doing it, but I don't know. It's like a switch has flicked and I can't turn it back on again. I *hate* that the shooting has taken another thing from me, but it's just not the right fit for me anymore." She paused. "I have no idea what else to do, though."

"Would you go into another form of healthcare?" Paula suggested, and Fiona shook her head. "I just think I don't need to be around so much death right now."

"You'll find something perfect for you," Rosie said optimistically. Fiona smiled. She had a strange feeling of calm about the whole thing. It felt like Rosie's words were true. The right thing would come along for her, and she had a perfectly good job in the meantime.

"And you!" Paula said to Rosie. "I think we've found the perfect thing for you right here. You're a natural born mum." Rosie smiled, and Paula went on. "You wouldn't know she was your first. You seem so comfortable with having a newborn. I wish I'd been more relaxed when Jasmine was little. Actually, I was probably even worse the second time around!"

"Do you ever stop to think..." Fiona said, looking at Eliza, who was now curled up in Destiny's arms. She struggled to put her feelings into words. "I mean, this has been such an awful year for all of us, but here's something amazing that's come out of it. In ten years you'll probably look back and remember it as the year Eliza came into the world, rather than the year you lived through a shooting."

Rosie shrugged. "I think I'll always think of it as the year my sister died," she said, and Fiona wanted to kick herself. Because she hadn't really known Rosie until after Betty was gone, it was hard to remember the extent of the pain Rosie had been through. Rosie hadn't just gone through a shooting like Fiona had, as traumatic as that had been. She'd also watched her sister die in front of her. Of course she wouldn't be able to focus on anything else from the year when she'd been through so much, not even something as wonderous as her new baby.

"But," Rosie continued, "I'll also remember it as the year I had Eliza. And that's okay. Sometimes you have to take the bitter with the sweet."

The four women were silent for a moment, all looking at the tiny individual in front of them. Fiona realised the truth in her friend's words. When Paula reflected on the year, she would no doubt think about Ollie's injury and subsequent trauma. But Fiona hoped she would also remember how she and Jasmine had grown closer again, despite the difficult circumstances. Destiny would, of course, think about Luke, but she'd also think about Nate, and her university graduation and her new job.

For her own part, when Jacob had died right at the start of the year, Fiona had thought the whole year was cursed. The shooting seemed only to cement that fact. Now, though... She knew she would always think of Jacob and the shooting when she thought of this year, but she would also remember it for bonding her with the other women, for opening up her world to more friendships than she'd ever had before. And, of course, for Burleigh, who had added so much to her life.

The bitter with the sweet. It really said it all.

Epilogue

On an ordinary February morning, one year to the day of the coffee shop siege, four women gathered at a park near Alpine Shopping Centre.

It had been Paula's idea to meet that day, just as it had been her idea to meet in the first place in the months after the shooting. She had even suggested they meet at the coffee shop itself, as a testament to what they had all overcome. The other three had quickly vetoed the suggestion, though. Paula understood where they were coming from, but for her, the coffee shop no longer had the almost mythical significance it had held. It was just a place she sometimes saw on her way to work at the cinema upstairs. Sometimes she even parked near it now.

It seemed only natural, then, to suggest they meet in the park where they had all met for the first time. Once again, they all brought picnic food along to share. This time, though, the conversation flowed more freely, and they all laughed more. And of course, this time they were joined by a fifth member - little Eliza, wearing a cheery sunflower onesie and being passed around between the women like a doll.

"So," Fiona said as they all sat down. "Don't laugh, but I've come up with some question cards for you all."

They did all laugh, but with her rather than at her. Fiona had finally settled on her new career path. She was now studying to be a grief counsellor, and she couldn't believe it had taken her so long to figure out what it was she wanted to do. Between Jacob's sudden death and the shooting, she knew more than enough about grief for a lifetime. She was happy to be able to put her newfound understanding towards a good cause, and hopefully help others to process their own feelings. It had given her life a new purpose. She had always quite enjoyed studying, and she was working part-time doing data entry at her neighbour Katie's family business. It was exactly the sort of non-taxing work she needed while she studied in her time off. The greatest perk, though, was that she had arranged the time off for Italy before taking the job. Fiona was leaving the following Monday. Adam and Julian's photos and social media posts from their travels so far had only fuelled her enthusiasm. Her bags were already packed.

"So," Fiona said, pulling out the first card. "What do you think has been the most surprising element of your recovery from the shooting?"

There was a pause, with none of the women seeming to want to volunteer to speak first. Finally, Rosie answered. "Surprising... I think how resilient we all are. I mean, don't get me wrong, there are still days I could lie crumpled on the floor. But I think human nature means you keep putting one foot in front of the other, even when you don't think you can."

They all nodded, agreeing with the truth in these words. Fiona added, "It's not linear, though."

"How do you mean?" asked Destiny. She had arranged the day off from her cadetship, which she was loving, so she could be there with them. When her editor heard what she had been through the year before he'd instantly agreed to giving her the day off, on the proviso that she write a reflective piece about the first anniversary of the shooting. Destiny knew a lot of people wouldn't have wanted to do so, but she had relished the opportunity. It was her first big writing job since she'd started her cadetship the previous month, and it felt like a positive step to be able to put her thoughts about the shooting down in writing for an actual audience. It has been printed that day, but she didn't think the other women had seen it yet. She hoped it expressed both the horror of the shooting, and the process of moving on since then. Nate had proofread it for her before she submitted it and he said it was "excellent", but he wasn't exactly an unbiased critic.

"I mean, I thought it would be like a cold. You feel a little bit better each day. But I can feel fabulous on Monday and be a complete mess on Tuesday."

"Oh. Yep, been there," Destiny said. "I thought I was doing really well after Luke's funeral, and then Ed said that crappy thing to me and I was right back at square one. Worse than square one, probably. And like Ro said, I still have my days where it's all I can think about. I still miss Luke, you know," she added suddenly, as if someone had challenged her. "I know I shouldn't, since I'm with Nate now. But I do." Destiny and Nate were planning to move in together the following month. It was her first time living out of home, and the first time she'd been so serious in a relationship. She knew it was pretty soon to be moving in with him, six months into their relationship. But then, their whole relationship had been strangely accelerated after the slow burn that was her falling for him.

Nate had told her he loved her on their fourth date, and she'd surprised no one more than herself when she'd said it back to him. They'd slept together for the first time that night and that had been amazing, too. Everything had felt right with the world, and it had felt that way every day since. She couldn't believe her luck. Sometimes the best things in life took you completely by surprise.

"Of course you should," Rosie replied firmly. "It's different to a break-up. You and Luke had something special. Now you and Nate have something special. It's good to move on, but it doesn't mean you've forgotten all about Luke."

Destiny smiled at her, tears filling her eyes. "Thanks. Nate is really understanding but I sometimes feel like I can't talk to him about all of this, in case he thinks I'd rather be with Luke."

"It's not a matter of rather," Fiona said. "If I meet someone new, it doesn't mean I'd rather be with him, but it doesn't mean I'd rather be with Jacob either. You can love both of them at the same time." It was something she'd been giving a lot of thought to, since she was planning to join some online dating sites when she returned from her trip.

"Exactly," Paula said. "It's like having a second child. It doesn't mean you stop loving your first. Your heart just... makes room."

"Speaking of which," Fiona said, momentarily forgetting her discussion cards, "how is Jazzy going now?"

Ten weeks had passed since Jasmine gave birth. As planned, she had adopted the little boy out at birth. There certainly hadn't been any arguments from Brad, who had happily signed his rights away. Jasmine didn't get to choose his name, but she had referred to him before and after his birth as Alexander. The adoptive parents named him Sam.

Paula sighed. "That's a tough one. There have been lots of sleepless nights," she said. "Lots of tears. And that's from both of us. Actually, all of us." She had been surprised by how much Alfie and Ollie had taken on the burden of the child they'd given up, rather than just herself and Jasmine. The circumstances were awful, but she felt as though the entire experience had strengthened their family bond. "But he'll have a better life with his new family than we could have given him, and that's what really matters. We made the right decision." Since before Jasmine had given birth, she'd been careful to call it 'their' decision, 'their' baby, rather than Jasmine's alone. She had done that to make her daughter feel like the entirety of the responsibility wasn't on her, but it was also so true that it started to come naturally to Paula. It *was* their decision, in many ways. It *was* their baby. The adoption, and the consequences of it, affected them all, not just Jasmine.

"And you and Tim?" Paula asked Rosie. "How are the wedding plans coming along?"

Rosie smiled. "Slowly, but we finally picked a date, at least! Which reminds me…" She reached into her handbag and withdrew a Save the Date card for each of them.

If you'd told her a year earlier that she and Tim would not only still be together, but happily engaged, she wouldn't have believed it. When Betty had told her the truth about herself and Tim, a piece of Rosie had died. It was a minor miracle that they had managed to get their relationship back on track, but they had, and she was truly happy. She had done enough looking back. It was time to focus on the future.

"Do you have more questions for us?" Destiny asked Fiona a minute later.

Fiona shrugged and laughed in a self-deprecating way. "I do, but I'll hold onto them for now. I was thinking about making some kind of a speech, but I don't think any of us are up for that. I did think we should make a toast, though. I was going to bring some champagne, but you know, park." She gestured around as if to prove they were, in fact, in a park. "I didn't want to get arrested right before my trip." She pulled a bottle of sparkling water out of her cooler bag and poured it into four plastic cups. "What do we toast to?"

They looked around at each other. "To Italy," Rosie said, raising her cup in Fiona's direction.

"To Eliza," Destiny added.

"To the people we've loved and lost," Paula said.

She was referring to Betty and Luke on their anniversaries, of course, but also to Jacob, and to little Sam. The world was filled with all types of losses. And all types of gains.

"To friendship," Fiona said simply.

Rosie looked around at the other three women, and at her newborn daughter. She smiled as they joined their cups together in a toast. "To the future," she said, with tears in her eyes and a smile on her face.

ACKNOWLEDGEMENTS

I want to start off by thanking my readers. When my first book, *Having It All,* was published in 2020, I was blown away by the support I received from family, friends and kind strangers on the Internet. I was equally thrilled with the excitement I received when I started talking about the launch of my second book.

I owe a huge debt of thanks to my first readers – my sister and fellow author Gemma Johns, and my friends Brooke James and Sue Manning Krach. They provided me with gentle corrections, insights and encouragement about my writing, and their response to the book made me much more confident about putting it out into the world.

I also have to thank the rest of my family – my parents Noel and Sandra, my sister Melanie and all of my nieces and nephews – for the love and support they always give me.

And finally, thank you to all my friends for listening to me talk about my writing and for their patience when I obsess over the small details. It means a lot!

ABOUT THE AUTHOR

Larissa Johns has been working as a primary school teacher for over ten years, but she has never forgotten her love of writing. Her lifelong dreams were realised when her first novel, *Having It All,* was published in 2020. *Without Warning* is her second novel.

When she's not writing Larissa spends her time reading, watching far too many movies, drinking tea and binge-watching sitcoms on repeat.

She lives in Brisbane, Australia with her overly-indulged cavoodle, Indiana Johns.

Did you love *Without Warning*? Then you should read *Having It All* by Larissa Johns!

Primary school teacher Annie Yates has a great job and friends she can count on, but her love life has never worked out the way she wanted. If it wasn't bad enough that, years ago, she fell madly in love with Jack Delaney before realising he was gay, now her new fiancé has walked out on her. Her world has come crashing down. All she's ever wanted was security, love and a family of her own. Her plans for motherhood have gone out the door... or have they?

Jack, now Annie's best friend, wants to co-parent together. Plenty of women have babies and end up co-parenting, so what's so bad about starting out that way? This is a second chance she never expected, but nothing ever did go smoothly for Annie.

Is having a baby with your gay best friend a recipe for disaster, or could this be the platonic love story Annie had never imagined?